FIVE RIVERS
ON FIRE

TO - Sheila and Angie — two great
friends - Thanks for your support.
— enjoy —
" world peace and friendship "

Bashir
3/2012

FIVE RIVERS
ON FIRE

M. Bashir Sulahria

This is a work of fiction. Names, characters, places and incidents either are the product of the author's imagination or are used fictitiously, and any resemblance to any actual persons, living or dead, events, or locales is entirely coincidental.

Cover:
Design by Bradley H. Boe
Art by Julie C. Sulahria
Photograph by M. Bashir Sulahria

This book was printed in the United States of America.

To order additional copies of this book, contact:
Xlibris Corporation
1-888-795-4274
www.Xlibris.com
Orders@Xlibris.com
108856

CONTENTS

In Memory Of

The victims of 1947 Indo-Pakistan partition
As well as
All those who have suffered from religious hatred, genocide and
Ethnic cleansing
The world over

Acknowledgements

This story is the outcome of my fond childhood memories as I frequently traveled ten miles one way, mostly on foot, with my mother Hussain Bibi from Sialkot to visit my Aunt Rakhi, and her family in Rurkee. I am eternally grateful for that experience.

My heartfelt thanks to Joe Parks, Mark Bacon, Penny LeVee, Mari Applegate, Kathy Berndt, Esther Early, Matt Bayan, Jim Linebaugh, Eric Lamberts, Patricia Anderson, Dick Maximon, and Carol Humphrey who not only encouraged me to tell the tale, but thoroughly reviewed and provided constructive comments along the way.

I am indebted to my wife Julie, my first line editor, who painstakingly reviewed and edited the manuscript numerous times. I am also thankful for the love I have received from Julie, our son Taj, his wife Jessica, and their daughters Taliah and Daisy throughout this project.

I am greatly appreciative of Judy Carlson, whose diligent editorial efforts have helped to make *Five Rivers on Fire* a smooth read. I would like to extend special thanks to Professors Stephen Tchudi, and James Hulse for their generous endorsement of my work.

Last, but not the least, I admire the fortitude of our dog Zoey, who sat for days on end, faithfully wondering: when will it be finished.

Map of India and Pakistan

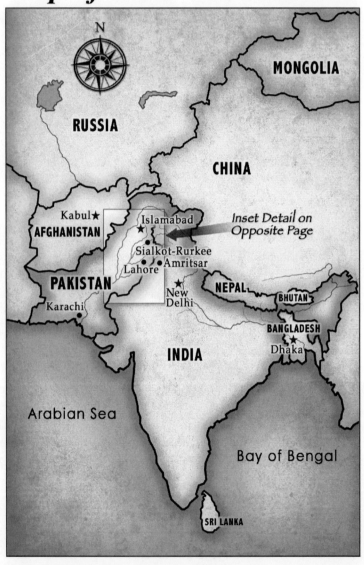

The Five Rivers of Punjab

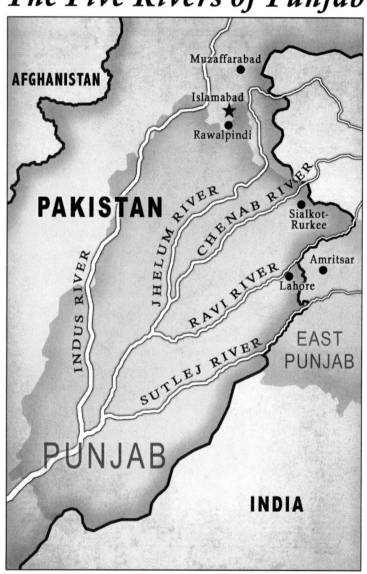

CHARACTERS

Fazal Din	Muslim shopkeeper in Rurkee
Rakhi	Fazal's wife
Karim	Fazal's son
Parveen	Fazal's daughter
Nazir	Fazal's brother
Sher Singh	Sikh farmer
Tara	Sher's wife
Makhan	Sher's son; Karim's best friend
Sarita	Sher's daughter
Aneel Gill	Sikh farmer in Kotli; Tara's brother
Zareena	Aneel's wife
Dalair	Aneel's son
Berket	Aneel's daughter
Shafkat	Wealthy Muslim landlord Rurkee patriarch
Jamal	Wealthy Muslim merchant in Sialkot Fazal's friend
Darshan	Hindu merchant Jamal and Fazal's friend
Gupta	Darshan's son

Part I

—1—

Sudden Talk

Turbaned Aneel Gill, a Sikh farmer, wearing a dagger on his hip, approaches the only shop in the village of Rurkee. His eyebrows form a deep ridge above his full-bearded, round, leathery face. Fazal, a Muslim, extends his arm, welcoming him inside the cramped shop of spices, food staples and school supplies. It is early March 1946.

"Aneel Gill, you're white as a sheet; the blood's drained from your face. What's wrong? What's bothering you, my friend?" asks Fazal.

"Can we talk in private?" Aneel whispers, while glancing back to make sure no one is nearby.

"Of course," says Fazal, quickly closing the door behind Aneel, while inviting him to have a seat. Pointing toward the floor cushion, he looks toward the open half door leading to the courtyard and loudly calls to his wife, Rakhi to make them *chai*—spiced tea.

"Fazal, I need more than chai. I need a smoke. Please ask sister Rakhi to bring the *hookah*. I'm scared. I need more than a cup of chai to calm my nerves," Aneel says, trembling, while holding his groomed gray beard in one hand and clutching the dagger with the other. Fazal leans over the half door and asks Rakhi to bring the hookah as well. Turning to Aneel, he raises his eyebrows and chides, "I thought you'd quit smoking."

"Yeah, I have, except I smoke when I'm upset. Today, I'm stressed out of my mind; I can't think straight. Hookah calms me down. You know that."

"I understand. I understand," says Fazal, squeezing his friend's husky shoulders.

"Brother Aneel, here's your hot chai and the hookah all fired up." Rakhi opens the top-half door and hands him the water pipe and two cups of hot chai.

"Thank you. Thanks so much." Aneel takes a deep breath and smiles fretfully. He frees his hands from the dagger and takes the tea tray and hookah from Rakhi. He hands one cup to Fazal and puts the other one beside himself. Sitting on the floor cushion, he grabs the hookah with one hand and puts the other near the mouthpiece and puffs like a drowning man reaching for air, filling the shop with smoke.

"Take it easy, Aneel. You're normally so quiet. What's up with you?" Fazal asks, waving away the smoke.

"My dear friend do you know that the village Narang is in turmoil." Aneel takes a few more drags, picks up the chai and half empties the cup in rapid slurps. He leans forward to gain Fazal's full attention and starts talking, his eyes piercing Fazal's, as his beard rises and falls with every gesture. His normally low, deliberate voice pitches higher. "Yesterday, a friend from Narang visited us. He said everybody is talking about partition; that it's coming. People don't trust each other. They're convinced India will be divided. Narang will become part of Pakistan. Hindus and Sikhs will be forced to move, leaving their valuables and property behind. Tension between Muslims, Sikhs and Hindus has been developing, now reaching an all-time high."

Aneel finishes his chai and takes a few quick puffs on the hookah before continuing. "Muslims are making life miserable for the Sikhs. They call them names, throw stones at their houses, harass women and hurl religious and ethnic slurs. They shout that Narang is going to be one hundred percent Muslim after partition, so Sikhs better leave the village. Muslim elders try to calm them down and struggle to put sense into their heads, but it's not working. Last Friday night a Sikh household was set on fire. The family barely escaped. The village knows the culprits. Unashamed, they refuse to admit their transgressions and openly pronounce that they can't wait for the day when Narang will be pure Muslim."

"Is the family okay, Aneel?" asks Fazal with genuine concern. His even keeled business tone evaporates.

Aneel takes another hit and continues. "I hope so. Nobody knows for sure. Two nights ago under the cover of darkness, the family, along with a number of others, left the village and fled east, hoping to reach a safe haven in India. Many Sikhs and Hindus don't want to leave and are buying weapons for self defense."

Aneel faces Fazal, whose mustache flinches as he listens. "Everyone isn't as accepting as you. I'm thinking about arming myself to protect my family. I'm getting another sword and will buy a rifle when I've the money. You know about my long-standing land dispute with Rifaqat. If Rurkee plunges into chaos like Narang, I'm afraid he'll do away with my family just to grab what little ground I've left to live on. What's going to happen here? I don't want to abandon my ancestral land. Fazal, are we safe in Rurkee?"

"Don't worry. As long as I'm alive, you and all Sikhs and Hindus will be safe. We all are Punjabis. We've lived here like brothers for generations. We won't resort to hate. I'll talk to Mr. Shafkat first thing in the morning."

Fazal stands and Aneel rises. He wraps his arms around the shorter man and pulls him into a tight embrace; he feels his friend's heart racing. He releases his grasp, holds Aneel by his shoulders and looks into his eyes and says, "Don't fret so much Aneel. We've better things to do: prepare for Vaisakhi—harvest fair and most importantly get your son—our son, Dalair married."

Relaxed a bit, Aneel acknowledges his friendship with Fazal by forcing a tight-lipped smile and a nod, while stroking his beard. The mention of these future events consoles him. He opens the door, steps into the deserted street and looks around. He takes out the dagger and dashes toward his brother-in-law Sher Singh's house located just two blocks away at the end of the alley. Fazal sticks his neck out of his shop and watches his anxious friend disappear into the darkness. He wonders if he can keep his promise, and then returns to his nighttime ritual of closing the shop.

Looking around, Fazal swells with pride, knowing that years of hard work have brought him success. He scans the merchandise as if to place each item anew. His flair for colors, texture and scale lets him orchestrate impressive arrangements. A few aluminum canisters hold mustard oil, *ghee*—purified butter, and kerosene. Wooden crates and big baskets store wheat and rice; glass containers brimming with dried fruit, and gunnysacks spilling over with onions, potatoes and garlic line the walls. He assembles them in a series of rows for display and accessibility.

Four feet above the floor, the shallow shelves rest on wooden pegs, making a border on three sides of the shop's mud walls. They support glass jars of candies in a variety of sizes, shapes and taste; cookies, peanut brittle and tea; aromatic spices like cardamom, cinnamon and cloves abound. Some containers hold herbal tea leaves, bulbs and roots plucked from medicinal plants. The aroma of spices and staples permeates the room. Assorted school supplies—pencils, papers and tablets are stacked to the right. Above the ledge hang pinwheels and different sized kites in a wild array of brilliant colors. Three plump floor pillows for customer comfort are stacked by the door. Fazal cannot help but admire his shop.

Upon hearing Aneel's anguish and disconcerting discussion, Fazal's latent fear about Punjab's partition plunges him into despair. "I may lose everything I've worked for all my life," he worries. For a moment Fazal yearns for his childhood, and recollects how difficult it was to convince his father that he would rather be a shopkeeper than follow his profession as a dyer.

Fazal remembers his father's hard work; how he created a myriad of patterns and colors by stamping the wooden blocks that fascinated him when he was a youngster. First, his father lightly dipped each block into a color and then marked the hand woven cotton material. He sat crossed legged for hours in front of a wooden platform, spreading the cloth tightly over it. He used an assortment of blocks, dipping each, just slightly into the dye pads framed in shallow wooden boxes. This profession had been in his family for generations. People spun cotton yarn at home, took it to the village weaver and then brought it to Fazal's father for dyeing or block printing. The villagers bartered for goods and services, and paid Fazal's father in staples of rice, wheat, corn and other farmed products for his work. Customers paid what they could afford or thought was fair. If they had bumper crops, he would get generous compensation. In lean years, he would barely get enough to support his family. It was a messy and backbreaking job that lacked enough pay to make a living. The family had lived hand to mouth, day by day.

Fazal did not want to follow his father's profession. It was too hard and uncertain. There must be better ways to make a decent living, Fazal had thought. Having no doubts, he was determined to open a small general store when he grew up, stocking the shop with items not available in the village and selling them at his asking price. Years ago, he had successfully convinced his father to convert his shop to a general store.

Haunted by today's conversation, Fazal begins closing the store. *No, no I won't; I will not lose my shop,* Fazal reasons. *I've worked too hard and long to build this business. Aneel is not going anywhere. Nobody is leaving Rurkee. It's getting late. I must get a good night's sleep before I make the trip to Sialkot tomorrow morning.* He closes and crawls back into the house courtyard, locking the half door behind him.

"You closed the shop early today," says Rakhi. "What's the matter? Are you feeling okay?" She looks at him with alarm. "Aneel Gill seemed very nervous. Is everything all right with Aneel and his family?"

"What are you talking about? Everything is okay, Rakhi. I'm hungry. Would you fix me supper, please?" asks Fazal irritably, without answering his wife.

Rakhi dishes out *saag*—buttered spicy mustard green paste; with two *chapattis*—a tortilla like bread. Fazal finishes his meal quickly, in silence. Rakhi knows, from hearing the murmur in the next room and the use of the hookah that the conversation was secretive and perhaps ominous. Fazal rarely shouts at her. She thinks of herself as a lucky and happy wife and mother, even though she must get by with less when business is slow. She comes to her duties willingly, enjoying a positive outlook on life.

"Would you like a glass of hot milk?" Rakhi asks, sensing that something is bothering Fazal.

"No thanks, I'm just tired. I'm going to bed. Besides, I'm low on supplies and I'd like to leave early in the morning for Sialkot. I need a good night's sleep for the trip."

Fazal lifts the curtain into their sleeping room and curls under the thick quilt, draping his arm over his head. Rakhi quickly puts the dishes away, and she hears him snoring. She feeds her son, Karim and her daughter, Parveen; then tucks them into another quilted *charpai*—woven jute cot. She stretches out on her *charpai*, and goes to sleep next to Fazal.

In the dark, two men sneak up to Fazal's shop. One douses the wooden door and window with kerosene while the other quickly lights a match and throws it into the shop.

—2—

Can't Tell

As the wood catches fire, the arsonists burst into laughter and keep pouring the fuel until the fire gets a definite hold. Engulfed in flames, the shop turns into an inferno. The smoke, fire and heat escape through the door and the window, while the eaves burn, producing tongues of fire and smoke. Flames consume the materials and merchandise.

"No!" Fazal runs to stop them. "Don't burn down my livelihood," he cries. He seems to run in place, feeling helpless. "Stop. Stop. Is anybody listening? Please, please, stop them," he yells at the top of his lungs.

Rakhi awakes, hearing the loud screams and pleas coming from her husband. She realizes Fazal is having a terrifying dream. She bolts from her bed, turns up the wick on the kerosene lamp and shakes him from his troubled sleep. "Are you okay?" she says grasping his shoulder with one hand while holding the lamp in the other.

"Someone set my shop on fire, Rakhi."

"No, no, your shop is just fine. You're having a nightmare, Fazal. Was it something Aneel said last night?"

"I don't think so."

"What was your dream? Tell me about it." Fazal rubs sleep from his eyes and swears her to secrecy before sharing the nightmare with her.

"I was coming back from the mosque after evening prayers when I saw a man splashing the front door of our shop with kerosene while another lit a match and set it on fire. Flames quickly engulfed the shop. I yelled at them, and ran toward them in disbelief, pleading with them to stop. Rakhi, I felt helpless and paralyzed. There were screams escaping from my lungs as if someone had pushed me off the roof top. The next thing I knew, you were leaning over me."

"Can you remember them? Who did they look like?"

"They had beards and wore turbans."

"Were they Sikhs or Muslims?"

"I don't know. It was dark. Muslims and Sikhs wearing beards and turbans look the same in the dark. Thanks to Allah it was just a bad dream."

"It's almost dawn. You can hear the roosters crowing, can't you? You better leave the *charpai* and get ready for your trip to Sialkot. You need to make a few more trips to buy supplies for the upcoming Vaisakhi fair, when you do so much business. We can always use extra money," she reminds Fazal, while walking with the lamp to the open courtyard kitchen. She puts on a small pot of water for chai and prepares breakfast, praying that her husband's dream will not come true. She serves Fazal his favorite morning food and wraps two spiced potato-filled *parathas*—pan-fried flat bread, for him to take. Fazal grabs the *parathas*, wraps them in rice paper and secures them in one of the bicycle gunnysack-saddlebags. He checks the tires for air, adjusts the seat and walks it outside through the courtyard door to the street.

"Rakhi, if I'm not home by evening, don't wait up. Just know that I have decided to stay with Jamal. Waking up so early from a bad dream has unnerved me. I'm already feeling tired."

He climbs on his bicycle and slowly starts pedaling. His broad shoulders move side to side, his head of cropped black hair resting confidently on his long, erect neck. Looking back for a moment he smiles and waves to his wife. She smiles and closes the door as he disappears around the corner in the dawning light.

The shopping trip to Sialkot is so routine that he can do it with his eyes closed; yet today he is tense. He can't erase the nightmare that plays constantly in his head. For a moment he looks up and breathes out a prayer into the blue sky, "Oh Allah, please don't let my nightmare come true. YOU and only YOU can save Rurkee from the forces of hate. Give us the strength to live in peace and harmony." Prayer eases his mind and soothes his soul.

As he rides through the fields, Fazal reminisces about his youth, recalling when his father worked as a cloth dyer and block printer right from the same shop. Fazal helped him mix organic powder dyes into the water filled barrels. He watched him boil the solutions over an open wood-fired hearth before he would dip the cloth and stir it with a wooden stick to make a uniform color. He fished the cloth from the cauldron, let it cool and wrung it out before spreading it on a clothesline for drying. As Fazal got older, he completed the job from start to finish, feeling proud to work alongside his father in block printing. He admired his father's speed as he reached into a big wooden crate and pulled out exactly the right blocks needed to create intricate designs and patterns.

During four years of school, Fazal learned basic writing and arithmetic. He chuckled as he recalled the day he decided to use his education, and shyly suggested numbering the blocks with indelible ink for easy identification. With a smile on his face his father said, "Go ahead. But remember that I can still pick out the blocks faster than you can, at least for now. Since I didn't go to school, I can't read the numbers anyway. You can do this on one condition."

"What's that?"

"When you get done, we'll have a competition," challenged his father, winking at him with his bright, deep-set eyes. His thin face seemed to bob perpetually while his scrawny hands reached robotically for the blocks, dipped them into the ink pads, and stamped colorful designs onto the fabric. Fazal wasted no time numbering the wooden grips to match the individual patterns, and challenged his father, only to lose. His schooling was no match for his father's experience. When his father died in 1940, Fazal became head of the household and took over the business. Now, he wonders if he is as good at his business as his father had been at his.

—3—

Rumors Fly

Fazal speeds up to cover as much distance as possible before sunrise. The early spring morning is cool, but the temperature shoots up once the sun appears. Rising vapors from the irrigated fields elevate the humidity, making the day hot and sticky. He reaches a steady speed, working his lungs to full capacity. His pace is strenuous, yet not overly stressful. He reflects on the past and ponders the future of his village. Absorbed in his thoughts, he is unaware of his surroundings and destination. He deftly negotiates the narrow, sinuous paths between the wheat, corn, barley and vegetable fields, occasionally wiping sweat from his face and forehead with his turban tail.

Fazal had limited schooling, yet he has learned how to read and write. Over the years, he has sharpened his literary skills by poring over newspapers and *Urdu* language periodicals. In Sialkot, he has befriended educated people and is impressed by some of his suppliers who keep abreast of current events, and, when not busy, have their heads buried in the local *Urdu* newspapers. He borrows the newspapers, flips through them, reads the articles that interest him and always gazes deeply at photographs of *Angrez*—the English, and wonders about them—ruling India so far away from their own land and culture. He had seen an English family only once, while visiting his friend who cooked for them in Sialkot. He faintly remembers that the family enjoyed a luxurious life style, residing in a grand bungalow. Called *Angrez*, they spoke an unfamiliar tongue and dressed differently. Their food was utterly plain compared to the indigenous spiced and curried dishes enjoyed by the locals. Fazal does not see the need for the *Angrez* to leave India, as they seem to run the country smoothly.

He would argue incessantly with his suppliers, "Nobody in my village has ever seen an *Angrez*. For them the rule of *Angrez* is just a myth and has no impact on their lives." The merchants would retort, with equal enthusiasm, "Indians would be better off without British rule. If the colonial yoke were cast away and the country was free, the people would be ruled by their own. Resources would be used for the benefit and betterment of Indians rather than siphoned off to England, which has made our country weaker and poorer."

"Maybe we do deserve independence, but what I don't understand is the idea of splitting the country in two, especially the Punjab. Why?" he asks. "In Punjab, we have lived side by side for centuries. Why can't we do the same after independence?"

While merchants prepare his orders, he discusses news with these well-informed businessmen. Since last year, the papers have been full of World War II stories, Indian soldiers fighting in far away countries and continents that he didn't know existed. More than half of the space is dedicated to the news and analysis about Indian independence and partitioning the subcontinent.

Fazal's innate curiosity and the frequent business trips to the big city, where news and rumors of Indian partition and division of Punjab flow freely, give him a prescient sense about what might happen. He knows more about Punjab's future than his fellow villagers, who are clueless about the pending chaos that could bubble to the surface at any time. Fazal keeps this to himself; he even lied to Aneel Gill to calm his fears. He hopes and prays that his village will not be affected. He feels burdened that he knows more about Punjab's impending partition than he has shared with his wife and friends.

These thoughts make him confused and uncomfortable. He has been riding the bicycle for almost two hours, when he suddenly realizes that he is on a paved road. Sialkot is a few minutes in front of him.

The approaching city and the city traffic require all of his awareness. He merges into the river of heterogeneous traffic, where pedestrians share the narrow paved road with animals, *tongas*—two-wheeled, horse drawn carriages, bullock and donkey carts of all shapes and sizes.

As Fazal cycles through the city, he senses an eerie calm. The bazaars are deserted. People lack their usual joviality; going about their business with cautious and guarded gaits. He speeds up, zigzagging his way through the bazaars, constantly ringing the bicycle bell, warning people of his unwavering haste. He takes short cuts, back streets, and alleys to arrive at Darshan's shop. He can't believe his eyes. His Hindu friend's shop is burned. Only the charred walls remain. Horrified, he bangs his fist over and over on his bicycle seat.

My nightmare was a premonition about Darshan's misfortune. It wasn't my shop in Rurkee that I dreamed was on fire; but it was my friend's business that was reduced to a scorched skeleton. He is terrified, yet he is drawn into the wall of rubble. He gathers strength and slowly opens the parched door. He needs to see for himself that Darshan is not inside, dead. The door creeks and opens partway.

"*Aslamo Elaikum, Bhai*, Peace be with you brother," says a voice, haltingly. The voice sends a frightful wave down Fazal's spine. His heart racing, he jerks around and is relieved to see his Muslim merchant friend, Jamal.

"*Wa Elaikum Asslam,* And peace be with you as well," murmurs Fazal, wiping sweat from his forehead.

"What happened here? Where's Darshan? Is he alive? How's his family? Who did this?"

"Let's go to my shop. I'll tell you everything," says Jamal.

Although Jamal is smaller in stature and walks with a limp, as a cultural courtesy he walks the bike to his shop as Fazal silently accompanies him. As they arrive, the two friends thump down on an old rattan shop bench. Jamal immediately orders his servant, a young boy of thirteen, to fetch two cups of chai for them. Jamal softly touches Fazal's shoulder and says sadly, "You know, events were rousing people up when you were here last month. The situation is getting worse each day, with ethnic beatings and throngs of rioters. Everyone believes India will be partitioned into two countries and that the Punjab will bear the worst of it. The newspapers say that *Angrez* plan to divide the subcontinent in the middle of next year and leave India for good.

"Hindus and Sikhs are afraid and don't feel comfortable living here. Hundreds have left the city convinced they'll be better off leaving rather than becoming part of a dangerous mass exodus later. Others still believe that partition won't happen and don't see the need to leave their homeland. There's unrest and uncertainty in the city. Some Muslims bully, insult, and even beat up Sikhs and Hindus. Sikh and Hindu youth retaliate; a perpetual cycle of violence. People are on edge. I'm afraid the simmering hate will spill over into unending brutality and revenge," Jamal speculates hoarsely.

"I understand, but where are Darshan and his family? Are they safe?" asks Fazal impatiently. Jamal rubs his silver *taviz*, an amulet that hangs around his neck, attempting to hold back his tears. "Darshan and his family fled eastward hoping to make it to India."

He puts his thumb and middle finger on his eyes and presses softly. He sighs and wipes his eyes on his shirt sleeve. The servant appears, dutifully handing them hot chai. They are not interested, and put the cups under the bench. Jamal takes a deep breath and turns to Fazal.

"Two weeks ago Darshan arrived at my house, his body sweating. He could barely speak, trembling with fright. He was incoherent and repeated nonstop that something terrible was going to happen to his family. I held him by his shoulders and pulled him forward to console him. I could feel his heart pounding, and helped him to a cot. He gulped down a glass of water and asked for a fresh smoke. My wife brought the hookah, which he inhaled as if it were food for a starving man. When Darshan calmed down, he turned to me, pleading, 'I know I'm a Hindu and you're a Muslim, but I've always thought of you as my brother. You must help me, and my family.'"

"'I'll give you all I can. You are like my family,' I said, assuring him that I would do anything.

"'Do you trust me, Jamal?' he asked.

"'Of course, I trust you,' I answered.

"'You must believe me. What I'm about to tell you is horrible but true,' said Darshan.

"'I've known you all my life, Darshan. You are an honest man. I know you'll tell me the truth. Go on, tell me what happened.'"

Jamal sighs and relates with tears in his eyes the story of Darshan. "It is difficult for me to tell, Fazal," says Jamal, "but I think you should know what happened, just as Darshan told it to me."

—4—

Rescue

Darshan told Jamal how it happened that night when he and his son Gupta were sitting on the veranda: They had, said Darshan, barely finished their supper when they heard loud screams. The high-pitched shrieks came from the nearby wheat field, punctuated by pleas for help. A young girl was in danger, and yelling at the top of her lungs for help: 'Help me. Please help me, please. They're going to kill me. They are going to kill me . . .'

"'Gupta, where are you going?' Darshan yelled, as Gupta stood up and put his hand to his ear.

"'Father, there is a girl out there who needs help. Don't you hear the screams?'

"'Yes, I do. But these are dangerous times, especially for us Hindus.'

"Before Darshan could finish his sentence, Gupta was out the door, running toward the screams. Somewhere in the wheat field he saw two boys, dragging the girl to the ground. They were upon her like hyenas snarling, 'Don't fight bitch. Submit or we'll kill you.'

"'Stop, Stop it. Have some decency. Don't harm her.' Gupta ran toward the attackers. He recognized the boys, and the girl. He ordered them to leave her alone. He shouted that they should let her be and go on their way. He assured them that he wouldn't tell a soul, not even her parents, if they promised that they would never do this again. The boys retreated into the wheat field. The larger boy grabbed a long stick, and the other picked up a machete they had hidden in the field. They came at Gupta. He couldn't believe what was happening. One grabbed hold of the girl's arm and the other demanded of her, 'Gupta was the one who was going to rape you. Wasn't he? You're lucky we got here in time to save you from this dirty Hindu.' The girl, terrified, said nothing. Her face drained of color.

"'Why don't you say something?' said one of her attackers. 'We know Gupta has been stalking you. He thinks being a big wrestler and the son of a rich Hindu merchant, he can get away with any crime.'

"'Not anymore,' screamed the boy with the machete; 'Sialkot will be pure Muslim soon, free of Hindus and Sikhs, who are *kafirs*—infidels. This infidel has to pay with his life. How dare he harass a Muslim girl?'

"'We are asking you one last time to tell us the truth,' said the boy wielding the stick. 'If you even think about protecting this scum, we'll kill you. Take a good look at him. He is the one who's been following you, and tonight he was going to rape you, wasn't he? Thanks to Allah, we heard your screams and got here in time to save you from this animal.'

"The girl raised her head, looked at Gupta, and adjusted her *dupatta*—chiffon headscarf. She then lowered her head in shame and whispered. 'Yes.'

"'Yes, what?'

"'Yes, he is the one who was about to rape me.'

"They ordered the girl to run home. 'Go on, tell your parents you were lucky that we got here in time to rescue you, save your honor, our honor and our community's honor. Remember what you said, and that it is the truth. If you don't tell the truth we'll kill you.' She rushed away and never looked back, disappearing into the evening darkness.

"Gupta knew instantly that he had been framed. The girl, even if she wanted, could not utter a word of truth, let alone defend his innocence later. He knew he was doomed, and darted into the shadows.

His two attackers chased him, wagging the stick and machete. He ran through the fields as fast as he could, his lungs pushing against his ribs; his heart pounding in his chest. Running like wolves, the boys overtook him, using the full force of wood and steel. He covered his head with one hand and used the other to ward off the beating. He felt unbearable pain from the constant stick blows, yet his eyes were on the machete, as he tried to defend his body from the blade. He took the punishment as long as he could. Exhausted, Gupta could no longer protect himself. In an instant, blood oozed from his left thigh and right wrist. Reeling from a jagged gash on his neck, he collapsed. The beating and gruesome neck wound must have scared the attackers. Afraid of being caught, they left him for dead, while Darshan waited anxiously for over an hour for his son to return.

"'Gupta, where are you? Can you hear me son?'" yelled Darshan nonstop from the rooftop. There was no answer. Scared, he scurried down, grabbed his brother, who lived next door, and set out to look for his son. In darkness, they rushed toward the screams. It wasn't the girl who was screaming, but his son who cried for help. The pleas grew weaker and then went silent. Searching the field, the brothers kept running and looking, until they came upon Gupta's body lying in a pool of blood. Darshan was horrified. His outrage turned into howling; he crumpled to the ground and gazed into space. 'Why? Why? Who would want to kill my son? Who, oh my God who, who would do this?'

"Darshan's brother wasted no time. He kneeled down, put his ear to Gupta's chest, and shouted, 'Brother! Brother, he is alive! His heart is beating; I can feel his warm breath. This is the time to act and act quickly. Each second counts. If you want to save his life, help me now!' Darshan took off his turban and tore it into three long narrow strips, bandaging the neck and leg wounds tightly. Darshan's brother, in a quick motion, hoisted the boy's body over his shoulder and ran toward the house. Darshan, frail and weak with shock, followed; puffing to keep up with his brother; watching to ensure the bandages held. As they neared their house, Darshan rushed to fetch the doctor. The doctor arrived, and after a quick examination opened his leather medical bag. He cleaned the cuts with warm soapy water, sterilized them with tincture of iodine, applied an antiseptic cream, and finished the treatment by dressing the wounds with thin muslin gauze.

"'It's a miracle that he is alive,' said the Doctor. 'He has lost a lot of blood, but the cuts aren't life threatening. Next twenty-four hours are crucial. Pray hard and keep a close eye on him. I'll check on him in the morning.' The doctor put his hand on Darshan's shoulder, reassuring him that his son would be all right. Darshan took the doctor's right hand in his, squeezed it gently and kissed it reverently, saying, 'Thank you, Doctor. Thank you.' Overcome with emotion, Darshan sobbed, his unchecked tears spilling onto the doctor's hand. Moved by Darshan's gratitude, the doctor could barely hold back his own tears. 'I'll see you in the morning,' he said as he left the house.

"Once the doctor had left, the attackers, along with the girl's parents, confronted Darshan at his front door, yelling and shaking their fists. 'You'd better pack up and leave. Take your fornicating family to India. We don't want infidels here. Sialkot is going to be part of Pakistan; the country of believers. Your son almost raped our daughter. You should thank your stars that these boys got there in time and saved her honor.'

"'But . . .' protested Darshan.

"'But what?'

"'My son is innocent. I know he is. He's the one who responded to the girl's screams.'

"'That's a lie, *kafir*.

"'It doesn't matter, anyway. We want you to disappear. Most Sikhs and Hindus have left already. All of you *kafirs* must go. The sooner you leave the better. You have two days. Two days only. We're warning you that if you don't leave, you won't have a house or your shop. Worse yet, you may not have a family at all.' The girl's father raised two fingers, signifying the two-day ultimatum. They all left, laughing.

"Darshan stood in front of his house, dazed, his eyes searching the dark sky. He staggered back into the house, barely making it to the cot where his son's half-dead body lay, struggling for life. He grabbed the cot leg, slumped to the floor, looking at Gupta's bandaged body. He put one hand over his bruised forehead and whispered, so as not to disturb him, 'My dear son, have faith and be strong. I know you're going to be all right. I'm here to take care of you. I'm keeping an all night vigil.'

"Darshan felt complete despair and isolation. Emotionally drained and exhausted from the trauma, he fell asleep, still holding onto the cot. It gave him some comfort knowing that his family and friends were around him, silently praying and monitoring the victim's every breath.

"Gupta made a remarkable recovery. In less than three days, he was breathing well, gaining strength and assuring his family not to worry. He told them that his body was beaten but not his spirit.

"Soon after this horrible experience," says Jamal, shaking his head at Fazal, "Darshan came to visit me, asking for advice. I told him he should go to the police and press charges.

"'I'm afraid to go to the police,' said Darshan. 'I know that I wouldn't be believed, and given the forty-eight hours notice 'to leave or else' I'm scared to death.' It took some time for Darshan to calm down.

"'I'm sorry for what happened to you Darshan,' I said, 'but I assure you that no more harm will come your way. I'll make sure that your family is safe. At Friday's prayer I'll talk to community elders and discuss the matter. It's only five days away. We'll send an influential Muslim representative to talk to the authorities. I'm confident that he'll be heard. You'll have protection and justice will be done.' Darshan embraced me, and before leaving, looked in my eyes and said, 'I trust you more than a brother, Jamal. We will lay low until Friday.'

"Friday never came," says Jamal. "The next morning, Darshan's shop was ablaze. I was among so many others who hurried to put out the fire, but it was too late. The fire was, without question premeditated. It appeared the arsonists used plenty of kerosene to douse the inside before setting it on fire. The crowd watched in horror, unable to save Darshan's property. The only thing we could do was throw water and dirt onto the adjoining shops to stop the fire from spreading. Darshan, hearing that his business had been set on fire, raced to the scene and tried to get into the shop, hoping to save some of the valuables. We pulled Darshan from the edge of the inferno and dragged him back to the street. 'Have you gone mad?' I said. 'You'll burn yourself alive. It's all over. Nothing you or we can do will save your shop.'

"'Yes, I've gone mad and I do want to kill myself,' said Darshan. 'First my son is nearly beaten to death, and now this. I don't know what to do,' he screamed, throwing his hands in the air. I grabbed his arms and ordered him to hurry home and bring his wife and children to my house. He shuddered for a moment, took a lingering look at what was his livelihood and, like a wounded animal, scuffled home. Soon, the family was at my doorstep.

"'Why? Why this much hate? What did I do to deserve this?' mourned Darshan.

"'I'm so sorry, Darshan,' I said. 'I was wrong. I didn't know that people's hatred had taken root so quickly. No time to analyze and understand their reasons; just think of ways to get out of here, and to a safe place.' Darshan lowered his head, having no choice but to go as far away as he could. As he went to get a tonga, his wife helped pack the few belongings they brought from their house.

"Haji Iftikhar, my uncle, volunteered to drive," says Jamal, "and wasted no time bringing his tonga to the house, where Darshan and his family, packed and prepared to leave, waited nervously. They hid their meager belongings under the seats, while my wife handed them a large package of food for the trip. Darshan extended his hand and dropped his house key in my hand. With teary eyes and in a barely audible voice, he whispered, 'Keep this Jamal. I leave my ancestral home in your care.'

"'I'll take care of it for a while,' I said. 'As soon as this partition matter is settled, you'll be back to claim what is rightfully yours.'

"Darshan climbed into the tonga, and, looking back, waved his hand. 'I know I'll never see you again,' he said, 'but I'll always remember you and your family, until my dying day.' Iftikhar climbed up, whistled his horse to move, and the family I had known since childhood disappeared in the darkness. The next morning, I went to check on Darshan's house. Only ghostly ruins and a charred structure remained. A few people gathered around celebrating. Someone yelled, 'Did you hear the news, Jamal?'

"I turned around to acknowledge a stranger, who came forward with a wicked grin on his face. 'Barely a mile out of Sialkot,' he said, 'they found Darshan and his family on a dirt road, along with the *tongawala*—tonga driver, murdered. The horse had been stolen, and the occupants' bodies were found near the tonga in a ditch.'

"'Oh my god,' I gasped.

"'This is what you get for helping an infidel, Jamal,' yelled another.

"I lunged, wishing I could pull their tongues out. I felt dizzy; my knees buckled and I fell to the ground unconscious. I remained home in bed for days before I had the strength to get up and meet you, Fazal. Sadly, my Uncle Iftikhar became an innocent victim, while trying to save my friend and his family."

Jamal rubs his amulet for a moment and reaches into his pocket. "Fazal, this is the key to that house. The house that was Darshan's life. I couldn't protect it or his family for even one day. I'm responsible for my uncle's death. How cruel and sad. I shouldn't have waited until Friday. I should have seen the immediacy; instead I failed miserably."

Fazal rises, extends his arms while his friend falls into a much-needed embrace, sobbing.

"I'm so, so sorry, Jamal. You've done the best you could; more than anybody could've done." Fazal trembles from hearing the shocking episode, and tightens his embrace, patting him on the back. Again, for the second time in a day he wonders if he and others can save Rurkee from the rampant violence.

"Well, my friend, it's getting dark and the *goondas*—thugs are roaming the countryside. It's too dangerous to go back to Rurkee. If you don't mind I'd like to stay with you tonight. I told my wife I might."

"Of course, Fazal you are welcome to stay with me any time you want. My home is your home. You know that."

It's a matter of only one night. I imagine my family will be safe during my absence, Fazal thinks to himself, hoping he has made the right decision.

—5—

Walled City

They walk in silence to Jamal's house, not a word said between them. Jamal's wife, sensing their weariness, greets Fazal warmly and serves them dinner. Fatigued and emotionally exhausted, they fall onto cushioned cots under the veranda and stare into the sky. Sleep eludes Fazal; he tosses and turns. The faces of Haji Iftikhar, Darshan and his family will not leave his mind. He cannot believe that Darshan and his family are gone, the innocent victims of an unthinkable atrocity. The perpetrators are still at large and perhaps will never be caught. Justice seems distant. He feels bad for Jamal who is left with unbearable guilt, feeling personally responsible for his uncle's death.

Fazal drifts into sleep as he gazes into the star-studded sky, washed by the Milky Way. He feels some solace in remembering his father telling him the Milky Way is the remnant of cosmic dust left by Prophet Mohammad's galloping white horse, as he ascends to the heavens to have audience with Allah.

Just before dawn, he is awakened by the *muezzin's* call to prayer. Soon after, atop the mosques' minarets, a dozen more join in, simultaneously calling the faithful for the Morning Prayer, in melodious Arabic.

"*As-Slat-O-Khar-Ul-Minin-Noom*, prayer is better than sleep," the message reverberates throughout the city. Fazal is not a Mosque regular. He is not a devout religious man, yet feels that he is spiritual. He tries not to miss the *Juma*—Friday prayer, and occasionally goes to the Mosque to say the Morning Prayer when he opens his shop early. He wants to answer the call, but this morning he is disheartened, and questions the actions of his fellow believers. He goes back to sleep and does not wake up until noon.

"I'm sorry. I didn't know it was so late," says Fazal.

"No need to apologize Fazal. Sleep is a great respite from pain. Let's go to the bazaar. We'll have breakfast there," says Jamal. They walk Fazal's bike, threading along a narrow street and arrive at Jamal's shop. The ancient city is coming to life.

Raja Sal built the city centuries ago and named it Sialkot, meaning Sal's abode. A centuries old walled city with a fort in the middle comes from an era when rulers built with two objectives in mind: controlling their subjects, and warding off attacks by neighboring rulers or hostile tribes. Even today, one can imagine the ghosts of ruthless rulers dancing with joy, as well as the cries of tormented prisoners, seeping out of dilapidated fort walls. The city thrived and grew into a commercial center, having trade arteries called bazaars radiating from the city-center fort. Each bazaar manufactured and sold specialized goods and services: cloth, gold, metal, spices, pottery and produce.

The city stayed unchanged until the British colonized the subcontinent in the eighteenth century. Throughout the country, they built and established military garrisons for defense, and housed the armed forces in cantonment areas. The city changed significantly as they widened the streets, improved transportation and linked this military establishment to Lahore, a city of one million, the capital of Punjab.

Jamal's son rolls up the metal doorway to open the shop early, arranges the goods out front and waits for customers. A teenaged assistant attends, waiting for orders. Jamal tells him, "Hurry to the corner shop and bring us hot breakfast."

"Okay sir," says the smiling young man.

"When we finish our breakfast, I want you to bring us the best *puris*—deep fried tortillas, paper-thin, and *halva*—sweetened cream of wheat mixed with butter and pistachio nuts. And don't forget the chai," Jamal reminds him.

"Aye, Irfan," Jamal tells his son, "as soon as your uncle and I finish eating, you can take his order and get together what he needs for Rurkee."

Fazal looks up and scans the bazaar more intensely than he has ever done before.

The shops on either side of the narrow road extend as far as he can see. Jamal's twenty-year-old son, who is wearing a blue *shalwar kameez*—baggy trousers and loose tunic, squats in the middle of the shop. A scale hangs from a beam above, swinging in front of him. Behind him sits the cash safe that looks more like an oversized metal piggybank than a cash register. The bright orange canvas awning, tied to the shop wall, stretches out to the other two corners, supported by bamboo poles that shade the merchandise stacked in front of the storefront.

On one side of the shop, foodstuffs of green lentils, orange split peas, black garbanzo beans, white basmati rice, wheat flour, golden chickpea flour and brown and white sugar fill large gunny sacks, all mounded as high as the goods' shape and density will allow. On the other side, colorful spices: red cayenne, yellow turmeric, curry powder, whole and ground red chili peppers, plus both white fine granular and quartz like rock salt are stacked in small sacks. The fragrant spices: cloves, cardamom, cumin, coriander, cinnamon along with tea and tobacco fill the aluminum canisters to the brim. Different colored and shaped inverted cones are visible, while cinnamon wafts over the setting.

Behind Irfan, the wall is stacked with cans and boxes of varying sizes, colors and forms, storing more items. The large canisters of mustard oil and kerosene fuel sit on the ground as if trespassing on the Bazaar, moving half way into the street. To complete the scene, Jamal's smiling son sits proudly, striking a youthful portrait-like pose, beckoning passersby to get the best products in the land.

Similarly, various displays draw attention to goldsmiths, cobblers, cloth merchants, tailors and barbers, along with other shopkeepers set up for maximum exposure to attract customers. Hawkers, displaying their wares and broadcasting their prices fill the street. Bicycles, rickshaws, donkey carts and tongas occupy whatever space is left. At times, the asphalt disappears as shoppers and sellers shimmy between the encroaching banks of shops. How people move in and out of the bazaar is a wonder. Courtesy and competition work hand in hand. Fazal turns to look behind him. His admiration for his favorite Sialkot bazaar is now marred by one shameful act of hatred: the charred ruins of Darshan's beautiful shop.

The slim shop boy sets a small folding table in front of the rattan bench and places the neatly wrapped food on plates. Fazal and Jamal eat quietly, without exchanging a word. No sooner do they finish the tasty brunch than the boy brings the *puri* and *halva* for dessert, and sweetened hot chai. Jamal asks Fazal what he needs to take for his shop. Fazal thinks for a minute and says he does not feel like taking much.

"I know you are heart-broken, but take some merchandise, at least some of the lighter items," insists Jamal.

"Yeah, okay. I'll take five pounds of tea, ten pounds of sugar and small bags of cayenne, salt, turmeric, cumin and cinnamon. I'll take some candy, definitely some candy, and a bunch of biscuits; that's what they eat when inflicted with fever. Hmm . . . black tea and crunchy biscuits. I sell them a lot. Lately, everyone considers chai the cure for every curse, including malaria. Even children have developed a taste for it, and often fool their parents with fake illnesses just to have chai and biscuits, normally forbidden to young ones due to caffeine and cost."

He packs the goods neatly and efficiently, arranging them inside the bicycle saddles. Fazal rechecks the packages, the air in the tires and then hops on the bike saying, "Put it on my tab. I'll see you in a few weeks and thanks for being a great friend. *Khuda Hafiz*, God be with you."

"Khuda Hafiz." Jamal waves, as is his habit, touching the amulet, while his friend disappears into the crowd, still mourning the murders of his dear Uncle Iftikhar and friend Darshan.

Fazal amazes people by the way he packs the saddle baskets and gunny sacks on his bike and skillfully pedals along the ribbon-like trails winding between the fields. Fazal can't wait to get home. Lost in thought, he compiles a mental checklist and rehearses what and how much he is going tell the people of Rurkee.

I'll share everything with my wife and friends. I'll tell them the whole story. The unrest in Sialkot; Hindus and Sikhs being harassed and victimized by Muslims, forced to flee eastward, hoping to cross the border not yet defined. I'll tell the entire tragic account of my friend Darshan; his family and Haji Iftikhar's brutal murder. I'll be the bearer of bad news and warn them that the storm of hatred has erupted and will engulf the city of Sialkot; and that our little village is in its direct path.

He arrives at the village. He feels it was a fast trip. Preoccupied with Sialkot's mayhem, and with a lighter load, he made good time. He climbs off his bike and rings the spring-activated bike bell announcing his arrival. His wife comes out running, greets him with a smile and helps him unload. He helps himself to a glass of water and lies down on the cot in the courtyard. Rakhi makes chai and brings it to him, only to find he has fallen asleep.

"Fazal, here is your tea." She nudges him awake. "How was your trip? You stayed, and I see you didn't bring many provisions this time. Is everything all right? How are your favorite businessmen, Darshan and Jamal?" she asks.

"Oh, everything's okay. Darshan and Jamal and everybody else in Sialkot are just fine and wonderful." He decides to tell nothing, nothing to his wife or anybody else. A lie, in this case, he thinks, is a virtue. He wants his village to be safe. He hopes the hatred will not reach his village and if they are lucky, it will just blow over, sparing it like a neighborhood outside the path of a tornado. "Anything new here, Rakhi? You and the children were okay in my absence? I was worried," he says, changing the subject, afraid to chance spilling the truth.

"Yes, we made it. It was a long and frightening night. Fazal, I didn't sleep a wink. Mobs clamored and horses rumbled until dawn."

"Mobs in Rurkee?"

"No, there were no mobs in Rurkee. The ruckus was some distance away. It was scary though."

"Oh Allah—I'm sorry, I should have come home. I promise you I'll never stay away again, not even for one night."

"Oh, one more thing, Makhan's mom, Tara came by to say that her brother Aneel and his wife Zareena are pressing to set a date for Dalair and Sarita's wedding. They are thinking sometime in September."

"That's only five months after Vaisakhi fair," comments Fazal, wondering what the next five months will bring.

—6—

Glimpses

Fazal Din rises early and opens the shop well before sunrise, just in time to give his son, Karim and his friend Makhan, a handful of peanut brittle, along with his routine advice. "Be careful, stay out of trouble, watch out for each other and study hard."

The shop is the meeting place for Makhan Singh, a ten-year old Sikh boy, and Karim Din, his Muslim friend since first grade. They look forward to Fazal's generous treats that make their long walk to school enjoyable. They eagerly skip along the dusty lane at six in the morning, heading to their fifth grade class in Chowinda, about four miles away along the railway line.

Fazal does not expect many customers at this hour, because his major mission is to unpack and stock the merchandise he has brought from Sialkot, fifteen miles to the north. Meanwhile, Rakhi, in one quick motion pulls out spindly firewood logs from the open hearth, smothering them into the ashes. Holding a hot pot with edges of her *dupatta*—head scarf, she decants the aromatic chai, a strong boiled blend of black tea, cardamom, cinnamon, sugar and milk into a cup while deflecting the smoke rising from the embers. She walks across the open courtyard, opens the shop's half door, and hands her husband the cup. "Hey, here's your daily dose."

Fazal just smiles while taking the cup. He sits on a well-worn thin cushion and leans against a thick pillow propped up against the shop wall. A kerosene lamp hangs by a cord from the ceiling. The turned down wick casts a glow into the dimly lit room. Recent rains and the north wind have chilled the early spring morning. To ward off the cold he folds his legs to his chest and snugly wraps a woolen shawl around his body like a mummy. Between his turban and the shawl, the face is the only part of his body exposed to the elements. He wraps both hands around the steaming cup, enjoys slurping the hot sweetened chai, taking comfort from the warmth radiating from the cup. Being up early, tired from the previous day's bicycle trip loaded with shop supplies, and emotionally exhausted from the news of Darshan's demise, he is half asleep.

Dreamily, he thinks of Karim and Makhan, who are on their way to school, and feels content, as they have opportunities he never had. He imagines that one day they will be successful men and will achieve much higher social status than he has ever had. He puts the unfinished cup down by his side to rest a few minutes. He tries to forget Darshan's misery and Iftikhar's brutal murder, hoping it won't be a forerunner to uncertainty and unrest in Punjab's division. Pushing fear aside, he manages happier thoughts for Karim and his friend Makhan's future. His half-closed eyes continue to droop until he falls asleep.

In dreams he is transported to a sofa, in an elegant living room within a bungalow style house. He is wearing a fashionable silk *shalwar kameez*—baggy trousers and loose tunic, a woolen cap and a pair of thick woolen socks that tightly fit in his shiny brown sandals. The sparse embers from the fire, lit the night before, still radiate soothing warmth from the black cast-iron wood stove standing against the brick wall. The early morning sunlight, streaming through the windows makes the room even warmer.

He looks outside. His gaze rests on the covered porch where a uniformed army driver is polishing the already well-cleaned car. Two whitewashed brick columns support the porch roof. The open sides form three spacious curved arches where the overhanging bougainvilleas rustle in the breeze. Beyond the lush green lawn, rose bushes line a nine-foot high brick wall that surrounds the bungalow grounds. Broken pieces of sharp glass embedded in the concrete cap keep out intruders while defining the perimeter of the stylish residence. He is overjoyed with the luxury. Satisfaction suffuses him because he is proud of his son's status. He waits for Colonel Karim to step into the car that will chauffeur him to his military headquarters. After the Colonel leaves he orders the servant to bring him a hot breakfast.

Fazal jolts back to reality when his wife opens the small creaking wooden half door that connects the shop to the courtyard. "Hey, Karim's father, are you daydreaming?" she says, jutting her arm forward. "Daydreaming doesn't get the job done. Here's another hot cup. Now get to work."

Opening his eyes, Fazal takes the cup and looks at the unpacked merchandise. Pushing up to his feet, he takes a quick inventory while sipping the steaming, milky tea.

I must be getting old, he thinks. *It seems only yesterday that I could make the thirty mile round trip to the city market, bring back the goods, unpack and shelve them the same day. But then,* he rationalizes, *I was only twenty and worry free, without a wife and two children to take care of.*

The family lives in the simple mud and straw house that Fazal inherited from his father. It has a flat roof and sits at the corner of two narrow dirt lanes. Up three steps, and through swinging double doors that pivot on creaking wooden pegs, is a spacious courtyard. On the right side is a covered veranda. Straight through the courtyard is the largest room, accessed by wooden double doors. A small patio on the left is sandwiched between a storage room and the shop in front. From the patio, sixteen earthen steps rise, partially supported by an arch that leads to the flat roof. A two-foot wall borders the rooftop for security and privacy. The cooking area nestles under the stairs. On windy or rainy days the open hearth, fired by wood and cow dung is pushed under the arch, providing limited shelter for Rakhi while she prepares family meals.

Fazal feels lucky to work next to his house. The small shop's window opens to the courtyard next to the pass-through half door. Another door opens to the street outside. When closed for business, Fazal locks the door from the inside and comes through the half door into the courtyard, locking it behind him for peace of mind.

Rakhi taps on the door and hands him his breakfast. At five feet, with a slender build, she has a small chiseled face. Always wearing a *dupatta*, she seems very serious when not being watched. However, when she talks, a shy wide smile welcomes friends, showing her perfectly even white teeth. The house is her domain, where she focuses, works enthusiastically all day and tenaciously fulfills her duties.

Fazal takes the *chapatti* plate—a round hand woven reed basket from his wife, turns up the lamp wick for more light, and sits on the floor mat to eat. The aroma of the food rising through the napkin makes his mouth water. He quickly removes the hand printed cotton napkin and starts eating his favorite breakfast: a plate full with *parathas* and a bowl of left over *saag*—spiced spinach paste cooked in butter. Holding the bowl with his left hand, he scoops up the *saag* and hungrily takes the first bite. He eats slowly and savors the last bite by wiping the bowl clean; washing down the breakfast with a full glass of *lassi*, a drink blended from whey whipped in water and salt to a frothy liquid, and swipes his moustache clean with his hand. A *paratha* or two every day with left over vegetables or lentil curry from the previous night's dinner usually is the breakfast. He slides the dishes into the courtyard and opens the shop door.

Fazal's strong, muscular body makes him a handsome middle-aged man. Almost six feet, he is very tall for an Indian male. He has high cheekbones; a slightly upturned thick black moustache enhances his bronzed face. He looks striking, and dresses well for a village shopkeeper. On special occasions, like *Eid*—a Muslim religious holiday, and Vaisakhi—the spring harvest fair, and for weddings, he wears a silk *kurta*—collarless long sleeved tunic, which gracefully drapes over a brushed cotton sarong that touches the gold embroidered curled-toe sandals. He completes the outfit by putting a well-starched sparkling, indigo, muslin turban upon his head, carefully adjusting its pleated tail on his back, becoming the handsome Raja.

While he waits for customers, he unpacks the merchandise, filling containers and stocking the shelves. Ready to sell, he opens the door, letting a swath of morning sun light on the floor, warming his thin worn out cushion. Fazal is open for business.

—7—

The Walk

Karim and Makhan are inseparable. They walk to school together every day. Karim wears a white *shalwar,* a light blue *kameez,* and well-used mended socks slipped into old sandals. His friend dresses in a red *kameez,* a straw colored *dhoti*—sarong, and curled toe sandals with thin socks. Both have shawls covering their heads, ears and neck, draping around their bodies and secured in front with a loose knot. These shawls are made of *khaddar*—a homespun coarse cotton that is soft to the touch but keeps the body warm on cool occasions. The straps of the two-pocketed khaki, canvas school bags are looped over their shoulders.

The boys leave the village by walking on a ridged path between the sweet-smelling wheat fields. It is so narrow that they walk quietly in single file. After thirty minutes or so, they come to a rutted, narrow dirt lane. Walking side by side now, they quickly resort to friendly horseplay. They push each other into the fields, grab and pull on shawls, while they sprint away from each other, their shoulder bags swaying back and forth. Soon other children from neighboring villages join the journey. They look forward to seeing Makhan's cousin, Dalair Gill, who is a seventeen-year-old tenth grader. He is glad to connect with them both and watches over them, without giving the impression that they are under his protection. By the time they walk for an hour and a half to get to school, the group swells to more than thirty students.

They see the school in the distance next to the railway station. The U shaped brick building sits behind the three-foot-walled courtyard. The headmaster's office and assembly hall is toward the front, while classrooms flank each side. School assemblies, games and athletics take place in the courtyard. Teachers frequently use the open space to hold classes on sunny days in winter and under shade trees in summer, which the boys really enjoy. The wrought iron entrance gate hosts a sign that reads:

KNOWLEDGE IS LIGHT
CHOWINDA HIGH SCHOOL

The school staff and 200 students are diverse. The headmaster is a Hindu, three teachers are Sikhs and the fourth one, as well as the school clerk are Muslims. Similarly, the students are Sikhs, Hindus and Muslims, representing the major religious upbringing of these youngsters. No girls are in the school. At this time, the prevailing thought is: 'Girls don't need an education.' — *and remains to this day?*

Chowinda's population is over ten thousand. Most residents live in mud houses, while prosperous farmers and merchants reside in comfortable whitewashed brick homes. Two major dirt roads intersect in midtown leading in and out of town. These unpaved town streets boast a friendly, noisy bazaar atmosphere. Goldsmiths, blacksmiths, shoemakers, cloth merchants, butchers, confectioners, fruit and vegetable sellers have their wooden-stall shops set along the roadway. They bring their wares daily and sell them to locals as well as to the shopkeepers from neighboring villages. Two imposing mosques and a temple dominate the Chowinda skyline. The mosques' minarets and the temple cupola can be seen from miles away.

At the edge of town and close to the railway station and the school, there are four small food and snack shacks. Adjoining these shops is a tonga stand where drivers with their horse-drawn carriages wait for fares. The majority of their fares are passengers disembarking from the train that stops twice a day. The tonga drivers wait endlessly, gossiping with the shopkeepers and drinking dark sweetened hot chai. When the train arrives, they rush toward the open platform soliciting business. Each one peeks intensely into a train compartment, looks back and forth, and even grabs the potential fare by the arm, constantly charming and convincing passengers that he has the best tonga with the best rates. As the afternoon train leaves, the snack stalls close, tongas disappear and school closes soon afterwards.

The colorful main bazaar at Chowinda stays open until late evening. The shops lock up late at night; the entire town goes dark with the exception of a few oil or kerosene lamps that dimly light the houses.

Today, teachers take advantage of the sun and hold classes in the courtyard, where the breezeless sunny day offers a relatively warm respite from the cool classrooms. Makhan, Karim, and other fifth graders study *Urdu*, history and math. In the last period, the students practice multiplication tables, chanting these tables repeatedly to commit them to memory. The intense rhythmic singsong is engaging, yet their ears are tuned to the closing school bell. As soon as the bell rings, they pour out of the compound and head home to their villages. School is over and Makhan and Karim walk briskly alongside Dalair.

"Hey, Dalair Gill, you're a lucky man. Soon, you'll be done with school. You won't be walking miles to sit in boring classes. You'll marry and work on the farm with your dad," says Karim.

"Get married to whom? I heard that my sister was getting betrothed to someone other than Dalair," Makhan teases.

"Why?" asks Karim.

"Dalair isn't good enough for Sarita. My sister is too pretty to be his wife," replies Makhan.

"I'm glad school is almost over. I don't care for it much," complains Dalair. "My dad insisted that I should at least finish high school. You don't need schooling to farm."

"You go to school only to chaperone us. As far as I am concerned, I wish you'd drop out, get married, and then we can be free of your supervision," teases Karim.

Makhan looks at Karim disapprovingly and turns to Dalair to say confidently, "I think Uncle is right. You should finish high school and go to college."

Makhan speaks carefully, gauging Dalair's reaction and continues, "You know what? I plan to get as much education as possible. After I finish here, I plan to go to college in Sialkot. It's a big city. There's a lot to learn and do in big cities."

"What are you going to do with all that schooling?" questions Karim.

"Oh. I'll be a big officer in the government. I need an education to become a big man and get away from this hard village life," says Makhan. Dalair gives friendly chase and pushes them both, showing disapproval of their teasing. Both keep a safe distance from him for a while.

Throughout these moments Dalair imagines looking into Sarita's oval face—seeing that slight dimple appear whenever she slowly breaks into a smile. Black sculpted eyebrows lift inquisitively above round, dark brown eyes when she tilts her head playfully from side to side, displaying her humorous nature. A gently pointed chin complements her wavy dark hair that barely shows under her *dupatta*. At five feet two, she reaches Dalair's chin. Fringed by long curling eyelashes, her eyes draw him far into the future. During this thoughtful respite, he dreams of their happy life together.

Makhan, on the other hand, likes school and pores over his books at night, warming his hands between his knees. At ten, he shows signs of muscle along his broad shoulders. Thick eyebrows above deep-set almond eyes and rounded cheeks express his serious nature, except when he laughs and dimples appear in his cheeks. Small furrows gather above his nose when he gets exasperated. His dark hair extends into a topknot.

Karim indulges in sweets, but is scrawny and limber with angular features. From his dimpled chin to the top of his forehead, his unkempt straight hair frames his face. His ears protrude slightly, and dense, slender eyebrows top his wide-set oval eyes. He has not given much thought to the future. He goes to school because it is mandatory and because it gives him a chance to visit his friends.

"No. No. I was only joking," says Makhan. "If you buy us some candy and peanut brittle from Uncle Fazal, not only will we stop bothering you, we can arrange a meeting with Sarita. We know when she goes to the well to fetch water."

Dalair ignores them both until they are on the outskirts of his village. Dalair lives with his dad—Aneel Gill, mom—Zareena, and his seven-year old sister—Berket, in Kotli, a small village close to Rurkee. Aneel Gill is Makhan's uncle, Tara's older brother. His home is modest, and has two acres of farmland situated between Kotli and Rurkee. He keeps a water buffalo for milk and a Brahma bull for plowing, drawing well water and irrigating the small fields of wheat, corn, vegetables and sugar cane.

As the three boys talk, and tease one another, the distance from school to home seems shorter. Before they know it, they are at a small, low-slung mud shed where Aneel keeps farm tools and equipment, next to his leased sugar cane field. Three men are busily setting up machinery for making sugar the next day.

"*Sat Sari Kal Apu*," says Dalair, giving the Sikh greeting.

"Hey boys, how was school today?" Aneel glances up while wiping his hands with an old rag, removing the grime from oiling the machine gears.

"It was lots of fun. We studied math and science," Makhan replies enthusiastically.

"Father, it was boring. I couldn't wait to get home," declares Dalair. "The best part is that tomorrow is Sunday, and you know what that means? No school tomorrow."

"Uncle, can I come and help tomorrow?" asks Karim, avoiding the school day assessment.

"Of course; Makhan's parents are coming early to help. It'd be great if you come along, too," invites Aneel. Wrapped up in work preparations, he thinks less about the turmoil in Narang, and is glad that he and his neighbors have always participated in each other's farming activities: haying and making sugar.

Karim and Makhan grab sugar cane sticks from the huge stack, cut and cleaned for milling. Dalair waits for his father to finish setting up the sugar cane press and they both head home before dark. Eagerly anticipating the fun of making sugar the next day, the two younger boys continue on to Rurkee. Makhan leaves his friend at the shop and dashes home, less than two blocks away.

—8—

Sweeten the Pot

Typically, for a village farmer, Sher Singh's house is built of the same materials as Fazal's, except it is larger and laid out differently. A spacious veranda occupies one side and a small barn is situated on the other while a great room sandwiched between two bedrooms connects the veranda and the barn. The open courtyard has a guava and two *sheesham*—broad-leaved deciduous cottonwood type trees, for shade. The yard houses farm animals in their designated stalls. The buffalo sits and regurgitates her cud. Roped to a stake, a Brahma bull looks weary from the previous day's plowing. A donkey munches on hay and stands next to a small two-wheeled cart. A goat, tied to the tree looks all around with amazement. The fodder and water troughs sit in the middle of the menagerie. On wintry cold nights, they all share the small barn. The whole yard looks like a petting zoo.

A *toka*—fodder cutter is a must for a farmer. Used for chopping hay, it occupies one corner under the veranda. Well water and outhouses are nonexistent, so everyone uses a communal well and fields for nature's call.

Makhan's mother, Tara wakes up at dawn every day. She hoists two fire-baked clay pitchers, holding them on her ample hips, and strolls to the communal well to draw water. A goatskin bag tied to a long rope is lowered with a pulley apparatus to draw the water from the well. She fills the pitchers and carefully stacks them on top of a donut rolled cloth cushion resting atop her head just above the pulled back bun. She carries the water pitchers home, carefully balancing them like a trained circus performer. Women visit, gossip and even arrange their children's marriages along the fields' pathways and while waiting at the well. Tara sits down carefully, unloads the pitchers one by one and places them on a squat wooden platform next to the open kitchen area.

Before cooking breakfast, she churns the butter and makes *lassi*. Her golden brown hands resemble root balls, toughened and chapped from years of these outdoor household chores. When she gently lays the flattened round dough on the hot pan surface, moving it around to brown the sides and steam bubbles to the top, breakfast has begun. Her husband, Sher, wakes up their children.

Tara prepares a large brunch for her family, her brother Aneel's family and about half a dozen other people who help extract the sugar-cane juice for making brown sugar. Pooling the voluntary work force from the village completes the process, from plantings and harvests to house construction, throughout the year.

Makhan and Sher wash up and start the morning chores. Sher feeds the animals, cleans up the animal waste and piles it on top of the dung heap. Excited, Makhan wastes no time getting the donkey cart ready for the trip to the fields. He feeds the donkey, waters and brushes him. He loves calling him *Tez*—the fast one, nicknaming the beast himself.

"It's going to be an easy, fun trip today, buddy. You have to pull us only a short distance, and as soon we get there you can lie around all day. Then you can bring us home in the evening," he whispers in the donkey's ear.

Tez wiggles his ears, acknowledging the good news. Makhan, while holding the rein in one hand and gently petting with the other, backs him into the cart. He fastens, cinches, buckles, threads and loops several leather straps, securely harnessing Tez. He double checks all the leather, and is pleased that his petting and talking has resulted in Tez's cooperation. The small flatbed cart is secured on an iron axle with a wooden wheel on each side. Three wooden panels drop into six holes as sideboards. He puts a bucket of water near Tez, slides his hand over Tez's head and says, "We'll be on our way soon."

Tara cooks generous portions of food—a meat-potato curry, pots of *halva*, fried and sweetened cream of wheat mixed with nuts and raisins and *pakoras*—chickpea flour battered vegetables, deep-fried in mustard oil. Sher checks that all the farm tools are put away and that the other animals have enough food and water. Makhan's sister Sarita stays home, while others hop onto the cart. Tara loads up the food.

Makhan drives the cart to Karim's place, where he is waiting outside the house holding two pinwheels that his dad has given him for the trip. He jumps up and enthusiastically ties the pinwheels on each end of the front sideboards. Makhan's father takes over the reins and orders Tez to go. Tez pulls the cart, first slowly, then gathers momentum, and paces comfortably, heading to Kotli's spreading fields. A bell atop Tez's head plume jingles as he trots along the narrow dirt path and the colorful pinwheels spin around, making the cart look like a carnival ride. Arriving at the field, Makhan frees Tez, who quickly wanders a few feet away and lies down under a sparse acacia tree, exhausted. Food and water is placed nearby so he can help himself at his own leisure. Aneel's family and helpers are already hard at work.

Men do the heavy work, while women stir the sugar juice pots and feed the crew. Sher and others gather up machetes and start sizing the sugar cane, piling the sticks near the press. A hand-powered press squeezes the sugar juice out of the cane sticks. The juice simmers in a huge cauldron on an open hearth fired by wood, cow dung and dried up sugar cane skins. As the concentrate turns to granules, the cauldron is emptied on muslin cloths for drying. As Tara, the short one, and Zareena, the tall one stir the juice, they notice that it is almost noon and the crew is tired, as they have been working since dawn.

"It's time for lunch, everyone. Stop, wash up and come get your food," they announce as they partially pull out the logs from the hearth turning the heat down.

The cool humid air, under a clear blue sky, sinks to the ground. The radiating heat from the open hearth warms their toes, while the sweet caramel scent of simmering sugar cane juice fills the area. Tara uncovers the food containers and lays out a buffet on the cart bed near the tree. The aroma, wafting through the air from the fried, buttered and spiced spread makes mouths water; their hunger intensifies. The sugar cane operation comes to a standstill. The men eat *parathas*, *pakoras* and pickles to their heart's content, and drink *lassi* from a communal bowl; the women and children follow. Tara uncovers the *halva* bowl and the team gathers around the fire to enjoy dessert. All sense that the crop is producing a lot of juice. They rattle off news about the weather, pending storms and the upcoming fair. Aneel heartily joins in. Although Narang is on his mind, he does not say a word.

After a half hour of rest, the work begins again. Makhan and Karim try cranking the sugar cane press on their own. They can only do this work under Dalair's strict supervision. Their help is more play than work. After a couple of hours they ask to go back home to Rurkee. Getting their wish immediately, each grabs a pinwheel and starts a brisk walk home. They blow fiercely, spin around and dash forward while holding the pinwheels in front of them like hand-held mirrors. The wheels spin wildly. Once at Fazal's shop, they plop down on the floor, leaning against the cushions.

"*Aslamo Elaikum*," they say, filling Fazal in on their wonderful day.

"Uncle, no candy for us today. We've had enough sugarcane and juice to last us a week," says Makhan.

As the men go back to work, Tara and her sister-in-law, Zareena, pickup, wash and stack the dishes. They take over stirring the cauldron. Zareena handles the spatula and Tara tends the fire. Zareena leans over the huge pot, asking Tara to push a log a bit farther into the fire. Tara complies and looks at Zareena momentarily, her gold nose stud sparkling.

"Tara, I think we should set a wedding date for Dalair and Sarita," proclaims Zareena.

"Wedding date?" Tara repeats softly, caught by surprise. "Sarita's father thinks we should, at least, wait another year," she counsels.

"Why wait another whole year?" asks Zareena, tossing her long braid over her shoulder.

"My husband feels we don't have enough money for the wedding," says Tara. "As you know, the last two years have been hard for people and harder yet for us. Due to the extended drought, the last two seasons haven't brought good harvests. It looks like a bumper crop this year, though. The rains have blessed us all," she notes. Remembering the dry clods of dirt, she is always hopeful that a new season will bring improved yields. "The tall corn stalks are loaded with cobs, and the dense sugarcane fields are ready to burst with juice. Look at the beautiful mustard that stretches as far as one can see. Your eyes see nothing but yellow. This year we expect a record crop to bring us all that we need for buying the rest of the dowry. We want a festive occasion, and to spend generously for the wedding activities. It'll be an unforgettable wedding for Sarita. My husband dreams of sending his daughter off with honor," Tara says, pulling her *dupatta* forward, then adjusting it back with her hand over her bun of tied hair. She squints up at her friend, shading her eyes from the sun. "We have worked on Sarita's dowry from the day she was born. You know that a girl's parents start saving for the wedding even before she takes her first step. Not a day goes by when we don't think of our daughter's future. We worry constantly, and are so happy to have ended our quest to make a good match. My dear Zareena, nearly everything is bought except the gold jewelry. The cost of the gold these days is over the top," explains Tara, her glass bangles jangling when she thrusts her arms toward the fields. "With God's blessing, this harvest will give us the money to buy the pure gold jewelry."

"Dowry? Sister, don't worry about the dowry. You're giving us your daughter. If that isn't enough, what is? What else would we want? We're so looking forward to welcoming Sarita to our family. We're so excited and can't wait to show off the prettiest daughter-in-law Kotli will ever have. Dowry! Dowry comes from worldly things that have no feelings and cannot provide love. We get what's in our stars. God gives and God can take it away. Worldly things come and go. It's the love and friendship that really matter." Zareena eases Tara's anxiety by touching her hand gently and giving her an assuring squeeze. "Tara, please don't worry, I know what you are saying. When we got married, people weren't greedy. It was the match and the family that mattered.

An yea - dowry... men have to be paid handsomely to agree to wed a lousy woman...

Of course, a small reasonable dowry was offered to honor the tradition and to give the newlyweds a running start. Nowadays some parents are greedy and put unreasonable demands on a girl's family. Dowry can be a good thing, if it's free of greed and demands."

"Zareena, I know it too well. My niece married into a well-placed family in Chowinda. She has been married over six years and has two beautiful children. Even today, she is picked on, harassed and abused. Her in-laws taunt her, call her names, and beat her. They constantly remind her that she didn't bring a decent dowry and that she's lucky her husband hasn't sent her back to her parents. She's emotionally shattered. Whenever I see her, she can't hold back the tears. She is miserable and blames herself, not her husband or his family. She's not the only one; there are so many others like her. I don't want this to happen to my dear daughter." Tara chokes with emotion. Even knowing Zareena for years, these fears still percolate through her thoughts.

"What are you talking about? I know this happens more than people realize. But we are one family. I promise you that if my son even once looks at Sarita with angry eyes or touches her abusively, I will poke his eyes out and break his hands. Let's set an early date so that I can bring my daughter home." She nudges Tara's hip to cheer her up.

"But Sarita is our only daughter," says Tara. "We would like to give her the best. Besides, what will people say? 'Sher did not marry-off his daughter. He just pushed her out of his life.' I know you don't care about these things, but these centuries old traditions just stick to us. We want to hold our heads high on the special day." Tara, soft of heart, looks at Zareena with misty eyes and squeezes her hand, conveying more than gratitude. "Thank you my dear sister. Promise me that you'll go with me to Chowinda to see the goldsmith. I'm not that good at bargaining," she confesses.

"It's a deal. You select the design and I'll do the bargaining," says Zareena in jest, her dimpled chin revealing her pleasure at the thought. They look at each other. Smiling is not enough. Spontaneously they hug each other and agree to pressure their husbands to set a September wedding date. Emotionally unsteady, but feeling light from their mutual love and understanding, they resume their neglected tasks.

As he looks toward his wife, Zareena and sister Tara, Aneel asks Sher, "What are those two up to? Knowing them, they're cooking up something, and it's more than sugar juice," he remarks wistfully.

All work until dusk. Tara is right about this being a good year. Sher gathers pots and pans, and then helps Tara onto the cart. They wave goodbye as he orders Tez, "Take us home to Rurkee." Tara sits quietly, lost in her daughter's wedding plans and hopefully bright future. Sher looks back one more time and says, "Aneel, see you tomorrow, bright and early." Aneel waves back, wondering how much Sher knows about the turmoil and unrest in Narang. Did Fazal tell him anything?

—9—

Changing Tunes

March's spring shows benevolent, life-giving signs. Greenery abounds. The wheat, corn, barley, sugar cane and mustard fields are taller and greener than last year. Dainty yellow flowers climb the mustard stalks. Deciduous trees, growing spottily in the fields, have branches loaded with white buds. Some are half-open and poised toward the trees' canopies. Many birds have appeared with their numbers increasing daily. They perch, flutter from tree to tree and occasionally dive into the fields for food. Melodious mating calls fill the air.

Abundant rains have filled the small pond at the edge of the village. Two old swarthy banyan trees spread mightily over the pond. The night's light drizzle mists the pastoral scene. The morning sun creeps into the blue sky. Fazal looks up to admire the day and opens his shop. After dusting and rearranging a few items, he sits down with a cup of chai. Since the weather is quite pleasant, he wears only a cotton *dhoti* and a shirt. Folding his legs into a yoga position, he grabs the shop ledger, adjusts his *dhoti* and leans over the paper work resting on his lap. He checks the inventory and makes a shopping list. He especially takes a close look at the back of the ledger and studies the names of people who owe him money. Business is brisk this morning. In the first two hours, he has a number of customers spending significant amounts. He welcomes a great business day.

Shafkat Hussein, on the way to the village's largest farm, enters the shop and extends a greeting, "*Aslamo Elaikum*, Fazal Din."

"*Wa Elaikum Asslam,*" Fazal smiles.

"What a beautiful day," says Shafkat, a Muslim farmer who owns twenty acres of productive farmland next to Sher Singh's. Most have only an acre or less. Shafkat's spread boasts a water well, equipment and animal shelter, a dozen farm animals, two work horses and an Arabian stallion. The three resident sharecroppers add to his standing as a respected figure in the community.

At five-foot six, slightly overweight and in his mid forties, he has a round face, thick eyebrows and a wide forehead that looks even wider due to his receding hairline. A well-groomed short, gray beard and moustache cover most of his face, making his nose look smaller. He dresses in fancy clothes and turbans, riding his horse, while inspecting his farm; always pushing his workers to exert themselves for longer hours. He likes stopping frequently at Fazal's for chats.

Having the largest house, and full time live-in domestic help, Shafkat displays an air of importance. Although Fazal is better off than most villagers, he is no match for Shafkat's wealth and status. Yet Shafkat is impressed with Fazal and has genuine respect for qualities he secretly admires. He envies Fazal's successful business, and his knowledge of politics, along with his musical skill—his ability to direct the village *bhangra*—Punjabi folk dance team for the Vaisakhi fair. Even more, he envies Fazal's well-known ability to ride a fully loaded bicycle. Shafkat is a natural on horseback, but is terrified to even think about getting on a bike. Today, he decides to have a serious conversation with Fazal.

"Welcome. Welcome. Please have a seat," Fazal says, pointing to the cushions on the floor.

"Thank you." Shafkat sits down and gets comfortable by leaning his left elbow on two stacked pillows, holding his chin with the other arm against his chest.

"So, how's business? How's my sister Rakhi?" Shafkat says 'sister' as a respectful gesture commonly used by men to address the wives of their friends.

"She's fine." Fazal pauses, opening the side door and calling in the same breath, "Aye Rakhi, Shafkat sahib is here. Please make us a pot of chai."

"How is our scholar, Karim?" Shafkat asks.

"He's fine too. He and Makhan are at school. They are such close friends. They can't stay away from each other. You couldn't tell them apart if it wasn't for that big hair bun on Makhan's head."

"You mean *kes* and *kanga*?" says Shafkat, referring to the young boy's hair bun and the wooden comb. Sikhs proudly wear five items to distinguish themselves from others: *kes*, body hair never to be trimmed or shaved; *kanga*, a wooden comb tucked in the bun of head hair, usually gathered and tied into a knot; *kirpan*, a dagger hanging at the waist; *kara*, a steel bangle worn on the right wrist and *kachera*, special boxer shorts worn at all times.

"Yeah," chuckles Fazal.

Rakhi brings a steaming pot and two cups, and hands the tray to Shafkat with one hand while adjusting her *dupatta* with the other, "Brother Shafkat, how's everybody in your family?"

"They're good. Thanks for the hot drink," Shafkat acknowledges, and turns to Fazal, resuming the conversation.

"Fazal, I ran into Rifaqat yesterday. You remember Rifaqat, don't you?"

"Yes, of course. How can I forget? That *badmash*—rascal, who is a blight on his family and has given our village a bad name. He's the one who forcefully usurped a piece of Aneel Gill's land last year. Aneel is still mad, and madder yet that he doesn't have the money to hire a lawyer to reclaim it."

"Yep, he's the one, Fazal. He told me, with a wicked smirk, that as soon as Aneel and the other infidels leave, he's going to take over the rest of their land. He had the nerve to ask, 'You wouldn't mind Mr. Shafkat, would you? You have enough land. For you, a couple of acres is nothing, but it certainly would make a difference for me. Will you help me when the time comes?'"

"'Help you?' I yelled. 'Don't expect a shady deal from me. How do you know that Punjab will be partitioned? Moreover, even if it is, how can you be sure that Aneel and his family will just leave?'" I yelled louder, and he just walked away as if he knows something I don't.

"Fazal, you're a smart man. I've seen you bent over the newspapers you bring from the city. You go to Sialkot for business, meet, and talk to many people. If any one does, you have a finger on the political pulse and are tuned into current affairs. What are these rumors I hear about the *Angrez* leaving India?" Shafkat asks quietly, thrusting his chin forward, while holding the hot cup with both hands.

"Now that the big war, World War II, is over, the British have agreed to free India," responds Fazal.

"Do you know when? And who is going to rule India after they leave?" asks Shafkat sitting up straight.

Fazal concentrates. "I don't know for sure, but the Indian Congress insists that the sooner the British leave the better. I suppose the Congress Party would be in charge once India is freed."

Shafkat raises his eyebrows. "But what about the Muslim League?"

Fazal recalls an article. "The Congress Party is asking the Muslim League to merge with the party and form a joint government to rule India. But the Muslim League firmly demands a separate homeland for Muslims, a Pakistan."

"How will that happen?" asks Shafkat. "Do we know where the dividing line is going to be? Is Rurkee going to be in India or Pakistan? Will Muslims, Sikhs and Hindus be forced to leave their ancestral land?" He tentatively puts the emptied cup on the floor.

"I don't know the answers and I don't think anybody knows what's going to happen," Fazal notes with apprehension.

"Fazal, keep your eyes and ears open. People are hearing things and are getting nervous. The Rifaqats of Rurkee are getting bold and brazen. People are nervous; they would like to know. You can help us," says Shafkat while stroking his beard. "In the meantime, let's keep it quiet and plan something fun for the village."

"What do you propose?" queries Fazal.

"We should schedule an evening of *Heer Ranja*. It's been a while since Karamat, the singer, has come to our village to do the honor. He has a wonderful, melodious voice. I think we should invite him soon. Late March or early April would be a good time, I think. Let me know when and I'll send him a message," directs Shafkat.

Heer Ranja, the epic Punjabi love story, is filled with small vignettes, along with profound wisdom about the hopes and hurts of real life. The story, revered by all, is written in Punjabi poetry. Each year, once or twice, at night, people assemble and listen to the recitation, sung in a ballad-like rendering. Karamat, the village favorite, sits on a cot and holds the book, lit by a kerosene lamp, singing out the selected and requested lines to the crowd. Villagers sit on the ground, mesmerized.

"Shafkat Sahib, this year, I want to do something different. I'd like to surprise you and the rest of the village. Let's not invite Karamat. Instead, I'd like to bring a gramophone and play *Heer Ranja*," exclaims Fazal.

"Gramophone! Nobody has seen one. I've heard about it but I've never seen one. Do you have any idea what it is?" questions Shafkat.

"It's a small box that *Angrez* have invented to make music. They play it all the time. Shafkat Sahib, it is an amazing box. You just wind it up, put a disc on the rotating turntable and lower the needle arm onto the record. Wow! Music starts pouring out of the box like magic. The first time I heard it, I thought it was sorcery. I've contacts in Sialkot. I'm certain I can borrow it for a few days. If it's all right with you, I'd like to bring it and surprise the village." Fazal looks for approval.

"Well, my friend, if you can arrange it, that will be some treat. I'm sure everyone will be thrilled. I know I'll be."

"All right then. It's all settled. Spread the word. Instead of Karamat, *Angrez* will sing the *Heer* this year." Shafkat makes a cheer, showing his white teeth as he pushes the mustache across his lip and raises his arm in delight.

Shafkat chuckles and walks out of the shop saying, *"Khuda Hafiz."* He turns around and says with a smile, "Karim likes to come to the well with his friend Makhan to play around. Tell him he is always welcome. Actually, I love to see them both. They're good boys and always helpful in keeping the ox going."

"Thanks, I'll let them know."

"*Khuda Hafiz.*"

"*Khuda Hafiz*", replies Fazal, in good spirits, waving his hand. The word flies around the village that Fazal is bringing a magic box that sings *Heer*.

The oncoming summer dries the air. The days are hot and nights are warm and pleasant. Men, women, and children start gathering in the *daira*—a communal area next to the half-acre pond. A small brick mosque sits at the water's edge. The old spreading banyan tree forms a luscious green canopy. This popular place gives shade for people spending hot afternoons taking a siesta, while children play hop, skip and jump, hide and seek and the daring ones climb the tree despite adult warnings. Wooden plank and rope swings dangle from tree branches. *Daira* literally means circle. People come to sit in a circle and listen to the village elders who discuss important issues, make decisions, resolve community disputes and occasionally gather for fun. Across the pond, a gold domed Sikh Temple's shimmering reflection seems to reach across to the mosque. In this *Daira*, a small wooden table covered with a hand crocheted cloth sits next to a cot.

People anxiously await the gramophone's arrival with an air of disbelief. Fazal arrives. Carefree, Makhan and Karim sprint ahead of Fazal, parting the crowd. Fazal walks his bicycle, carefully balancing a metal trunk that is secured to the back carrier. Shafkat is sitting on the cot. He offers a smile and says, "Let's see what you have for us, Fazal."

Fazal stops next to the table, lowers the stand and pulls back the bicycle until it balances. He opens the trunk lid, picks up the box and carefully sets it on the table. The whispering crowd hovers in silence. People lean forward. Some stand on their toes craning their necks to catch a glimpse of the singing box. Fazal opens the top, winds up the spring and attaches the horn shaped amplifying device. He picks up the *Heer Ranja* record to wipe it clean with his sleeve. He looks at the crowd, asks for quiet and puts the disc on the rotating turntable. Fazal carefully lowers the microphone needle onto the disc. The crowd huddles together. There is pin-drop silence. All eyes are fixed on the box and some in the back cup their ears for better reception. A few scratchy moments later, a man introduces himself and starts singing the *Heer* story.

No one stirs until the record finishes playing. When it ends, people push their way to the table. With curiosity, they look at the box and inspect the side. Some even peek under the table, seeking the source of the sound. Many turn to Fazal asking, "How does it work?"

He tells them, "They hire an artist to sing in a room. As he sings, the *Angrez* captures his voice and packs it onto the disc. This special needle is then used to release the voice."

"But if the packed voice is released, why does it come out again and again when you play the disc," question some.

"I don't know the answer to that. It just does," answers Fazal irritably.

The amazed crowd is impressed by the invention but does not like the hollow, scratchy and one-dimensional singing. They express their wish that next time they want Karamat to come and sing the *Heer*.

—10—

Vaisakhi

Flat roofed Rurkee houses are built with mud, straw and sun-baked adobe bricks. The houses stand in solid lines along a network of narrow, irregular dirt lanes and winding dead-end alleys. Rurkee is level, except at the edge of the village, where a small *tibba*—plateau, rises fifty feet above the plane; a small lookout, reached by two spiral flights of stairs, sits atop. From this raised ground, Fazal can clearly see nearby villages. Fields surround the entire landscape.

Fazal loves climbing the plateau. On a warm April morning, Fazal stands at the highest point, scanning the scene—360 degrees. He spots and recognizes at least a half a dozen villages, naming them to himself. Farther out, he sees scores of villages that look like unfocused, abstract paintings. Mud adobe houses, scattered about the vast wheat fields, and surrounded by trees—lacy acacia, lofty *sheesham, peepal* and banyan, lay below the northern snow-capped Himalayas, which touch the sky. While they appear closer than the nearest village, the towering mountains are hundreds of miles away and rise over twenty-five thousand feet above sea level.

Fazal is the most knowledgeable villager; yet when asked about those giants and the sparkling white stuff, he responds, "Those are *pahars*—mountains, and the white shiny stuff is *berf*—ice."

"What is *berf?*" someone questions further.

"It's frozen water. I've seen it in the city. It comes in big blocks from the factory. How do they make it? I don't know."

Rurkee's moderate temperature rarely drops below freezing. The land is blessed with a year-round growing season. Fazal looks to the east, focuses his eyes and spots a clump of trees standing by a flat piece of land. He sees the water well and a small stream that is more like a wash than a watercourse. This site sports the Vaisakhi—harvest fair, every year. "Today is April first," he murmurs to himself. He slides his thumb along each finger joint, counting only thirteen days remaining until the festive annual event. After glancing around one more time, embracing the countryside, he jumps up and strolls back to his shop. He imagines pulling together his *bhangra*—dance team.

Fifty miles away in Punjab's capital—Lahore, Fazal's twenty-four-year old younger brother, Nazir, has become a successful cloth merchant. Success did not come easily for him. After a number of hardships and trying his luck at several jobs, he now owns a modest shop in one of the busy bazaars. Whatever he does and no matter where he is, he makes sure to attend the Rurkee Vaisakhi fair. Each year he helps his brother with the dance troupe, and more importantly concocts ingenious ways to vend merchandise at the fair to make some fast cash. His mind is always active with moneymaking schemes, thinking of new ways to sell and make profits.

Lahore's vendors sell block ice, while others use it as a refrigerant for cold drinks, fruits and chilled deserts, which impresses Nazir. Some make good money selling ice cones in a variety of colors and shapes during the hot summer months.

The block ice melts slowly if it's wrapped in a gunnysack. *It should last even longer if I wrap it more than once,* he imagines. He decides to surprise his brother and the rest of the people this year by bringing ice to the fair. The villagers have never seen ice. Himalayan snow-capped peaks are a mystery to them. Nazir is convinced the novelty and newness will make him money. Business is in his blood.

After practicing for a month, Fazal's *bhangra* team is one of the best. It has won many first prizes over the years. He has an eye for color, an ear for the best dance beat and an innate talent for choreography.

He naturally chooses striking costumes that burst with color, creates rhythmic dance moves, and selects the ideal music to showcase the free spirited choreography that unites the team in perfect harmony. He strives for perfection, incorporates new moves and constantly changes routines each year. The spectators have come to expect new steps and fresh routines. When it comes to costumes, he is the master. He selects the materials and uses his dyeing and batik talents in coordinating the turbans, *kurtas* and *dhotis* in dazzling colors and patterns.

To take his mind off the current restlessness and the rumors of partition, he immerses himself in preparing the dance team for the fair. He promises himself that his team will be number one this year. He gathers his nine-member male team to the house and lays out the plan, assigns vibrant costumes; and then describes the unique props: ankle bells, steel bangles and patterned sticks. The team eagerly shakes the bells and holds the sticks high in the air, moving them rhythmically to imagined music.

"Keep it a secret. This year, we're going to have not one, but two drummers as well as a tambourine player who'll be accompanied by one of the best *chimta*—metal tongs three feet long that clang together with the players' hand movements. I assure you the music will be rich and very rhythmic," he tells them excitedly. "Dalair is the leader. Follow his directions. We don't have much time. The rehearsal is five times a week and starts next Monday after sunset at the *khoo*—water well."

Dalair is seventeen. His five-foot ten-inch stature makes him tall for his age. With a well-built, strong muscular upper body, a chiseled almond face adorned with short youthful whiskers and a budding moustache, he stands out in a crowd. His soft brown eyes gaze engagingly. A traditional gold colored, tightly pleated Sikh turban caps his head covering the top of his ears. He wears a *kara*—steel bangle, on the right wrist and gold rings dangle from his ears. He is an excellent dancer. His respectful demeanor toward adults blends easily with an outgoing personality among his peers. Handsome, hardworking and dependable, he willingly helps others. He could display an air of self-importance, but his quiet reserve sets him apart. Sarita secretly admires these qualities and cannot wait to be his wife.

Knowing the importance of performing well, Fazal works tirelessly with the dance team for many evenings, and appoints Dalair to direct rehearsals in his absence. He knows how much people look forward to Vaisakhi. The day before the fair, life becomes hectic and the village buzzes with excitement. Adults and children alike anticipate the next sunrise, going to the carnival, shopping to their heart's content, eating delicious fried snacks, playing games, enjoying rides and watching the horse and cattle show. Vendors and merchants travel long distances to mark the best space and set up shops and stalls on the fairgrounds. They want to be ready, and are poised to attract the very first customers when the fair opens the next day.

On this same afternoon, in Lahore, Nazir stands by the delivery platform in front of an ice factory. He holds the pick-up voucher in one hand and squeezes his chin with the other, mesmerized when the workers guide the ice blocks down the narrow hall. A worker appears near the platform, tilts the two steel containers and dumps the two and a half by four-foot thick blocks on an aluminum surface. Nazir hands him the receipt, and with the help of the tonga driver slides the blocks to the side, wraps them in the gunnysacks and loads them into a waiting tonga that takes him to the railway station. He wraps extra gunnysacks around the blocks for additional insulation, gets them loaded onto the night train and arrives in Chowinda the next morning.

A tonga brings him to the fairgrounds just before sunrise. He finds a reasonably good spot, pitches a tent, extends a colorful awning into the bazaar lane, throws extra blankets on the blocks and lies down for a quick nap. He is confident that an early opening is not necessary. Business will be brisk when people get thirsty, as the day gets hotter.

Vaisakhi arrives on a warm morning, without a breeze in the air. The sun rising beneath clear blue skies heralds a long, hot, early summer day. A makeshift city has sprung up at the fairgrounds. A two-to-three-block long dirt lane gives the appearance of a bazaar that has numerous shops and stalls displaying a variety of merchandise. The shops show staples, aromatic spices, clothes and fabric of all imaginable colors, women's hair and make-up products and sparkling glass bangles painted in silver and gold. Some carry nothing but women's adornments, especially perfumes, gleaming bangles and henna. There are toy stores. Among the shops, food stalls aromatically beckon customers to eat *naans*—leavened oven-baked bread, *kabobs*—skewered barbecued meat, *pakoras*—fried fritters, *dals*—lentils, meat curries and everybody's favorite drink—*lassi*. Some specialize in sweet meats like fresh *jalabies*—a sweet fried pretzel and *halva*. People gather in twos and threes, holding a flat hot bread and *kabob* in one hand while breaking off succulent pieces of meat with the other and scooting them into their mouths. In between mouthfuls and telling rumors, laughter and fun abounds. Excitement is in the air.

Close by, numerous rides, including the popular Ferris wheel and the Death Well have sprung up. Nazir manages to stake his place just at the end of the bazaar, close to the carnival games and rides. This area features half a dozen games that are a major attraction for young boys and girls. Further away from the bazaar shops and rides are the hundreds of cattle and horses corralled for sale and trade. At the very end is a broad, well-leveled playing field for horse and camel races, *kabaddi*—a tackle game, and the *bhangra* dance competition.

By mid-morning the day is already hot. The fair comes alive. Men yell, barter and trade livestock. Women chatter, buy clothes, fabrics, makeup and new household gadgets. Children and young adults spend their allowance on rides, toys and novelties in the dusty lot. Everybody buys food and drinks. As the day gets hotter, people crowd Nazir's stand while others wait in a long line. No one has seen ice, so it is a mystery. Nazir's beige *dhoti* and gold colored *kurta* flutter around his slender five-foot nine-inch frame in the afternoon breeze, while he hawks his ice breathlessly at top of his lungs.

"This ice came from those soaring Himalayan peaks. I brought it myself. It's cold and will quench your thirst on this hot day." The black-corded silver amulet around his neck shines, complementing an exuberant smile. He is convinced that he will make more money than ever before at this Vaisakhi. He hopes to save the extra funds, and move closer to an engagement with a lovely young woman in Lahore, or from the village. After all of his work and schemes, he dreams of starting his own family. He uses a carpenter's planer rapidly, to shave the ice from the block, and pushes it into parrot-shaped metal molds.

He puts it on a stick, and then douses green and yellow sugary syrup over it, handing it over to the next customer.

"Here is the parrot of paradise for you. Next please," he smiles. He was right. Business is brisk. He is making money. People line up and want to hold the parrot of paradise and taste the sweet, colorful ice cone. At midday and early afternoon, it gets very hot. Movement slows down at the fair. The crowds thin out, people take siestas in tree groves, and the ones who live close by go home to rest.

In late afternoon and early evening, the fair comes to life, again. Karim and Makhan arrive. Sarita and her girl friends join the crowd. Fazal chuckles, watching his brother make money selling a new concoction. He joins in helping him sell the parrots of paradise while the dance team, along with his son and Makhan go on to enjoy the carnival.

Dalair has two things on his mind. One, he wants to lead and win the contest this evening. Second, he wants to see Sarita as many times as possible. His parents and family arranged his engagement and marriage, so he is not allowed to see his future wife openly. Driven by his innate desire and outgoing personality, he has managed to sneak messages, token remembrance gifts and even love notes to Sarita. The Vaisakhi fair is a perfect venue for this love-struck young man to see his beloved. Usually the adults, within limits, accept and intentionally ignore such encounters.

Among dozens of others, Dalair and Sarita crowd into the best perfume and bangle stall. They pretend not to see one another, although they are standing only a couple of feet apart. Eyes fluttering and hearts pounding, they look around to make sure no one is watching them.

"Sir, will you please show me that Jasmine perfume?" Dalair asks the vendor, while sneaking a look at Sarita. "Smells good, it must be a favorite with most young ladies," he says to himself, still glancing at Sarita. Sarita nods her head approvingly.

"I'd like to buy that, and would you wrap it in red rice paper?" he asks the shopkeeper. As the seller wraps the perfume, Sarita selects two silk handkerchiefs. She raises one of them to her lips while winking at Dalair.

"No," Dalair nods his head disapprovingly. She lifts the gold scarf to her mouth and raises it further to her eyes, peeking seductively through the silk.

"Yes, yes," he nods his head approvingly.

Dalair pays for the perfume and Sarita buys the gold silk scarf. They turn around and get lost in the crowd. He hands her the Jasmine perfume, while she puts the beautiful silk in his pocket. After a quick embrace, their bodies brush, infusing them with feelings of love before disappearing into the carnival crowd.

"See you at the *bhangra*," whispers Dalair.

Her eyes wide open, Sarita blows a kiss and disappears, looking for her girlfriends. They look back longingly at each other from a distance. Two lovers, forbidden to meet, and yet they skillfully steal a moment to be near one another. This is the closest they can get to each other without putting family honor on the line. Dalair, on cloud nine, and filled with excitement, joins his friends who are watching the *kabaddi* match in the same field where the dance competition will be held in the evening. All are staunch fans of this sport and dream of becoming the best *kabaddi* player of all time.

Kabaddi, a century old sport has eleven players on a team. They wear nothing but skimpy handmade shorts and huddle in a group, waiting for the challenger from the opposing team. The spectators roar as a challenger walks across the middle neutral line, set between two dirt clods, then runs to the back boundary, turns around and faces the entire opposing team. With strength, speed and agility, he touches one of the players. Simultaneously, any member of the defense can tackle the player. Once the challenger and the defense player have made physical contact, the rest of the team peels off to watch. The crowd goes wild. Now, it is between these two. The defender makes the tackle and the challenger gets away or breaks the tackle in the allotted one minute time. When the defense player is unable to tackle, he is out of the game. The fully tackled team loses the turn. Best of five wins the game. The game is simple, no sports equipment required, yet is great fun and excitement for spectators and a wonderful way for young men to show off their strength and agility. Rurkee's team falls to a neighboring village, so Dalair leaves and heads home to get his dance team assembled. For a moment, he visualizes Rifaqat getting tackled and leaving with a bloody nose.

The *bhangra* contest signals the end of the fair. Although early evening, the weather is still very hot. Most teams have performed and been rated. Dalair's turn to lead his team in the finals has arrived. His nine-member team is poised and the drummers, tambourine and the *chimta*—tong player get underway. They start softly with a slow beat so the dancers can accelerate their movements once the music gets louder and faster.

The rhythm picks up; the team splits into trios. They shuffle and swirl so their colorful costumes make them look like pinwheels. The music is loud. Spectators clap to the music. Dalair gets in the middle and the rest twirl and dance around him, until their bodies and costumes spin in perfect harmony. Dalair looks into the crowd where Sarita is standing with her friends. He winks at her. She winks back with a smile. Dalair raises his hand, all five digits spread apart to indicate five months until the wedding. The Rurkee team wins. Fazal joins the frenzy and they carry him on their shoulders and dance around awhile before putting him down. Nazir, grinning, joins his brother and shows his profits from selling the parrots of paradise. Victorious and exhilarated, Dalair merges into the crowd that is returning to Kotli. Rifaqat appears out of nowhere, knocks him down and sneers, "Watch it *kafir*, watch where you're going." Dalair gets up, ignores Rifaqat and sprints away, fuming.

—11—

Storm Brewing

Fazal takes his brother, Nazir, to their prominent childhood knoll, the *tibba*, both admiring the stretched-out plane and fondly recalling their youthful exploits, playing two by two on this hillock. Chasing squirrels, lizards and small critters into holes dug beneath the shrubs that dotted the fragile slopes, they explored each nook and cranny in their private refuge. Thumbs jetted marbles in all directions under the lone acacia tree that gave filtered shade from summer's searing sun. They never missed an opportunity to climb atop the small lookout, reached by twenty earthen steps that spiraled from the floor.

Squatting down, they gaze in different directions. "The Vaisakhi is over," says Nazir.

"How are things in Lahore?" Fazal asks, ignoring his brother's comment.

"What do you mean?"

"You know what I mean, little brother. The looming partition intended to split Punjab. Hindus and Sikhs are heading east while Muslims are coming west. In Sialkot, people are terrified. There are riots, fires and even killing of the innocent," he blurts out.

"People have been killed?" queries Nazir, absently gazing into the wheat fields.

"You know more than you're telling me. Lahore is a city of one million Muslims, Sikhs and Hindus. It's the capital of Punjab and the planned border is less than fifteen miles away. What's really happening? I want to know. I worry about you. Are you safe there? Maybe you should consider moving back, staying in Rurkee until the strife is over." The younger Nazir turns toward his brother with misty eyes. He places his thumb and forefinger at the bridge of his nose, gently pushing against his covered eyes to hold the dammed up tears.

"What's the matter? What's eating you up?" Fazal leans over, gently removing Nazir's hand from his face. The dam breaks and tears stream down his cheeks. Fazal wraps his arms around him. "You can tell me anything, anything." Nazir's lips quiver. His lament turns quickly into heaving sobs. His tears fall onto Fazal's hands, clutched tightly around his. Fazal slides his hands from around Nazir's. Looking into the distance, he whispers. "Things aren't good in Lahore. Partition is certain; rumors are that it'll happen sometime next year. Lahore is a mess right now. Chaos is everywhere." He turns toward his brother.

"You are right," says Nazir, holding back the flow of tears momentarily. "Hindus and Sikhs are leaving and Muslim refugees are coming in droves from East Punjab."

"Why were you so upset? A grown man crying! I haven't ever seen you like this. Thanks to Allah you're safe. All you can do is protect yourself, your friends, and as a decent human being, help non-Muslims who desire flight to their future country."

Nazir breaks down again and lets out a deafening scream. "That's the problem, brother. I'm not a decent human being. Something I was involved in haunts me and I feel despicable for what I did. It's too late. I willingly witnessed a horrific deed myself. I'm so ashamed." He wipes his face across his sleeve, cleaning off mucus and a few tears left on his cheek. With tears and emotions drained, he feels weak, yet has an uncontrollable urge to relieve his heavy heart. He looks toward the horizon as if to pinpoint the division line that will supposedly separate the two countries. His confession unravels:

"Late one afternoon I was at home, wondering about the chaos that's replaced Lahore's usual calm. People scurry toward the border only to meet others heading the other direction. Random fires and lootings abound. Murders and rapes are happening in Lahore. Why is this going on and when will it end?

"Just before *Maghrib*—the evening prayer, I heard a knock at my door that startled me. I bolted up, unlocked the door, and opened it a crack to see who was there. One of my friends was standing outside with another young man that I didn't know.

"'*Aslamo Elaikum,*' I muttered.

"'Meet my friend, Majid,' said my friend. 'People call him *Churri*—dagger. You know what that means. I feel protected when Churri is along.'

"I waved them in. They looked backward, making sure nobody saw them before walking inside. I pulled them in, locking the door behind. Still standing in the courtyard and without wasting a minute my friend said excitedly, 'We're going on a mission and want you to come along for some fun. You know a number of Hindus and Sikhs have fled their homes, leaving valuables behind. The abandoned homes are full of clothes, jewelry and even cash.' Before I could open my mouth, he continued, 'Remember widower Patel, the rich Hindu businessman who lives near your house with his old father and a teenage daughter?'

"'Yes,'" I replied.

"'We have information that last night, they fled to India. Isn't that great? The fewer non-believers in Lahore the better, as it makes the city pure and provides us with more opportunity. We're heading to Patel's house. Everything and anything we want is there waiting for us. We want you to come along to get your share.'

"'But that's not right. It's wrong. It's looting,' I argued.

"'It's not looting. It's taking from an infidel. Besides, we'll be taking what's rightfully ours. People say that these Hindus got rich, comfortable and powerful on the backs of poor Muslims. Our leaders have been telling us that for centuries. They monopolized businesses, exploited our labor and used deceitful money-lending schemes to enslave our brothers. We want you to join us in claiming a small token of what's ours.'

"'What if we get caught?' I whispered. I don't know why, but I said it. I was wrong even asking. I should've just refused.

"'We won't get caught,' said my friend. 'Nobody's there, Nazir. It's so chaotic all over the city. There are hardly any Hindu or Sikh police officers. Only a few Muslims are policing the city and they can't be everywhere. Besides, the law looks the other way when it comes to confronting the infidels. Don't worry Nazir. See, what we have here is our own personal protection—Churri.'"

Fazal sits motionless—all ears, and listens anxiously to his brother without making eye contact. He finally turns his head and looks squarely into Nazir's eyes and asks, "You didn't join them, did you?"

"Brother, I should've stopped them or at least refused to go. My scruples left me while greed propelled my body. I locked my house and went with them. No harm in looking, I thought. Maybe I'll bring home something I need. What I won't get, somebody else will claim. Just a small offense, I rationalized." Nazir looks the other way to avoid his brother's frightened gaze, and pauses before continuing his story.

"We followed Churri. After walking half a block, we turned into a narrow, winding alley. It was brick-paved, with gray-water in open drains on both sides, and lined with multi-story houses side by side. Wooden or iron doors led into small courtyards, where ornamented wooden balconies and elegant wrought iron railings hung from expensive homes.

"We turned down the alley and passed by a couple of shops filled with general merchandise, but no customers. We wove through a dusty intersection where a half-dozen children played soccer, oblivious to the danger, ignoring the evening darkness; kicking a well-worn scruffy ball. Side stepping a water buffalo, sitting stubbornly in the middle of the alley chewing her cud, we hurried past a *tandoor*—commercial clay oven, where a few people were buying freshly oven-baked *naan*—flat, round bread. The normal bazaar atmosphere had changed; people were afraid and stayed secluded inside their houses. I was nervous, yet I followed the others. After sneaking through a couple of narrow alleys, we arrived at Patel's house.

"'This is the house,' Churri said excitedly."

"What happened next?" says Fazal, interrupting Nazir's narrative. "Did they go in? You didn't barge in with them, did you?"

[handwritten margin note: Not exactly a normal conversation →]

"Listen to me, brother. It didn't end there. It got bad; really bad." Nazir looked at his brother regretfully. "I'm so ashamed."

"Go on. Hurry up. Tell me how it ended," urges Fazal.

"Churri stood in front of Patel's house, and we were right behind him. The ornately carved wooden door refused to open when Churri pushed it forcefully; the door was locked or latched from the inside. His furious pounding went unanswered.

"'Somebody's in there,' we exclaimed, while looking behind, hoping we were not being watched.

"'No. No. I'm sure they've gone. Patel must have locked the door and climbed over the courtyard wall before fleeing; a smart idea to make people think that somebody's inside the house,' said Churri, while climbing the low wall. In an instant he was in the courtyard, swinging the door wide open; he waved us in. He quickly latched the door and turned to us with a sinister laugh, extending his hand for high fives. No one was there. My pounding heart slowed down.

"'I told you so,' grinned Churri.

"We looked around. Next to the front door was a sizable living room. We peeked through a window and saw nothing but expensive furniture. The anxiety and thrill of hunting an unknown treasure took over. Across the courtyard were two rooms, each having a door and a window. A cement stairway led to the second story. No noise. No sign of life; there was dead silence. Encouraged, Churri took a peek in each room, and seeing nothing but darkness, ran upstairs.

"From the start, Churri acted like a leader and was now definitely in charge. We followed him upstairs and landed on a veranda in front of two rooms overlooking the courtyard. He opened the door to one of the rooms. Holding up a flashlight, he lit the kerosene lamp and set it on a table. We squinted and adjusted our eyes to see the contents of the room.

"'Check out the loot in here,' Churri exclaimed.

"On one side, two cots draped with satin sheets rested on a fancy *kalin*—hand woven rug. Colorful pillows and tasseled bolsters were everywhere. Locked steel cabinets lined the other wall. Several posed family portraits hung on the wall. It seemed like the occupants had just stepped out and would return at any moment.

"'Let's get to work and break open these treasure chests and pile up what we want to take,' clamored Churri exuberantly. We found a hammer and a steel bar in a box on the veranda. Like blacksmiths, we pounded on the locks, latches and hinges to break open the cabinets.

"'We've only one hammer and a steel bar. You guys keep on working. I'm going to check the rooms below.' Churri issued his orders as he dashed out the door.

"After Churri had left, we ransacked the room. Suddenly we heard screams coming from below, one deafening scream after another. We darted downstairs and entered an open room, met by a shocking sight. An old man lay wounded; sprawled on the floor, bloodied and unconscious, while a teen-aged girl cowered on a cot across the room, her clothes tattered and torn from her body—clear evidence of a vicious rape. Apparently the girl and her grandfather had been hiding when Churri discovered them. As I entered the room, clutching a silk suit and half a dozen gold bangles, stolen from the steel cabinet I'd broken into, Churri stood beside the girl, staring into her glazed eyes, while holding a knife against her throat. He turned to face me, tying the string on his gaping *shalwar*. The silk suit and gold bangles slipped out of my hand and landed at Churri's feet. Overcome with revulsion and fear, I stumbled down the stairs and ran from the house as fast as my trembling legs would take me. I locked myself inside the house for days, wondering, *what have I done?*"

His story concluded, Nazir looks to Fazal beseechingly. No words are spoken as Fazal embraces his brother. Arm in arm, they descend from the lookout in silence.

—12—

Winnowing

Nazir and Fazal awaken to the aromatic breakfast that Rakhi has prepared for Nazir. After a quick wash, Nazir joins his brother on the straw floor mat laid down on the mud floor next to the kitchen. Rakhi hands them each a plate holding an onion and cilantro omelet, along with a woven basket containing stacked *parathas*—flat, round layered pan-fried bread in purified butter tucked into a cloth to keep warm, mango pickles and two large glasses of *lassi*—a yogurt drink churned frothy smooth.

"Brother, I'm so sorry about what I've done." Nazir looks down shamefully, while breaking off a piece of bread.

"One can't undo what is done," says Fazal. "*Shaitan*—Satan is always out there leading people astray. We have to battle him constantly, and fight temptations. I know you have a good heart. When you go back, you can help others in need. Find other Patels, protect them and do everything in your power to lessen their pain on their journey to the Promised Land." He pauses for a bite of food, turns to his brother and says, "Look into my eyes; I want you to promise me one thing."

"What's that?" asks Nazir.

Fazal offers a stern warning. "Like a typhoon, I know a dangerous partition mania is brewing. I have seen clear signs in Sialkot. Lahore could be in the center of this storm. Nobody, except for a few of us in this village, knows about it. Sikhs, Muslims and Hindus have lived here side by side for generations, accepting one another. They know nothing about *Angrez* or partition and less about leaving their homes against their will. As you know, in Rurkee we practice our faiths differently; yet we have come together cheerfully to celebrate our joys and willingly share our sorrows, regardless of beliefs. I know the storm is imminent. I pray to Allah that the typhoon's destructive path spares us, saving Rurkee from the misery of division. You must keep this to yourself, and don't utter a word to your *bhabi*—sister-in-law or to any one in Rurkee."

"I understand. You have my word."

They finish breakfast. Nazir hugs his brother warmly before thanking his *bhabi*, for the delicious breakfast, and sneaks a good sum of money that he made at the Vaisakhi fair into Rakhi's hand.

"Khuda Hafiz, God be with you," says Nazir, waving his hand good bye. He hops on the tonga that takes him to the Chowinda railway station, where he will catch the evening train to Lahore. Fazal and his wife hurriedly climb the stairs to the flat roof of their house. As the tonga turns the corner and comes into full view, they wave their hands, smiling sadly. *"Khuda Hafiz. Khuda Hafiz,* God be with you."

Fazal blocks the early morning sun by putting his hand over his forehead, sheltering his eyes, and admires the ripe wheat fields that extend as far as the eye can see—wheat stalks swaying in the gentle breeze, interspersed with alfalfa, patchy acacia and *sheesham* trees.

"Fazal, what are you looking at?"

"Oh. My dear, I'm admiring the bumper crop our village is blessed with this season and dreading the backbreaking work our farmers have at harvest."

Rakhi hears the comment, accepting it at face value. She heard the brothers talk in between their bites of breakfast and realizes that Fazal has purposely evaded her question. She cares deeply for her husband, admiring his abilities and flair, but wishes he could share the heavier burdens of his heart with her. The unease he shows intermittently has her concerned about the future.

Dalair's family has about two acres of wheat to harvest. It is unusual for farmers to pay in currency rather than borrowing and bartering labor, which is the common practice. Dalair and Aneel eagerly help every farmer in the village. Today it is their turn. At dawn, a dozen or more farmers with sharpened sickles gather at their field and form a line. With Dalair and his father in the middle, they spread out and begin at one edge of the field while sitting on their heels; they swing the sickle, cutting the wheat. Each person makes a small pile as he moves along. A couple of people follow behind, picking up the piles and stacking them until they repose naturally. It is a hot, sweaty backbreaking effort. The team works hard until late morning before they take a break.

Aneel's wife, Zareena, stays with her brother and Tara the night before the harvest. She, along with Tara and Sarita, get up at dawn to prepare pots of meat curry, *pakoras*, fried potato or cauliflower fritters, and churned pitchers of *lassi* for the crew. When all the food and drinks are packed, the two mothers pick up the provisions and are about to leave, when Sarita asks, "What about me? I helped. I want to go as well." Both women look at her mischievously. "You can't go," they tease; "Dalair is there. You'll wed him soon. It's not proper. What'll people say?"

"But . . ." Sarita protests.

"No ifs, ands or buts young lady," retorts Sarita's mother and heads toward the field where tired and hungry men are waiting.

Dalair does not expect Sarita to come; yet his heart throbs just in case her mother brings her along. He knows that gender separation is strict and even more unyielding after an engagement. The mothers arrive at the field just in time for the men's break. One of the young men turns to Dalair and says, "You weren't expecting Sarita to show up, were you? Well, you'll just have to wait now. It's only a few months before she becomes your wife." Dalair walks away, hiding his embarrassment.

During the harvest season, village life becomes hectic, and the countryside turns picturesque. The stalks piled high form wheat temples. Men and women work side by side, separating the wheat from the shaft by thrashing bundles of stalks on dirt mounds. The hay-like mixture of wheat grain, chaff and fine straw winnows into the air when reed baskets are hoisted by hand above their heads—almost nonstop—to separate the grain. They haul the wheat home, sieve and store it for market.

Aneel and Dalair toil over a week, and are ready to wrap up the harvest work when they hear shouting. "Hey, Aneel Gill why the fuck are you working so hard? What's the use? You will soon flee to India, leaving all this land behind for me," yells Rifaqat, strutting at the edge of the field.

Dalair clutches his *kirpan*—dagger and runs toward Rifaqat. His father does not know it, but Dalair is fully aware of Rifaqat's animosity toward his father over the land he has forcibly taken from him. "I am going to kill you. I am going to kill you," shouts Dalair as he sprints toward Rifaqat. A young man of quiet demeanor—Dalair, with pent up anger against his family's archenemy, has gone mad.

"Dalair, please stop. Somebody stop him. Son, don't. He's just stirring up trouble. Please don't play into his hands," pleads Aneel as he races after his son. Rifaqat positions himself with his *lathi*—fighting stick and provokes Dalair further, shouting, "Come on, you son of a *kafir,* come on."

Instantly, others with sickles in their hands follow Aneel, who rages at his son, "Don't kill him. Wait for us. We'll beat him into pulp." Rifaqat had not expected the others, who were mostly Muslims, to take Aneel's side. He quickly takes off running, while the other resume their work. The confrontation is over in an instant; the challenge, insults, reaction and Rifaqat's departure have taken less than five minutes.

"Father, what's going on? You know more than you tell me. Rifaqat is getting more blatant and belligerent. First Vaisakhi and now this; I swear on Guru's head that the next time he challenges me, I'll give him a fight he'll remember for the rest of his life."

—13—

Well Connected

The sun shines brightly, heralding another hot April day. Three of Sarita's friends come to her house. They surround her in the courtyard and whisper giddily as if to impart a secret. "We want you to come along to Mr. Shafkat's *khoo*—water well and tell us all about your wedding plans." Hoping to get a positive answer from her mother, Sarita throws in an extra incentive, offering to do the laundry.

"That'll be great. Also, before you return, please fetch a pitcher of water. I didn't bring enough this morning," says Tara.

"Of course mother, I'll do that gladly."

Sarita puts soiled clothes, a bar of soap and a two-foot long, three-inch round stick in a bed sheet. Pulling the four corners together, she ties them into a knot, then hefts the bundle and places it gently on her head. Barely bending to stay balanced, she swoops up a clay pitcher to rest on her hip. She wraps her hand around its neck as if holding a baby.

"Hurry back and don't be late."

"I won't," says Sarita while walking gracefully, balancing both the bundle and the pitcher on her small frame. She and her friends head to the well. Like Sarita, one is carrying a similar load, while each of the other two carries a water pitcher. The four walk in single file along the narrow path, to the *khoo*, that cuts through a vast, green, knee-high mustard field laden with cheery yellow blooms that sway back and forth in the late morning breeze, as if mimicking the four friends walking. Upon their arrival at the well, the girls shed their burdens and quickly huddle for gossip. It is a rare opportunity for these young girls to talk, and contemplate their futures freely. Around others, especially their parents, they are shy and reserved in expressing feelings, so they look forward to going to the well for private time.

"Sarita, tell us, when's the wedding? Has the date been set? We're all very excited. We've our wedding clothes and can't wait to show them off." Her friends tease, while Sarita blushes and turns her head away without answering. She notices one of Shafkat's farm hands checking the ox, making sure it is fit and ready to go to work. He lifts one ox foot at a time, looks for small rocks; and then gently runs his hand through the ox's mane to ensure that the harness and blinders are comfortably snug. She hears him talking to the animal.

"Buddy, I know you're tired. I am too. We've been working since sunrise. Just a couple of more hours, then we'll be done. I'm going to check the fields and ditches for leaks and debris. When I get back, you'd better be moving. Wheat needs water." He smiles, and whispers into the ox's ear. He whistles, ordering the ox to start moving, picks up a shovel, laying it on his shoulder, and walks along the irrigation ditch, disappearing into the wheat field.

Wells are very expensive and only a few can afford them. Shafkat is one of those who has a productive well on his farm. Occasionally, Sarita's father leases water from him. As the ox moves, the well comes to life. The wooden gears creak and the animal sets a slow plodding pace. The sound of droning gears, along with that of brim-full clay jugs releasing a waterfall into the wooden trough takes Sarita back to her childhood.

She was only eight when she stood at this very spot with her family. A sizable crowd gathered to enjoy a feast and *dohl*—drum music. Mr. Shafkat personally distributed garbanzo basmati rice pilaf. He presented baskets of sweets, just for the taking. People took turns peering carefully over the edge into the thirty-foot deep hole of standing water.

"Father, how did they know where to find water?" asked Sarita shyly.

"See that tall man over there smiling and standing proud. He's a Shaman."

"The old bearded man in fancy white clothes and a silk shawl?"

"Yes. Yes. Mr. Shafkat gave him those clothes and showered him with hundreds of rupees. He's a very smart man with an extraordinary power. Three weeks ago, Mr. Shafkat hired him to find a site for a successful well. Carrying only two willow sticks, this sage walked for two days, crisscrossing Mr. Shafkat's land back and forth, pondering, praying and looking for water. This is the exact spot where he stood declaring, 'There is your water. Dig here.' He asked Mr. Shafkat to join him in blessing the site and they raised hands in prayer for the successful, sweet water well. You see Sarita. He was right. The well diggers went to work and they hit water at less than thirty feet. Today, we enjoy the food and festivities."

"Where does the water come from?" asked Sarita, tugging at her father's shirt.

"I don't know. But they say that, in the middle of the night, the elves who live underground bring buckets of water from the ocean and quietly fill up the well," replied her father, matter-of-factly.

"But how do they breathe?"

"They are very tiny, like little fish and don't need air," said her father, looking at her persuasively. She believed him. "Maybe I can barter or lease water when the well is completed and functional," he murmured, pulling her by hand toward the pilaf and sweets.

A few days later, work started on the project. Several men lowered a round heavy wooden platform, slightly smaller than the hole into the shaft. Laborers lowered the bricks for the masons inside to line the wall. As the circular platform sank deeper, the well diggers excavated as deep as possible to make the well deeper and dependable. According to myth, the entombed platform released a dreadful echo, as if someone had taken their last breath. It is believed that the living tree that gave birth to the platform had been buried alive deep into the well for good, producing the mournful sound, just as the myth had decreed.

The *khoo* is the nerve center for the farm, and a place where the owner, his employees and others gather, gossip, bathe and conduct business. Next to the well, Shafkat has built a small barn; a storage shed for tools and hay, along with a room for his workers, where cots, sheets and pillows and a hookah welcome all. The well is more than a water source. Women get water and do washing while they visit, at times poking their heads into the small rooms, making sure that nobody listens to their gossip. Next to the old banyan tree's towering canopy, Shafkat has planted numerous trees and shrubs around the facility, making the well an inviting place.

"Sarita, are you okay? Are you napping? You haven't answered us. We want to know if your wedding date has been set." Her friend giggles and pinches her, snapping her out of her daydream.

"Look. Look. There is your love, Dalair, coming this way!" exclaims the other girl, pointing in the opposite direction. Sarita believes them. Her heart misses a beat as she turns to look, but sees no Dalair. It is Sunday, so there is no school. She came hoping to see him.

"In September, that is when the wedding takes place. Dalair graduates in June and my mother makes the money from the wheat sale to buy the jewelry. September sixteen is the date."

"That's coming up quick. Soon you'll leave us and become a married woman," her friends chime.

"It's getting late," says Sarita. "I'm going to get in trouble if I don't hurry. Help me with the washing."

Sarita places the garments on the wooden board, swipes them with soap, hand rolls and beats them with the stick one at a time, turning each over occasionally, while hand sprinkling it with water. Her friends dip the soapy garments into the water, rinse and wring them out, then spread them lightly over the ground and shrubs for drying. They talk animatedly about the wedding preparations while the clothes dry.

Laundry done, dried, folded and packed, they fill the pitchers with water. Sarita picks up the dry laundry bundle, balances it on her head and jerks the water pitcher to her hip, securing it immediately by her arm. Content with the social outing, and caught up with the girly gossip, they walk cheerfully home in a single file.

"Aye, Sarita. Girl, you look beautiful," shouts Rifaqat across from the mustard field. "Where is your *Ranja*—Romeo Dalair? Tell him that I'm looking for him." Terrified, Sarita and her friends pick up the pace, ignoring Rifaqat, while all the time hoping that he was not coming after them.

—14—

Vows

and there it is...

A boy's birth is a blessing and a cause for celebration, while the baby girl's arrival is a burden and a life-long worry for the parents. When boys become adults, they provide for elderly parents and bring home brides with the bounties of dowry. Sarita's parents love her dearly and from the day she was born, her mother has saved and sewed for her future.

Tara goes into the back room and unlocks the *paeti*—a sheet metal trunk, lifts the lid and admires all the hand-sewn garments and embroidery she and Sarita have created over the years for the wedding. Lost in thought, she reminisces that not long ago Sarita and Dalair were only small children. One evening, when she was visiting her brother Aneel in Kotli, she admired how Dalair and Sarita played and chased each other. "They'll make a very cute couple, Tara. What do you think?" asked her brother.

"I accept."

"Accept what?"

"*Veera*—brother, are you proposing that Sarita will be Dalair's bride when she comes of age?" she exclaimed excitedly.

"*Behn*—Sister, that's okay with my family. Then it's settled; a done deal. My wife's dream has come true."

It is widely believed that the future rests in heaven and predestined relationships hang in the stars. As arranged marriages are universal, families work constantly to make these connections succeed. Often children are spoken for early in their lives for marriages.

"My dear wife, what are you doing standing in front of the open trunk," asks Sher, putting his hand on her shoulder. Startled, she turns and smiles. "Nothing. I'm just thinking that Sarita has grown up so fast and there's not much time left until the wedding day. I'm worried about how much we have to do to get ready for the special day."

"Don't agonize, dear. You've accumulated nearly everything for the dowry, except the jewelry. We've been lucky this year and will make a lot of money from our crops. Take Zareena with you to the jeweler and buy whatever you need."

Tara and Zareena invite Sarita, who happily accompanies them to the Chowinda market. They stroll around, looking leisurely at the glittering window displays before entering the shop that is located in the middle of the gold bazaar. They have always bought wedding jewelry at this particular shop. The owners have served Rurkee families for generations.

"*Namaste.* Come in please. A warm welcome to you, my sisters. Sit down and make yourselves comfortable." The owner gestures by folding his hands in front of his face; then quickly releases them and points towards a cushioned wooden bench that leans against the wall. Even before they sit down and utter *Namaste* in reply, he asks them, "What would you like to drink with *mithai*—sweets? *Lassi,* milk or mango juice? On the other hand, maybe chai? Chai is a favorite drink these days. Even children are drinking it. What will it be?"

"We'll have milk." Zareena decides for both of them. "Chai is too addictive and *lassi* is too cheap. It's time to splurge." *Although he's our family jeweler, he's going to make a small fortune from us today,* she thinks to herself. The jeweler's teen-age son and apprentice, so well trained, darts from the shop and returns quickly with a plate full of *mithai* and two glasses of milk.

"Thank you," the women say in unison, taking the milk and the plate from the boy. Relaxed, they sit back against the wall, silently admiring the intricate golden necklaces, earrings, ring sets, along with the forehead pendants. Many patterns and designs intrigue them.

The narrow, mirrored, two-room shop holds a bench and a glowing glass display case showing three shelves of twenty-four karat gold jewelry. On the bottom shelf, pendants and necklaces lie freely. Made from pure gold or studded with precious topaz, lapis, rubies and garnets, they gleam. Sparkling bangles are bundled together in sets of six or more, stacked neatly in open red velvet boxes on the second shelf, vying for the shopper's attention. The top shelf contains earrings, hairpins, nose rings and studs, intentionally laid on top of a black velvet cloth to amplify their luster. Behind this counter the owner sits, with a business-like courteous smile, while constantly studying his customers, whose eyes focus on the display case. The women lean forward, pointing at one design and then another, nodding approval or disapproval, whispering back and forth to one another.

A narrow door opens to the back room. Here, the owner's son busily works on a bangle, hammering out a delicate filigree design. This work area houses the small coal-fired furnace; crucibles and the tiny goldsmith tools are scattered on a worktable. A refrigerator-sized iron safe keeps additional inventory. Peeling plaster leaves pockmarks on the whitewashed shop walls and ceiling. A solitary wall calendar showing a picture of Hindu god Shiva decorates the shop.

"Brother, please show us these two necklaces, those six bangles and the hair clips that are in front of you," Tara suggests, pointing, while placing the empty milk glass on the counter and reaching for another sweet. They lean over the items, looking, feeling and occasionally tilting a piece to capture the light. They select two necklaces, one pendant, two sets of earrings, a nose ring and a dozen bangles.

"We'll take these," says Tara holding the necklaces in each hand and admiring the other selections, beautifully spread out on the counter.

"What do you think Sarita? Do you like them?"

"I like them very much. No, I love them. Thank you, Mother, thank you Aunty," Sarita utters, blushing.

"Good choice *Behn*," smiles the goldsmith.

"Good choice *Behn*, you say. We know how to shop. Listen to me and pay attention to what I'm telling you," exclaims Zareena. "Make sure these items are sized exactly and get the best polish. Don't you dare pick our pockets. Charge my sister an honest price. If you don't, I guarantee you'll not be our family jeweler anymore."

"Don't worry. As always I'll be reasonable and charge you the best price."

"Okay, then. We'll be back next week."

"Next week it is."

As they walk out, they are not surprised to see that a tonga waits to take them back to Rurkee. They hop on and look back momentarily as the driver orders the horse ahead by slicing his crackling whip through the air. The shopkeeper rests one hand on his chest while waving with the other, and says with a toothy grin, "My treat! See you next week."

Just two weeks left until the wedding. Although all the arrangements are in place, Tara and Zareena worry, going over the checklist of food and festivities, guests and gifts each day. They always find something that needs a little more attention.

September fifteenth arrives. It is the *mehndi*—henna night; the most fun filled affair for Sarita. Her girlfriends, aunts and neighbor women gather at her house on this calm and cool evening. While her mother and aunts prepare food, the two dozen girlfriends gossip on courtyard *charpais*. All the animals, including Tez, are tethered in the barn. Swept clean, the courtyard and veranda boast multicolored streamers and small triangular pennants strung overhead, blowing gently in the evening breeze. A few well-cleaned kerosene lanterns hang, ready for lighting after dark, making the courtyard exotic and festive. A red and gold embroidered satin sheet drapes one cot. Marigold garlands, along with a sprinkling of red and yellow rose petals, provide more decoration at the spot where Sarita takes her place of honor for the henna ceremony.

"Let's get going, bride," says Sarita's best friend, while grabbing her hand and pulling her towards the special cot. Some of the girls sit on the cot's edge while others tilt forward around her. Sarita sits shyly, yet leans comfortably against a silk bolster, her legs dangling. An aunty presses the thickened henna paste into a tapered paper tube. The girls slowly squeeze the green paste onto Sarita's hands and feet, taking turns to create intricate filigree designs. When finished, the girls indulge themselves, applying the henna on each other's hands. A couple of them make sure that Sarita's shirtsleeves and *shalwar* bottoms stay well above the decorations until the wet paste dries completely. They giggle, make jokes, and tease her while singing ceremonial songs that are silly or serious, in concert with the beat of a *dholki*—small drum.

Although it is a 'girl's only' event, Karim and Makhan join in, uninvited, constantly teasing and deriding the girls. Rakhi, who is helping Tara, occasionally shoos them away, but they manage to reappear. The girls try to ignore them, but in reality, they rather like their playful presence. The aunts serve a simple meal of rice and lentils, and then distribute sweets, money and gifts to all the women who helped. The girls continue to drum the *dholki* while the rest sing along to their heart's content. As it gets late, Rakhi rounds up Karim and asks Tara how many guests are going to stay with her.

"Just two families, a total of six," answers Tara.

"Okay, send them over. All the beds are made," says Rakhi, grabbing Karim's hand to take him home. On this special occasion, the host family cannot accommodate all the guests, who have arrived from afar. The neighbors' festive communal courtesy exemplifies their customary hospitality toward the guests. The hosts provide the best beds for sleeping, and after a hearty breakfast the next morning, they assemble for the wedding celebration.

A less elaborate *mehndi*—ceremony takes place at Dalair's house. His sister pastes a dollop of green henna paste on her brother's palms while the gathered circle of family and neighbors sing along to a drumbeat. They honor the groom by tossing money into the air, while the hired help quickly collect the rupees. Once the rice and lentils are served, sweets are presented and congratulations and blessings are exchanged, they all retire and eagerly wait for the next day.

At Aneel's home, the family and guests rise early. All are excited and dress in their traditional finery for the occasion. After sunrise, Dalair sits on a wooden stool while his mother, sister, and aunts gather around for the *khara*, a pre-bathing ritual that wards off the evil eye.

Each woman takes a bit of yogurt mixed with mustard oil and rubs it onto Dalair's head. They sing songs, give money to the poor and pray for his successful marriage. Dalair is embarrassed and annoyed.

"Mother, how long do I have to sit here? Let's hurry up and be done with it," he urges her irritably.

Zareena motions to the village potter's wife, who stands by, waiting for the order. She puts down five fire-baked clay plates in front of the groom. Dalair gets up, jumps on the plates, crushing them all. The ritual is complete. The evil eye has been cast off. Dalair takes a quick bath and gets ready for the next ceremony, *Sara Banai*. He gently pulls a silk *kurta* over his head. He adjusts his shoulders so it drapes above the gold colored *dhoti* that gracefully touches the matching curled-toe gold shoes. He sits down on a cot while everyone, now dressed in their best wedding clothes, gathers around him. His mother, father and sister stand next to him. Aneel reaches for a cloth bag, takes out a beautiful and sparkling muslin turban, kisses his forehead and proudly, with a sentimental smile, puts it on his son's head. Then his mother ties the *sara*—a semi transparent face covering, suspended from a golden headband, with silver and gold tinsel filaments hanging below the chin, around his head. Dalair's sister, Berket, ties a *Ghana*—a tasseled strand, twined from home spun yarn with small-multicolored fabric pieces sewn on, around his right wrist. She has made this herself with devotion and care. Dalair, moved by sisterly love, gives her a *piyar*—head pat, while sliding a few silver rupees into her hand. Rose and marigold garlands are laid around his neck. One by one, the guests line up to shake his hands and gift him with an undisclosed amount of folded money. He thanks each person, handing the money to his father and waits restlessly for the next ritual.

Soon Dalair is escorted to the *Gurdawara*—Sikh temple, where the *Giani*—priest, is waiting. His family walks by his side and others follow the loosely knit procession. He enters the temple, bows his head and prostrates himself, touching his forehead in front of the *Guru Grunth Sahib*—the holy book, the living guru. After the priest's blessing, he is ushered back to the house where the wedding party waits outside.

An ornamented and tasseled horse awaits him. The master helps Dalair atop. Dalair sits comfortably in the saddle, carefully adjusting the sheathed sword that dangles from his right hip. He looks like a Sikh warrior, ready to bring his bride home. His sister Berket springs out of the crowd, throws a beautiful shawl over his shoulders and offers him a glass of milk while holding the reins, blocking his way, as if to stop him from going. He knows the custom well. He takes just one sip and offers her some money. She smiles, saying it is not enough and insists on more. He happily gives in to her demand.

By now, the Kotli neighborhood children have gathered in front of the band. Their eyes are on Dalair's father. Aneel removes a bag full of coins from his shoulder. He reaches into the bag, takes a handful of coins and tosses them high in the air to the expectant children. The airborne coins sail above Dalair and the band, reaching the children. Like soccer players, they lunge, jump and scramble to catch as many coins as possible. This is the cue for the wedding party to move. The whole procession travels toward Rurkee at a steady pace, with Dalair atop the ceremonial horse. A trio made up of *dhol*—drum, a foot-long wooden reed instrument called *shahnai*, and six inch round brass clappers, plays upbeat folk tunes, leading the way. The guests follow the horse, led by his master. Children jump and wave at Aneel, enticing him to throw more coins. He tosses a few more handfuls before closing the bag. Cheerfully, the children peel away, counting their loot and waving boisterous goodbyes to the wedding procession.

Simultaneously at Sarita's house, family, friends and guests are up early. Fazal and Shafkat's families help. All the reception arrangements are finished. The men wait in the communal area under the boldly colored pitched tents, smelling the cooking food. At home, the women prepare for the ceremony, counting and displaying the entire dowry. Sarita's girlfriends appoint themselves to stand by her at all times. They help her to bathe, and dress her in gold-embroidered, red silk wedding clothes, apply the blended make-up, adorn her with the gold jewelry and adjust the *dupatta*—chiffon head shawl, to cover her forehead, showing utmost modesty. They scurry about her constantly, never leaving her alone until the groom and wedding party arrives. She sits still, breathing deeply, to take in all the colors, fragrances and people who joyfully surround her.

One of the men from the wedding party launches six powerful fireworks balls that explode thunderously high in the sky, announcing the arrival of the wedding party. Along with Fazal and Shafkat, Sher Singh issues orders to the men: "Get ready, get ready. Did you hear the boom? They're almost here. Line up the refreshments."

The party arrives. Dalair dismounts the horse; the band plays loudly while Aneel lobs coins to the Rurkee children who have waited since morning. Sher, Fazal and Shafkat walk towards Aneel Gill and Dalair. They set garlands around their necks, drape colorful woolen shawls over their shoulders, and reach out with firm, welcoming embraces. The rest of the men greet one another by shaking hands and embracing, all the while inquiring about their families. Everyone eats an abundance of sweetmeats, salty *pakoras*—potato fritters and *samosas*—deep fried triangular dough stuffed with minced potatoes; all accompanied by cold drinks and hot chai.

After refreshments, the groom, accompanied by his family and friends, is escorted to the Temple where the bride and her family wait. Dalair and Sarita bow their heads and prostrate themselves, planting their heads momentarily in front of the *Guru Grunth Sahib*. They sit side-by-side, facing the *Giani*—the priest. He recites the holy book, guides their vows and blesses the wedding. The bride's father takes the long end of a lightweight, pleated shawl that rests on Dalair's shoulder and places it on Sarita's. She follows Dalair, holding the end of the shawl, as they reverently circle the *Guru Grunth Sahib* four times, each time stopping in front of the *Guru Grunth Sahib* long enough for the *Giani* to recite more verses from the holy book.

The formal ceremony over, Sarita and Dalair are married. Congratulations are exchanged, and the couple is showered with money. More sweets are distributed. Back in the tent, the visiting guests start eating a tasty and hearty rice pilaf, *naan*—leavened bread baked in a wood fired clay oven, and beef curry with *raita*—shredded cucumber and cumin yogurt, and a variety of chutneys. Milk, *lassi* and chai satisfy their thirst.

A few hours later all eyes are on Tara's house, where a large crowd, mostly women, gathers to admire the dowry that Sarita will take to her new home. Rakhi proudly displays two fancy carved cots, two sets of complete bedding—including flat pillows and round bolsters, a number of handmade crochet covers, cotton block-printed comforters, metal pots and pans, copper plates, bowls and glasses, a dozen *shalwar-kameez*, a milk churner, hookah, *charkha*—the spinning wheel, and of course the *paeti*—metal trunk for storage. Rakhi guardedly shows the gold jewelry for a very short time; then quickly takes it away for the bride to wear.

"The bride is ready. They're sending her off," says someone. The crowd rushes toward the courtyard door, joining a score of others already jammed in and waiting, just to catch a glimpse of Sarita. A girlfriend and her mother, along with Rakhi, are right behind her, touching her shoulder. They gently guide Sarita by the elbow. Discreetly bowing her head, she wears a red satin *shalwar-kameez* embroidered with *gota*—tightly plaited silver ribbon that shines and sparkles from the hand sewn diamond pattern. The matching chiffon *dupatta* drapes over her head and shoulders gracefully. Gold and silver sequined shoes complete the outfit. The rusty henna color compliments her gold jewelry. The twenty-four carat gold chandeliered necklace, earrings, forehead pendant, nose ring and six bangles on each arm glisten in the sunlight. Her light make-up and downward cast kohl-lined-almond brown eyes become misty. "Oh, ooh, she looks so beautiful," the women gasp sentimentally.

"She's the most beautiful bride I have ever seen," whispers Rakhi, turning to Tara.

"Thank you," says Tara "I appreciate all your help. You're the sister I never had and more than that you are my best friend. Rakhi, pray for my daughter's bright future."

"Tara, I see nothing but a bright future for our Sarita." They break down, embrace one another and cry on each other's shoulders.

"It is time we get going, Tara. People are waiting. Time to say goodbye," says Sher pulling his wife away from Rakhi. Teary eyed, he dries his tears with the tail of his turban.

As Sarita is ushered, by her mother, into the palanquin sitting outside, aunts shower her with *piyars,* hands delicately touching the top of her head, while girlfriends impart hearty and emotional embraces affectionately. Dalair's friends do the frantic *bhangra* dance, lifting their shoulders and arms forward, snapping their fingers excitedly in rhythm to the drum. Amidst tears of sadness and happiness, four men pick up the palanquin and follow Dalair on the horse while several other men carry the dowry over their heads. *What is this? The 7th century?*

Zareena and Berket, along with friends and neighbors welcome the couple at Kotli. The women and young girls, dressed in silky hot pink, yellow and orange *shalwar-kameezes,* gather in front of the bride and bridegroom. Three to five girls make a small circle and do the *Luddi,* a welcoming song and folk dance for the newlyweds. They sing, clap, twirl and hop, bringing one foot to the other while the rest clap vigorously. The dancers invite others to join, or pull in replacements. The waiting women happily move in, while the dancers peel out to give others an opportunity to show their talents. A wedding celebration is the rare time when women can express themselves freely in public through singing and dancing. They take turns and dance until exhaustion overcomes them. *whoopie!*

Zareena performs a few more rituals, pouring oil on the door hinges, offering them sugared water and drinking the rest herself, then swirling money around the heads of the newlyweds, before handing it to the poor and deserving. Other women join the custom. They ward off the evil eye and bless the marriage, hoping to bring the couple a long, happy life and many healthy children. *BOY*

—15—

Side by Side

The newlyweds move into a small bedroom that Aneel has added to his modest mud house. Two weeks after the wedding, on a bright sunny morning, Sarita finishes her breakfast and decides to take a little rest. She sits on a cot, props herself against the round, satin bolster and closes her eyes, soaking up the soothing late September sun. She thinks of her childhood. She feels very happy and, half asleep, lingers in thought:

I'm so fortunate that Dalair and I grew up together. We've secretly admired each other since we were children, and have become adults blissfully in love. Dalair has called me Heer—Juliet while I have called him Ranja—Romeo. I feel blessed and overjoyed that our parents arranged our union. Maybe they knew all along that we wanted to be together. Thankfully, it happened. Now, we are married and have our lives together. I will always love Dalair and both of our families, and take care of them until their last days.

"Sarita dear, you're sleepy already. Would you like to drink something," asks Zareena, tugging on her shoulder.

"I'm sorry. I'm sorry. I just dozed off. I should be serving you, not the other way around. I'll get a glass of *lassi* for myself. What can I get you, mother?"

"Nothing, Sarita, you just rest. After I get you a drink I'll do the dishes."

"No. I can't let you do that. It's been over two weeks that you haven't let me lift a finger."

"That's okay. You're a newlywed. This is your honeymoon. We don't let our brides do household chores until the henna color wears off completely. I hope my brother bought good quality henna so you can have a long honeymoon," smiles Zareena.

"Thank you, mother," says Sarita, blushing, and gives her a quick kiss.

"Would you like to take lunch to Dalair? He's been working the fields since dawn. He must be hungry. This is one chore I'm sure you'll love to do. It's all packed up and ready to go." Zareena points towards the package with a playful smile.

"Yes, of course. Thanks for letting me do something."

Sarita springs up, puts the food package atop her head and walks out the courtyard door. Thrilled, she walks from the village and weaves her way through fields of mustard and wheat while humming sweet songs of *Heer Ranja*. She cuts across fallow ground and arrives at the *Dehra*—farm center. A fired up hookah is placed in front of a dilapidated *charpai* that sits outside the latched mud shed. She opens the shed, puts down the food and goes out looking for her husband thinking, *Hookah is still hot. Dalair can't be too far away!*

"Aye *Sardar ji*, where are you? Can you hear me?"

There is no answer. She is worried. After walking along a few wheat fields, she arrives at a wide and dense sugar cane field.

"Aye *Sardar ji*, where are you? Are you out there? Can you hear me?" she shouts louder. There is no answer. She panics; her heart sinks and she yells at top of her lungs, "Dalair. Dalair are you all right? Can you hear me?"

"Yes, yes I can hear you. Wait for me right there. It won't be long. I'll be there in just a few minutes." Dalair shouts back from the other side of the field. Sarita is relieved. She watches Dalair as he appears from the other end of the field, holding a few sticks of sugar cane.

"It's not quite ripe yet. It won't be long though before it is ready for making sugar."

"*Sardar ji*, you are the farmer. How long will it take the sugar cane to ripen and be ready?" teases Sarita, tilting her head with a dimpled smile.

"I guess we have to wait three weeks or more before we can have the sugar making party." They smile at each other and walk single file along the narrow edge between the fields, returning to the center. As Dalair washes his hands, Sarita lays out the food. He is hungry and quickly devours the food. She pours a glass of water that he chugs down, handing the glass back for another.

"You must be starving. You work too hard."

"I don't mind. I love farming, Sarita, and I have a plan."

"Plan, what plan?" Sarita asks.

"I am going to work hard and save money. Eventually, I'll buy more farmland. Then some day, we'll even have a water well just like Mr. Shafkat's. We'll irrigate our fields in case of drought and won't have to depend on random rain. Farming will be fun and our income more dependable that way. And I want you to remember one more thing."

"What's that?" Sarita questions.

"I'll take back my father's land, which Rifaqat has usurped from him. My name Dalair means 'the brave one'. I want to hold my head high and take back what's ours. I want my father to feel proud."

"You have big dreams, my dear husband."

"Oh, yes I do. Look how hard our parents toiled. They've done well considering that they started from nothing."

"I'll work equally hard along with you to make your dream a reality."

"You're the most beautiful girl I've ever laid my eyes upon."

"I'm so lucky," says Sarita, blushing, with eyes cast downward; her heart throbbing.

Dalair lifts up her chin and locks his eyes onto hers. They stand, holding hands and smiling radiantly at one another. Their bodies pull together into a tight embrace. Quickly, they look to see that no one is watching and kiss passionately for a few moments before Sarita pulls away.

"I must be going. Your mother is waiting. I'll see you tonight."

"Tonight!" winks Dalair, beaming with a tender smile.

Sarita blushes. She quickly picks up the metal dishes, throws them in the basket and walks away, balancing the basket on her head. Turning her head, she offers a seductive smile. Dalair is almost giddy, and goes back to work the fields, as Sarita's unsteady legs walk her quivering body towards the village. She thinks fondly of a blissful life together. Dalair and Sarita have always been in love. They are happily married. Both families are pleased, get along well and frequently visit each other.

At one of their family gatherings, Aneel, Sher Singh and Dalair relax and smoke the hookah.

"Father, can I ask you a question?" inquires Dalair.

"Sure, son," says his father.

"The other day someone came by and asked me if we're thinking about moving to India. He went on, saying that as Punjab is divided, Sikhs and Hindus won't be safe in west Punjab. You know, *Badmash,* rascal Rifaqat has been saying the same for some time now. Is he right father? What do you and Uncle know about this?"

"My son, there's talk of partition. Some people are moving across the border. It's a personal choice. No one has to move if they don't want to. Mr. Shafkat and Fazal assure us that our area is safe and we don't need to leave our homes. I'm confident that we'll be safe. Don't forget that we have *kirpans*—daggers and swords for our defense."

"Okay father, I believe you. I just needed to ask."

"Dalair, don't share this conversation with the women. No need to worry them unnecessarily," Aneel says, getting an uneasy feeling himself.

"I understand," assures Dalair.

In early November, as earlier in the year, they come together to make brown sugar. Makhan and Karim, a little older and stronger are a real help. In winter, there is not much to do. Dalair keeps himself occupied on the farm caring for the animals, cutting and mixing fodder for those that are stalled. Sarita takes over all the household duties from her mother-in-law and in the long winter nights she crochets, sews and spins cotton yarn on the spinning wheel. As the seasons pass, they wait. After spring, comes Vaisakhi, the fair, which Dalair and Sarita anticipate with excitement. As a young couple, they will go together to have fun, eat, drink and shop until they are exhausted.

—16—

The Attack

"Open up, open up Fazal. Please hurry and come down quick," someone shouts, while knocking violently at the door. Fazal, clad only in a *dhoti* has just fallen asleep. He is on the roof top, sprawled on a cot next to his wife and children. He bolts upright and looks for his sandals. It is the middle of a hot night in May of 1947.

"Who's at the door?" he shouts. No one answers, while the pounding continues.

"I'm coming. I'm coming," Fazal shouts again. Slipping on his sandals, he slides into a thin muslin *kurta*, grabs his *lathi*—fighting stick, and heads towards the stairs.

"Be careful Fazal," Rakhi warns. "I know more than you tell me. Tara tells me about everything—the partition, the panic, their relatives, who have been chased out of Narang village. You don't know who's at the door. Maybe it's someone who doesn't like us. Non-Muslims are also on the rampage and retaliating, so watch out," says Rakhi, stretching to sit up on the cot, draping her *dupatta*, as a matter of routine.

Fazal glances at his wife, acknowledging her concern, and slows down a bit, steeling his body and mind for the unknown. He moves down the steps and cautiously opens the door a crack, only to see Sher

Singh on the other side. He swings the door wide open to admit his friend, who is shaking with rage.

"Hurry, hurry Fazal."

"What's wrong? What happened?" asks Fazal.

"You've got to come, and bring along Mr. Shafkat as well," Sher utters faintly, his broken voice mixed with muffled sobs.

"Tell me. Tell me now so that I can tell Shafkat." Fazal grabs his arm and hurries toward Shafkat's house.

"Less than an hour ago, Zareena sent a message that her family has been attacked in Kotli. Dalair and Sarita are gravely wounded. She needs help. We've got to go. I'm outraged and scared at the same time," he screams.

Shafkat grabs his loaded rifle, and runs to the barn. Incensed, he yells at the top of his lungs, "We can't let this lunacy go on. We must stop them and get the culprits." He saddles two horses, giving one to Sher, and motions Fazal to jump behind him. With Shafkat in the lead, they gallop quickly out of Rurkee, leaving a trail of dust. They arrive at the outskirts of Kotli, sickened to see the fields on fire. Numerous houses are ablaze. They hear people screaming and yelling for help. "Why? Why?" they shout.

"This is much worse than I expected," cries Shafkat, raising his hand and signaling Sher to slow down. They approach the village of Kotli cautiously, shifting their eyes; hoping to spot the offenders. They arrive at Aneel's house, tie the horses to a tree and run through the open door. The courtyard is packed with angry men and wailing women. They push their way through, only to witness a scene of horrifying carnage. Two bodies lie on a cot under a blood soaked sheet. Zareena, kneeling on the floor, rests her head on one of the corpses, her arms spread across the bodies, as if to protect them from further harm. Half a dozen women sob, their *dupattas* partially covering their faces. They crouch around Sarita's blood soaked body.

"Oh my God, oh my God, don't tell me my Sarita's dead," Sher gasps, pulling back the sheet and crumpling to the floor. He lets out a deafening shriek, seeing Dalair's and Sarita's lifeless bodies punctured with stab wounds and sword gashes. A single gunshot has pierced Dalair's chest. Leaning over the cot and cupping his hands around his daughter's head, he plants a gentle kiss on her cheek. He runs his hand over Dalair's head, combing back his hair, planting a soft kiss on his forehead. His legs weakened, he collapses next to Zareena and pulls the grieving mother to his chest.

"Sher, I couldn't protect your daughter. I'm so sorry." Zareena keens, her broken words barely discernable; her voice hoarse from crying.

"It's not your fault. What happened? Where's Aneel?" Sher asks gently, muffling his sobs while holding Zareena tightly.

It is almost dawn. The morning light, increasingly bright, overtakes the darkness of night, improving visibility. As Sher gets up, he realizes a few more women are on the rooftop, watching in shock and silence. He spots Aneel, whose head, hung in sorrow, is sitting at the edge of the cot, his legs limp, his feet resting on the ground. Shafkat and Fazal are sitting beside him, holding and comforting him. Sher hugs him tightly and asks, "What happened? Who killed our children? They've been married only a few months and still honeymooning. I'll find the murderers. I swear I'll kill them with my bare hands."

Shafkat takes Sher's hands in his, while Fazal holds his shoulders, and helps to calm his body, which is overwhelmed with shock.

"We'll get them and bring them to justice. Tell us, how did it end so tragically?"

"We were sleeping," says Aneel, clearing his throat as if to swallow, and running his tongue over dry lips. There is a long pause.

His friends wait patiently. "Take a deep breath. Take your time," they encourage him. He starts to talk slowly, dryly; almost with a sense of resignation, his stocky frame collapsed into his heart.

"We were in bed. My wife and I were on the rooftop, while Dalair and Sarita were sleeping in the courtyard. I woke up hearing loud shouts warning that our village was being attacked. I looked toward Sialkot and saw fields and haystacks burning. It's still dark and I heard several men on horses heading our way. Quickly, the word spread and half of the village was on the rooftops looking and wondering. People panicked. Sikh and Hindu families knew they were the targets. Some locked their doors and hid, while others got swords, daggers, knives and fighting sticks. A dozen horsemen, maybe more, neared the village.

Most of them had their faces covered, rifles cocked, swords drawn, shouting to kill all the *kafirs*—nonbelievers."

Aneel pauses; wiping tears from his face, he continues. "I ran downstairs and shook Dalair out of his bed. He looked around and ordered us to hide in the back room along with his wife. We did what he asked. He wasn't afraid and believed that a few *goondas*—hooligans were out looting and causing a ruckus. He assured us that we'd be all right. He gathered his sword and *kirpan*—dagger, locked the door, dimmed the kerosene lamp and hunkered down in the storage room next to the front door. Soon the commotion and screams got louder and closer. I was afraid. We held our breath, waiting and praying for the storm to blow over. Later, people told me the *goondas* went wild, knocking down doors and robbing families of their gold and precious possessions. If people resisted, they pushed them aside, beat them and even left some of them wounded. The victims were all non-Muslims.

"Soon two of the *goondas* were at our doorstep, knocking incessantly and ordering us to open up or else. Nobody stirred, not even Dalair. The masked intruders kicked open the door. Dalair stood up too and tried to reason with them. One pushed him aside and yelled, 'Where's the rest of your family?'

"'They're not here,' Dalair answered.

"'You're lying,' the other shouted.

"'If they don't come out soon and bring all the money and gold, we'll kill you. You have two minutes, *kafir*.'"

"'Please don't kill him,' begged Sarita. 'Take all the jewelry I have, or whatever else you want. But don't hurt him.' Sarita ran out pleading, taking cover behind her husband.

"'I want you,' taunted one.

"Dalair went insane. Pulling his sword forward, he attacked them with full force. He endured hit after hit hoping to shield his wife, while she took severe blows trying to protect her husband. She fell screaming, terribly wounded. She was bleeding profusely; almost dead. Dalair lunged at the *goondas* like a wounded lion, waving the steel furiously, trying to knock them down. One assailant yelled, staggering forward. 'He's going to kill us.'

"'Go get your god-damn gun,' screeched the other.

"The intruders dashed out the door and were back in a split second, one of them pointing a rifle at Dalair. He raised the barrel and emptied the bullet into my son's chest. I saw all this through a small window. I should've come out. I should've bought a gun. Old age and fear was my poor excuse for inaction."

"Don't blame yourself. It's not your fault. You would've been dead too, had you intervened. Besides, Dalair would never have let you come out to face the monsters." Sher rubs Aneel's back, offering what little consolation he can.

"Dalair fell, slumped over his wife's body, and gasped for breath. The vigilantes jumped on their horses and disappeared into the darkness, joining others on the run. We ran to the children, but neither moved. I could hear the bastards proclaiming, '*Pakistan Zinda Bad*—long live Pakistan. *Hindustan Murda Bad*—death be to India.'

"Neighbors came pouring into the courtyard. They put Dalair and Sarita on a cot. They remained unconscious, their eyes closed, barely breathing, while some tried to revive them, and others attempted to stop the bleeding. In the midst of crying, screaming and sobbing, the couple took their last breaths. Someone pulled a sheet over them. The screams and crying became louder and more intense. My wife couldn't cry any more. She just stretched her arms over our beloved children and lay there as if she were dead herself."

"Did you recognize any of those men, Aneel? Was Rifaqat was one of them?"

"I don't know. He could've been. I can't say. It was dark, chaotic, and their faces were covered."

Shafkat, having failed to quiet the crowd, fires a shot in the air. The crying and wailing stops. He addresses the crowd. "Listen, and listen carefully. This is atrocious. I feel as if my own two children have been murdered. I want to find and jail the culprits. However, that won't be easy or even possible. As you know by now, because of Punjab's partition, there is panic and uncertainty. Half of Sialkot is in ruins. Our neighbors are subjected to arson, rape and now murder. Our community was safe until now. At least, I thought so. On behalf of all our Muslim brothers—and I'm sure that Fazal would agree—I must tell you, we cannot guarantee your safety, or protect your property.

"I propose we form a posse to find these criminals, who have, in the name of religion, pillaged and plundered, giving Islam a bad name. We'll do our best to protect you. However, I urge you to consider leaving. We'll protect, with our lives, anyone who wants to stay. Those who want to leave? I'll personally see that you have safe passage across the border. Think about your future plans."

As the village patriarch, Shafkat continues. "The grieving families have given me permission to arrange the funeral today after sunset. We all know that Muslims bury their dead, while Sikhs cremate theirs. Although we have lived like brothers and sisters, and have come together eagerly to share each other's happiness and sorrows, we haven't participated in each other's funerals. This time, I urge my Muslim brothers to make an exception and show up for the cremation. We'll give Dalair and Sarita their last rites and say good bye with honor and dignity. Pay your respects to the slain, and send a strong signal to the criminals that we stand shoulder to shoulder in condemning such atrocities, regardless of religion.

"Gather your strength and spirit. Help and look out for each other, and most importantly stand by the victims' families in their grief. No parents should be alone to bear the terrible burden of burying their children. Fazal and I are going to Rurkee. I'll bring Tara back; she will be devastated by the attack on her daughter. It might be wise for Fazal to stay with the son, who is too young to understand the violence."

Fazal climbs up behind Shafkat, who spurs the horse forward. "Where are we going Shafkat?"

"Fazal, I have to make a quick stop," says Shafkat, heading for Rifaqat's house. Once there, Shafkat pounds at the door nonstop until Rifaqat's wife appears.

"Where is your God damned husband?"

"I don't know Mr. Shafkat. He left yesterday morning to see his brother and hasn't returned yet," replies Rifaqat's wife, shaking with alarm.

"He hasn't returned?" Shafkat spits out the words.

"No, he hasn't. He never tells me anything. He comes and goes as he pleases. Something's the matter?" she asks.

"You tell him that I'm looking for him." The frightened woman nods and closes the door.

"Shafkat, you don't think . . . ?"

"Maybe. We definitely want to find out."

When Tara arrives at Kotli to view the death scene, she motions for someone to pull back the sheet. She wants to see for herself, still hoping that someone else is under the cover. She lets out a dreadful scream, and wails, releasing bottled up emotions and tears all at once. She throws herself on the cot and sobs until her lungs make no sound. Tara thinks of her son, left behind in Rurkee with no knowledge of the horrific attack which has taken his sister's life. She is thankful for Fazal, who must break the awful news to Makhan. She counts on the presence of Makhan's best friend Karim, and his favorite Aunt Rakhi to help the boy absorb the pain.

At Rurkee, Fazal prepares himself to convey the horrible news of Sarita's death to her young brother.

"Uncle, what's going on?" asks Makhan, sensing pain and apprehension in Fazal's expression. "Where are my parents? Why is everyone upset and sad?" Makhan questions incessantly, until Fazal tells him the news. The young boy is shocked, unable to fathom that his sister and her husband have been killed for no reason.

Fazal takes the boy into his arms, presses him against his chest before releasing him from a prolonged fatherly embrace and explains discretely, yet lovingly, the reasons for chaos and misery. "Makhan, conflicts have erupted, and unfortunately Dalair and Sarita were at the wrong place at the wrong time. It's said that bad things happen to good people. They were such good people, Makhan. You should know that they have joined their Maker and that their spirits rest in heaven." Fazal puts his arm around his shoulder, and takes the boy home, where Rakhi enfolds him in her arms as if he were her own son. Karim looks on, stunned; his face expressing disbelief.

On the same day, friends help the grief stricken parents prepare Dalair's and Sarita's bodies for their final journey. They wash the bodies and dress them in their best attire before laying them on cots under clean cotton sheets. Their bodies are covered with roses and marigolds. The people of Kotli and Rurkee come to pay their respects all day. Just before evening, the loved ones hoist the cots on their shoulders and take them to *shamshan ghat*, the cremation ground. Teary-eyed men, confused children and wailing women follow.

Dalair and Sarita lie next to each other on the *ghee*—soaked sandalwood funeral pyre. As the sun sets, their fathers, Sher and Aneel, light the wood. Makhan and Karim, holding hands tightly, stand next to Fazal. Soon Aneel and Sher join them. Their saddened faces glow, as the flames and smoke rise, shrouding the dead. Makhan looks beyond the pyre blankly, unable to believe that loved ones are being cremated right in front of him. The sullen and frightened people of Kotli and Rurkee, Muslims, Hindus, and Sikhs alike, gather to pay final respect.

Two days later the families return, rake up the bones and reverently put them into urns, hoping to someday to take them to the sacred waters of *Haridwar*, the ultimate resting place. The grieving families, numb with shock, wonder if they will be the next targets. Should they stay or flee?

—17—

Pulled Apart

Frightened, and reeling from the tragedy, Aneel and Zareena—with their daughter Berket, move to Rurkee to live with grief stricken Sher and Tara, and their son Makhan. They comfort each other, while passionately feeling the need to stand united. Rurkee is incident free, yet Sikhs and Hindus are fearful, especially after the carnage in Kotli. They visit Fazal's shop, talking incessantly for hours, asking for advice.

Fazal recalls the words of Mr. Shafkat: "We'll protect you with our lives, but as the situation spins out of control, we can't guarantee your safety. We'll help you if you decide to leave."

During an evening meal, Aneel and Sher contemplate their future. The two men take turns smoking the hookah, while Tara and Zareena wait for the conversation to start. Makhan and Berket lie on a bed staring blankly at the ceiling. They are quiet and aloof, still shocked by the evil deeds. As children, they turn inward, knowing they will not be asked for their opinion.

"We should leave," says Aneel, exhaling a big puff of smoke.

"Leave?" Sher snaps, looking at him, in surprise. He grabs the hookah and smokes for a minute, frantically blowing clouds of smoke that nearly fill the room. "We can't leave. This is our home. This is the land where our ancestors dwelled and made a living for generations. We've friends here. Did you forget that just last week we buried our children here? You say leave? I can't do that," says Sher, making the case angrily.

Stillness hangs in the smoke filled room, interrupted only by the gurgling water filtering the smoke. Sher sucks in a long draught before handing the hookah back to Aneel. Aneel pauses, and then makes his case, point by point. "These days, one can't tell the difference between a friend and a foe. It's not our doing, but the fact is we've been thrown into chaos. Even Fazal and Shafkat can't assure our safety. We've suffered enough. We should plan to leave, and leave quickly before it's too late," he says emphatically, while taking his turn to smoke.

"What about our property and possessions we've worked so hard for all our lives? Our animals—especially our animals. What are we going to do with them?" says Sher despondently.

"Sher, I don't know why you're even thinking such thoughts. We can't roll up the land and carry it with us. Animals need food and water. The possessions will draw attention to our escape. What good are worldly possessions if we're dead?"

"My dear Sher Singh," argues Zareena, "listen to Aneel. What matters is that we make it to our future homeland alive."

"I agree. We should leave and go to India," says Tara, looking at her husband anxiously.

Sher knew in his heart that they needed to leave, but required a nudge. He nods in agreement, "Okay, let's get on with it."

"Maybe it's for the better. I can't bear any further loss," whispers misty-eyed Tara, while looking at Makhan and Berket, who are fast asleep, unaware that their destinies have changed forever.

The next day the parents break the news of their leaving to their children. Berket appears unconcerned, while Makhan becomes petulantly quiet.

During the next two days, Fazal and Shafkat help pack the essentials, and develop an escape plan. On Tuesday evening all gather at Shafkat's for a farewell dinner. Though the feast is elaborate, the atmosphere is somber. Hardly speaking a word, they eat quietly. After picking up the floor mat and shaking out the crumbs, Rakhi puts the dishes away and brings chai to everyone. Makhan has disappeared with Karim. The two best friends are distraught over their impending separation.

"Where are the boys?" asks Rakhi, while serving the tea.

"They were here a minute ago. They ate with us. Can't be too far away," Fazal says calmly.

"We've got to get going soon if we are to follow our plan," says Shafkat emphatically. "We'll give the boys a few more minutes." They drink tea without looking directly at one another; stealing occasional glances, and seeing only sad faces and teary eyes. They know this is their last time together, and they will never see each other again.

An hour later, the boys aren't back. "We'd better look for them," Shafkat observes, with concern. Sher and Fazal search their homes but come back empty handed. Now, everyone is nervous. They look frantically, searching everywhere—their homes and Fazal's shop. Panic sets in.

"The *Khoo*; they must be at my well," says Shafkat. "That's their favorite hangout. Fazal and I'll go." He exhales confidently. He climbs on his horse and gallops toward the well, while Fazal runs to his house to get his bike. They race to the well, constantly looking in all directions. They search each room at the well, every corner and under each cot without success. Their hearts sinking, they start to turn back when they hear a rustling in the thicket behind the barn. They tiptoe to the brush and see Makhan and Karim crouched in the bushes. Their hearts pounding, they order the boys to come forward. The boys crawl out, holding hands, with their eyes lowered.

"I don't want to leave. I can't and won't abandon my friend," Makhan cries out, hugging Karim. "My family can move to India but I want to stay with Karim."

"Son, everybody is worried sick, especially your parents. They're all waiting anxiously for you to come home. It's best for you to go with your family, where you can be safe and pursue your life's dreams," consoles Fazal, pulling the boys apart. Makhan tears the *kara*—steel bangle from his wrist and slides it onto Karim's right arm.

"This is one of the most sacred things I own," says Makhan. "I'm giving it to you as a symbol of my friendship—to remember me by, forever. Last night I knew that our move was coming. Maybe in the future I'll come back to see you, or you'll come to visit us in India. Promise me that you'll come," Makhan pleads, hugging his friend emotionally. His tears turn into sobs.

Karim nods. "We'll see each other again, I promise." He clutches Makhan, tears rolling down his cheeks.

Shafkat separates the boys, and lifts them onto the horse, while Fazal follows on his bike. They gather together at Sher's house, only to say good-bye. Before the leave-taking, Shafkat inspects his horses; grooms their coats, examines their hooves for sores and stones, and rechecks the harness.

"They're ready to go. Fazal will ride with you," declares Shafkat, handing one of the horses to Sher. Meanwhile, Tara and Zareena go inside the house one last time and come out, each holding an urn in their hands.

"My dear sister Rakhi; if you don't mind, we'd like to leave our children with you," says Tara. "If we don't make it across the border, they will be safe with you. If we do, I promise you that we'll be back in Rurkee and will take Dalair and Sarita to *Haridwar*, the holy place for ashes on the Ganges. This tragedy will be temporary . . . you'll see."

"I pray that you're right, and hope we'll see you once again very soon," answers Rakhi. She brushes away her tears with her *dupatta*, and takes the urns. Tara and Zareena kiss and hug her, while the three women cling to one another, sobbing.

Tez has been fed, watered, harnessed and checked for travel worthiness. He is ready to go. The two women, Berket and Makhan get on the cart and squat down next to a few bags of clothes, food and a sack full of fodder for Tez. Shafkat softly jabs his horse, spurring him to move. Aneel tugs the reins and Tez dutifully pulls. Sher and Fazal, on the other horse, follow behind. They all look back at their friends, waving farewell until their faces blur and disappear into the darkness. The spiritless and hunched bodies of the passengers blend with the bundles of provisions on the cart bed. They have no more tears to shed.

Shafkat surprises the travelers by stopping at his well. "We're stopping so soon?" Aneel asks, while reining in Tez.

"Fazal and I need to discuss our travel plan and escape strategy," replies Shafkat, while Fazal unloads a bag and spreads its contents on the cart bed. He removes two old patched *dhotis* and tattered *kurtas*, handing them to Sher and Aneel, and instructing them to do as they are told. "Here you go. Please change into these. Hand me your turbans and *kangas*—wooden combs, and let down your hair," he tells his friends, who raise their eyebrows in surprise at the orders.

"Why must we give you our turbans and *kangas*?"

"I've thought long and hard," explains Shafkat, "and I'm convinced that it's much safer this way. From here, until we cross the border, you're traveling as *Pir Malangs*—Muslim holy men, with your wives and children. Your wives and Berket don't need to change. Looking at their clothes, one can't tell them apart from Muslim women. However, we need to disguise your appearance a little. Taking off a turban is not too much to ask under the circumstances."

"Wearing a turban is our religious duty and a symbol of honor," reasons Sher. "We've always respected you with or without your turban. As you've known for some time, it has become a target of hate. When we get to the other side, I'll insist that you put your Sikh garments back on," says Fazal as he replaces Makhan's turban with a beautiful Muslim *topi*—cap, and pulls him close, in an assuring embrace.

"Son, it's just a matter of one night."

As Sikhs transformed into Muslim holy men, they regroup and resume the journey. Shafkat sprints back and forth, scouting and making sure no trouble is in their path. Tez slowly clip-clops along, while Sher follows. Fazal looks out keenly and listens for danger that might lurk in the shadows. The caravan travels over narrow dirt paths, taking the back ways. It is hot, very still and eerie. As they skirt around villages and pass through the countryside, they see more burned homes; damaged and charred fields, some of which are still smoldering. Clear signs of turmoil, uncertainty and peril mark the mass exodus of Sikhs and Hindus. They are more than half way to their destination when Shafkat senses danger. He gallops back, ordering the caravan to stop. Three masked men on horsebacks approach.

"*Aslamo Elaikum*," says one.

"*Wa Elaikum Asslaam*," replies Shafkat.

"Who are you? Who are these people with you? Where are you going?" questions the second. The mothers, frozen with fear, discretely enfold Makhan and Berket within the bundles. Stooped over, they remain lifeless.

"My name is Shafkat Hussein and that gentleman is Mr. Fazal. He is one of my best friends. These are our *pirs*—spiritual leaders, and their families. We're escorting them to Chubara to attend an important *Urs*—a holy gathering. Despite the unrest, they insist on going, as they've never missed the annual gathering for twenty years. It's so dangerous out here with this Partition and all, Fazal and I have decided to escort them." Shafkat speaks confidently, while keeping one hand firmly on the rifle hidden behind him. Shafkat stands tall and firm. It boosts his courage to know that Fazal has his hands on his sword, while Aneel and Sher firmly grip their *kirpans*—daggers, concealed under their *dhotis*—sarongs, which they did not give up during the transformation. *→ translated repeatedly already*

"Shafkat Sahib, aren't you from Rurkee?" asks one of the horsemen.

"Yes, yes. I'm from Rurkee."

"We've heard a lot about you. You're well known, and a respected landlord there."

"Thank you for the compliment."

"We're sorry to interrupt your journey, and apologize for stopping you, but it's very treacherous out here. Sikhs and Hindus are fleeing. Some of these *kafirs* are dangerous, especially the Sikhs. You want to watch out for them. They're violent and mean. Don't hesitate to kill them if you have to. If you don't, they will kill you."

"Thanks for your concern and warning," says Shafkat. "Believe me; we're keeping a very close eye out for them."

"*Khuda Hafiz.*"

"*Khuda Hafiz,*" answers Shafkat. All are relieved, as the absence of fear calms their nerves.

"We're keeping a close eye on those Sikhs!" murmurs Aneel, pulling Tez's rein. For just one moment they all chuckle, even under the terrifying and unpredictable circumstances.

"Shafkat, how do you know about the *Urs* in Chubara?" asks Fazal.

"I don't. I just bluffed. Besides, there is always an *Urs* somewhere."

It is nearly dawn and they are very close to their destination. They resume their journey, and just after sunrise, arrive in Chubara, a village that sits just at the presumed border of newly created countries: India and Pakistan.

Refugees move across the border in both directions, looking at each other resentfully, their eyes filled with suspicion and hate. They carry meager belongings. They are tired, hungry. Shafkat wastes no time. As they huddle to say good-bye, he pulls out a small package from his horse satchel and hands it over to Aneel. It contains a bundle of money and six gold bangles. Aneel, overcome with emotion, looks up and says, "This isn't necessary."

"You'll need money to settle in your new land," says Shafkat. "And the bangles are for Berket. Put them on her hand on her wedding day and tell her it is the gift from Rurkee. She should remember her roots and know that she'll always be a daughter of Rurkee." He turns to Sher and says with pride, "I'm impressed with how you handled that horse. The horse likes you, and he wants to go to the other side of the line and settle with you in East Punjab. You'll take care of him won't you?"

"Line, what line? They can draw a line on the ground to try and separate us," says Sher, biting his quivering lips. "But we are bosom brothers, nursed by our mother—Punjab. No one, I mean no one can draw a line through milk. We'll always be together, if not in body then in spirit."

Fazal hands back the turbans and *kangas* that were stowed in his bag. He places one on Makhan's head, while the other two put theirs on. He says with a smile, "See, I told you that we'd send you off with honor!"

They give one another a quick and firm embrace, relieved, yet so sad at the same time. Fazal jumps up behind Shafkat, who turns the horse around and urges him forward. The horse sets off quickly, leaving a trail of dust; racing full tilt, as he carries the two men back to Rurkee.

—18—

Beyond Border

The family wanders aimlessly around Chubara until they see a banyan tree, where a few refugees are huddled together. They squeeze alongside them and mark a small space with blankets. Tired and confused, they feel as if they have been picked up by a dirt devil and dropped under the vast tree canopy. Momentarily, they forget their village and the arduous journey, and focus on their family's survival and future. The disappearance of Shafkat and Fazal in a swirl of dust lingers in their minds.

Makhan frees Tez from the cart and puts out fodder. Tez quickly eats, and slumps down. Sher ties his new friend, the horse, to the tree's aerial root and gives him a generous portion of feed, which he promptly starts to munch.

"Eat up, my friend. You're so deserving; thanks for carrying us across," whispers Sher, while patting him from head to tail. Sher and Aneel tell their wives they are on the safe side. The women feel assured enough to tell the children to relax, and make them believe that they are safe.

Tara spreads the food that Rakhi packed for them out on the cart bed. They eat quietly. After having been uprooted and thrown into unfamiliar territory, their bodies require nourishment, and they must keep their heads clear, to work out their situation. With bodies fatigued, minds numbed and stomachs full, they fall sound sleep.

At noon, the sun's direct rays sear their faces, causing the adults to spring up from their slumber. One after another, they awaken to the harsh surroundings. Makhan and Berket remain asleep, and will never know that Tara has moved them numerous times for better shade.

The red haloed fireball accentuates the sweltering heat and rising dust. The smoldering houses and fields have generated a thick smoky haze that covers the horizon. Fly ash and dust devils whirl in the distance.

A night's rest and nourishment jump-starts the thinking process. Realizing their dreadful predicament, the parents gather strength and decide to move on and find a place they can call home. If not for them, at least for their children, they must go on.

"Look around Aneel," says Zareena, shaking his shoulder; trying to bring him out of his melancholy. "We're not alone. Did you notice that other families are just as haggard as we are, sharing the same canopy? They are all Sikhs. Our very own."

Aneel gives his wife a faint smile, and acknowledges her optimism. "The turbaned men, speaking Punjabi, put me at ease, and give me hope for our future," he says, squeezing Zareena's hand. "We must move on."

All these families, thrown together in common misery, take shelter under the centuries old banyan tree. They cook and clean in open make-shift kitchens, wash in uncomfortable and inadequate privies—hastily erected with sticks and sheets—and sleep in the open. They sit for hours sharing their painful predicament. They have all fled their homes and native villages for reasons they cannot grasp. Most can name someone in their family who has been brutally murdered or raped. Not many, but some have escaped without witnessing such atrocities. The Chubara villagers, uncertain of their own safety, having been too close to the border, or not knowing where the border lies, come to help, courageously and generously.

The bewildered refugees contemplate what to do next. Their emotions vary. Some swear revenge; some hope to go back to their homes, and others sit traumatized, in a state of numbness.

Occasionally, reasoned thought rises through the angry and confused mind; a realization that life must go on. One must leave the past behind, look ahead and move forward. Aneel and Sher decide they will travel further east the next morning.

Zareena and Tara feel robbed of life. Their eldest children gone, they talk quietly about the loss, crying softly, hugging one another and looking at the two children left in their care. Tara finally says, "These two are the gold, our treasured spark of hope rests with them and their future." Zareena nods in agreement.

At dawn the next day, they are on the move again. Aneel hands Tez's reins to his nephew. Makhan obliges and helps his mother, aunt and cousin onto the cart bed. He pulls the reins and whistles for Tez to go; his uncle and father on the horse follow close behind. Tez, rested and burdened with one less person, eagerly pulls, and steadily picks up speed.

The warm morning heralds another hot day. Haze hangs in the air. The two families head east without a destination in mind, and distance themselves as far as possible from the imaginary border that someone has drawn on paper. They decide to travel east all day and settle in the very first village they come across at the end of the trip.

Unlike the night before, when they saw hundreds of people on the move, today they do not see a single soul. It's quiet and eerie. A sinking sensation pervades their bodies; yet they push on. Nearing one of the hundreds of irrigation canals, dammed and diverted from the five rivers that run through Punjab, they see a narrow bridge spanning the massive embankments.

Tara looks up and sees large birds buzzing near and over the bridge. She yells at her husband, while pointing to the sky, "What's that? Why are there so many vultures? Something isn't right." Alarmed, she scans the eastern sky.

The men leave the family under the shade of *sheesham* trees and jump on the horse, galloping toward the canal to investigate. As they arrive near the canal, they smell a foul odor. It gets stronger as they near the embankment. They tie the horse and quickly, yet cautiously climb the embankment. Their *kirpans* drawn, they stand at the top to look. The smell is too pungent to bear and the sight too horrific to witness; they cover their faces and noses with their turban tails.

Under the bridge, between the first pier and the abutment, the site of an unimaginable massacre comes into focus. Hundreds of Muslim men, women and children lie murdered. Beaten with staves, stabbed with daggers, cut down with machetes and swords or shot at point-blank, bodies scatter the land. Men have been executed, women's arms and necks gashed while they covered and clutched their babies and small children against their bosoms. Scores lie dead next to their parents, while others are strewn about haphazardly. Bodies are heaped at random, full of wounds, cuts and bullet holes. A few corpses float in the water, possibly dragged by carnivorous animals. Wild canines have torn into some, vultures have picked and pulled at the human flesh; the rest hover above to return for more. Attackers have eliminated both young and old, cutting down them like weeds.

Aneel and Sher are sick to their stomachs. They turn away from the scene and vomit until their eyes are red, and their noses are sore, having nothing more to evacuate. Putting away their *kirpans,* they dash down the earthen embankment, jump on the horse and race toward the *sheesham* trees. They are relieved to see that their families are safe. Their wives have waited anxiously, while the sad and weary children sit quietly.

"What's up ahead? You look scared!" cry the wives, gripped with fear. The men grab their wives' arms and pull them away from the children so they will not hear.

"We have a terrible problem. A number of Muslims have been killed and their bodies are scattered under the bridge," says Aneel. "I'm afraid that the villains are still lurking around. It's not safe to take the bridge. We must find another place to cross the canal." He lies in order to keep their wives from seeing the carnage.

"We'll go further along, and find another crossing," says Sher. "Beyond those trees and thickets, I can see a village, across the canal. There must be a crossing," he suggests, blocking the sun with one hand and pointing upstream with the other. Makhan helps his passengers onto the cart and orders Tez to follow his dad. They weave their way through the fields and soon arrive at the crossing. Sher was right. A narrow bridge spans the canal leading to the village.

"This is it. We are too tired to go any further. This is our Promised Land. We shall make our new home and future here," exclaims Aneel.

The rickety old and narrow bridge sways slightly. First, Sher walks his horse across. Then Aneel carefully moves Tez and the cart to the other side. The children and women follow. They regroup, then dash toward the village as fast as the horse and Tez will take them. For the first time in many days, the family is unafraid. Their happiness drives them to approach the village like thirsty travelers who have seen mirages for days and finally arrive at a clean, cool spring.

The village is slightly larger than Rurkee. More than half of the houses are burned, charred, or in piles of rubble. Smoke, and a foul smell hang in the air. Stray dogs roam aimlessly. Only a few people, mostly turbaned men, are out attending to animals and doing farm chores. The two families, having been through so much, are not surprised to see the lifelessness of the village.

A short distance off stands a beautiful, small building. "There's the *Gurdawara*—Sikh temple," exclaims Makhan, pointing to a yellow flag fluttering atop the golden cupola. Sher knocks at the temple door. The door opens and the bearded temple priest, wearing a milk white *kurta and dhoti,* and a matching turban over his jet-black hair stands on the other side.

"*Sat Sari Kal,*" says the priest, folding his hands and showing his sparkling white teeth.

"We're refugees from Rurkee."

"*Gee Aiyan Noon*—my heart welcomes you."

"We left our homes and lands, and have been traveling for days. Two of our children were murdered. We have no place to go. We need help," pleads Aneel.

"You are my brothers. I consider your family as mine," says the priest. "I know you've suffered. There are others who have fled Pakistan and made it here to Rahim Pura, and call it their home. I'm *Giani,* Kirpal Singh and I welcome you. Today, you'll be my guests and tomorrow we'll talk to the *Numberdar*—village representative, Diljeet Singh, to see how we can help you start your lives amongst us."

Kirpal hugs the men and children warmly and pays respect to the women, bowing his head and smiling gently. He helps them tie the animals on temple grounds, making sure that they have ample water and feed. Holding the children's hands, he walks them to his private residence, located within the temple compound. His wife and family kindly invite them into the courtyard of their small brick home. They wash, eat and fall onto the cots, sleeping soundly until the next day when they meet the *Numberdar*, Diljeet Singh. After listening to their tragic tale, the *Numberdar* tells them that half of the village is empty.

"There are no Muslims in Rahim Pura. They all left two days ago. I don't think they had a chance. I've a feeling that none of them made it beyond the canal. They may have been killed, or perhaps have escaped to the west. Other than a few Hindus, our village is purely Sikh now," says the leader. "You must go around the village to choose the houses you would like for your families. I'll see that provisions are brought for you and your animals." Sher and Aneel have mixed feelings when they claim two houses spared from arson and fire.

Sher surveys his home. A Muslim family appears to have left in a hurry, leaving everything behind. In the corner of the great room stands a low wooden platform, upon which lies a *Jai Namaz*—prayer rug, with Mecca woven into it. On top of the prayer rug rests a carved walnut stand supporting an open Koran—the Muslim holy book, its pages transcribed in beautiful Arabic calligraphy. Sher thinks of Fazal and Shafkat, recalling how they revere the Koran, just as Sikhs revere the *Guru Grunth Sahib*—Sikh holy book. Muslims perform *woozoo*—ablution, before even touching the Koran, and always place it high above everything else in the house. Sher does not know how to perform the ablution, yet unconsciously washes his face and hands, picks up the Koran, slips it into its green cloth cover, kisses it reverently and places it high on a wooden ledge, made especially for the holy book. He sits down at the edge of the wooden platform. Mulling over his simple life, crushed by horrific experience, Sher is forced into a moment of anguished soul-searching. For the first time in his being he digs deep, and tries to make some sense out of all the misery.

I know I was born a Sikh and that Nanak, the first Guru laid the Sikh foundation right here in Punjab. I have never traveled outside my village until now when I've become a refugee. I remember hearing that India is a vast country of different climates, cultures and creeds. I know that besides Sikhs, there are Hindus, Muslims, Buddhists and even Christians in India. I've no idea where they come from. How did their religions come into being? All I know is that they were born into their faith just as I was born into mine. Why split India into two countries? Why can't faiths coexist and the followers live in harmony, as we lived in Rurkee or at least I thought we did? I would like to know, he murmurs under his breath.

why not do away with "faith" of any kind?!

"What are you doing, Sher?" asks Tara.

"Nothing, nothing at all," he rasps, turning around so as not to reveal his tortured face.

—19—

Train

Fazal has not been the same since he helped his friends across the border. It maddens him that it was fellow Muslims—turned into hooligans, who murdered the young newlyweds in cold blood. He is upset that his son's best friend was snatched away and forced to travel with his family to an unknown destination. He is depressed about the uncertain future of his family and his beloved village, Rurkee. He has aged, and a sullen face has replaced his ever-optimistic smile.

"I know the reason why you've been depressed," says his wife gently when giving him his afternoon chai. "Nonetheless, we need to pick up the pieces and move on, Fazal. You've a family and business to take care of."

"I'm sorry, my dear. You're right, we must move on."

"You haven't been to Sialkot for weeks. Get a good night's sleep and go to Sialkot to see your friend Jamal tomorrow. That'll do you good."

"You're right," agrees Fazal. "I'll visit Jamal and find out what's going on in the city. Besides, I need provisions for the shop. Thank you," says Fazal, forcing a smile.

After breakfast the next morning, Fazal grabs his bike and heads to Sialkot. He has done the ride hundreds of times, and lets his mind wander. Lost in thought, he reflects on what has happened over the last few weeks. Dismissing thoughts of a nightmarish future, he journeys mechanically, little of the trip registering in his thoughts. Seeing the eerie city skyline, his mind awakens. As he bikes through the city, he sees nothing but devastation. Sialkot is a ghost town. Parts of the city, where Sikhs and Hindus had lived, are in ruins. Burned buildings, vandalized homes and businesses lay in rubble. Broken doors and windows swing open. Stray dogs sniff for food. The city that once teemed with life is nearly dead. Very few people, mostly Muslims, are outside. They look scared and run necessary errands quickly. Fazal speeds up and arrives at his friend's shop, one of the few that is open.

"*Aslamo Elaikum.*"

"*Wa Elaikum Asslaam*, brother Fazal," Jamal answers, getting up to embrace his friend, pushing his turban back slightly.

"You are open for business!" says Fazal.

"What business? Nobody is doing any business. Only a few frightened souls, desperate for food and basics, venture out. I'm here to protect my business. If left unattended, I'm sure it would be looted or even set on fire. My son and I take turns. This is our companion and protector." He points to the rifle.

"What happened to the city?"

"Don't ask, Fazal. People have gone mad. They have forced Sikhs and Hindus to run toward the Indian border. Many killed. Muslims killed, too. A cycle of violence reigns.

"I knew it was getting bad. But when did this hell break loose?"

"Things weren't bad here until the terror train arrived from Jammu about two weeks ago."

"Terror Train?"

"You didn't hear about it?"

"No. Remember, I live in a small village called Rurkee."

"I'm sorry. I understand," says Jamal. "Well, sit down. Take a deep breath and listen carefully to what I'm about to tell you. It'll be two weeks tomorrow since I, along with so many others, went to the railway station to receive Muslim refugees, scheduled to arrive on the 1:00 p.m. train from Jammu. We waited for hours on end. There was no sign of the train. The stationmaster told the waiting crowd that communications were down, perhaps severed, and he had no idea where the train was, or if it would arrive at all."

"Did the train arrive that day?"

"Oh, yeah, the train arrived. Much later, about 6:30 p.m., the train pulled up to the platform and screeched to a sudden stop. I could see the sparking wheels as the engineer braked, trying not to overrun the platform. The engineer swung open the cab door and ran towards the stationmaster's office screaming. 'There are dead and wounded in there. Hurry up,' he pleaded as he pushed through the crowd pointing to the train, while the stationmaster ran right behind him. 'I was completely helpless. I couldn't do a thing except run for help.'"

"Dead and wounded?" gasps Fazal.

"It was a long train that stretched the full length of the platform," says Jamal. "There must have been ten cars or more, all smeared and smudged with blood. The caked blood was clearly visible in and around the doors and windows, indicating a blood bath. By now we could smell the nauseating odor of blood and flesh escaping from the train."

"Oh Allah, have mercy on us," says Fazal, stunned; staring at Jamal. He removes his turban and places it on the floor, while listening intently to his friend.

"The crowd waited no longer. People lunged toward the train and swarmed like ants, opening the doors and windows. It was a ghastly sight and the unbearable stench permeated the senses like toxic fumes."

"Please tell me there were not many casualties," says Fazal, looking squarely into his friend's eyes. Jamal removes his turban, setting it in his lap, and tightly holds his silver amulet.

"Not many casualties? It was a massacre. More than a quarter of the passengers were dead and the rest sat lifeless, shocked from grief, slumped against their loved ones. Men, women and children hacked to death indiscriminately. Young children stabbed to death while clutching the bosoms of their murdered mothers."

"Oh, Allah, I don't believe it."

"People gathered around the engineer, who was telling the stationmaster what happened." Jamal explains, relating the engineer's account:

"'This morning,' the engineer had said, 'I was ordered to take a special train from Jammu at about noon to Sialkot with a run time of no more than two hours. I was extremely glad when I learned the train was a special one, as I would be taking hundreds of my fellow Muslim families across the border to a new Pakistan. Families boarded the train with their loved ones, carrying only meager belongings, reluctantly leaving their homeland, yet relieved and happy to be leaving uncertainty and danger behind. As I powered the steam engine slowly forward, I looked back and saw the guard climbing up the caboose with a folded green flag, while passengers were waving teary goodbyes and the children were happily smiling, just to be riding the train. As I cleared the station, I steamed full speed ahead. Less than fifteen minutes into the journey, I slowed down to stop in front of the warning red signal, waiting for it to clear. Next thing I knew, two Sikhs, who were hiding in the bushes climbed up the engine. One of them put a gun to my head, while the other, rattling a sword, ordered my assistant and me to move away from the controls. They tied us up, gagged us and demanded silence—or face death. Quickly, they motioned to others who were hiding in the fields, ready to attack. 'Hamla Karo, Attack,' yelled one of them.

"'Scores of young, turbaned Sikhs came out of hiding, forcing their way into the train, and went on a killing spree. I could hear babies screaming, wounded men moaning and women crying—asking for mercy. But, to no avail. They cut down people like corn stalks. It seemed like an eternity, but took only a few minutes to finish the gruesome and surely premeditated act. Suddenly, there was total silence. I couldn't hear any more screams, not even a moan, just a ghostly dead silence. The leader took the handkerchiefs out of our mouths, while his partner untied us. He pushed the rifle butt into my ribs and ordered us to look back, forcing us to see the bloodied train, and ordered us to go.'

"'Don't stop until you arrive at your destination,' shouted the gunman. 'Tell Muslims that this is the payback for what they're doing to Sikhs in Sialkot, and consider this a special gift from us to your new country, Pakistan.' He yelled at the top of his lungs as he climbed down the cab and ordered his men to disembark from the train. I couldn't do a thing. I felt helpless. My hands gripped the controls. I opened the steam full throttle and soon the train raced ahead at full speed. People and places along the rail line were nothing but ghostly blurs. I imagined Sikhs hiding in every field. I don't know how or when I got here. It seemed an eternity. Next thing I knew I was trying not to over-run the platform in Sialkot. I was having a nightmarish hallucination. I'm sorry . . . I failed in my duty. I'm really sorry. I couldn't bring my passengers safely to Sialkot.'

"At that point," says Jamal, "the exhausted engineer broke down and sobbed hysterically."

"Oh Allah, give Muslims patience," exclaims Fazal.

"Patience," repeats Jamal. "While most of the people helped the survivors and appealed for calm, others—mostly the young men, shouted for revenge. A small group of angry men grew into a mob, left the station, and quickly followed a self-proclaimed leader, who was shouting, 'Kill all the *kafirs*, especially the Sikhs. Kill them all and burn their houses and businesses. Don't let them get away alive. We must avenge the train massacre.'"

"'*Allah Ho Akbar*, God is great,' shouted the leader. '*Allah Ho Akbar*,' shouted the mob that followed.

"Fazal, in no time the mob grew," laments Jamal. "The young men grabbed guns, swords and machetes, mounting an attack against Sikhs and Hindus. They torched houses and burned down their businesses. Innocent Sikhs and Hindus fled, while some took refuge with Muslim friends. Two days of mindless rampage reigned over the entire city. They even killed a dozen Muslims who tried to stand between them and the victims. Pleas for forgiveness went unheeded. Hundreds were killed, while others fled toward the border. All the charred and burned buildings and vandalized houses you saw on your way into the city happened on that terrible day when the terror train arrived in Sialkot.

"You want to know more?" asks Jamal cynically, while fiercely rubbing his amulet.

"There is more?" says Fazal, his face taut with anger.

"One of the young Hindus pleaded that he always liked Islam and would be happy to convert, if his life was spared. One of men asked him to say the *Kalima*—the credo, first of the five pillars of Islam that is mandatory for the converts to recite in order to become a Muslim. '*La Illah Ha Illalla Mohammad Ur Rasul Lulah*, There is no God but Allah and Muhammad is his prophet,' repeated the scared Hindu, hoping that his life would be spared. Fazal, one of the ignorant fools insisted that he couldn't be a real and true Muslim, unless he was circumcised. The mob carried him on their shoulders like a log and took him to the barber who quickly circumcised him, unmindful of his horrifying screams, while four men held down his squirming body. Fazal, the next day they found him bled to death, the final act of conversion. I'm no scholar, but these ignorant men can't even read the Koran, let alone understand its message. For them conversion is not complete without circumcision, as if Islam is no more than the cutting of a little male foreskin. It is tragic, isn't it?" asks Jamal. "What about Rurkee?" he questions, putting his turban back on his head. "I hope you're lucky and your village has been spared from the violence."

"Not really. We've seen our share of tragedy," says Fazal, detailing all the wrongs he has seen. "It's not only Sialkot people who have gone crazy. The entire country is engulfed in flames of hate and is on the brink of total destruction."

"Have you seen this?" says Jamal, holding out a newspaper.

"No. What is it?" replies Fazal.

"*Haftawar*, the Weekly Newspaper. Look at the front page. Read the headline and study the map below it," says Jamal handing over the newspaper and pointing to the map with his forefinger. "Do you realize that there are going to be two Pakistans?"

"Two Pakistans! I thought the Muslim League was fighting for only one Pakistan."

"It's going to be one country Fazal, but with two wings: East and West Pakistan separated by a thousand miles of India. Bengal, just like the Punjab, will be divided in two. The Muslim majority in East Bengal will become East Pakistan, while one third of West Bengal will remain part of new India. Just as in Punjab, millions of refugees, both Muslims and Hindus are fleeing in both directions. Riots have broken out. Bengalis have pitched their battles along ethnic and religious lines. Reports of unimaginable atrocities—rape, murder and bloodshed, are there on the second page. The *Angrez* have not even left yet. It is rumored they are leaving in August or September of next year. That's when we'll have the independent India and Pakistan," concludes Jamal.

Fazal reads the headline and quickly scans the map of India. "I don't need to read the details. I believe you. It's too much for me to handle. I have to go." Fazal gets up, and hugs his friend. "I better be getting home," he says. "My wife's alone and these are dangerous times."

"Take the newspaper. I'll get the latest one next week. You can read it at your leisure."

"Thanks and *Khuda Hafiz*," says Fazal, while taking the Weekly and climbing onto the bike.

"Say my regards to my sister Rakhi; love to your children and stay safe Fazal," shouts Jamal.

Fazal looks back for a moment, acknowledging the farewell. He pedals on hurriedly. The train massacre has unnerved him. He has a hard time balancing his bike as he imagines *goondas* hiding in every field and lurking behind each tree.

—20—

Muhajir

Arriving home, Fazal quietly eats a small supper and falls into bed. At noon the following day he is still asleep. His wife knows that unless afflicted with sickness, he always rises early to open his shop. She knows that his trip to Sialkot did not go well. She makes lunch, puts it on a tray and approaches his bed. She nudges him with one hand while holding the breakfast tray in the other.

"Wake up, Fazal. You've been sleeping a long time. I brought your favorite food," she says, softly pulling the cover from his head. Fazal springs up, sitting forward on the cot; he rubs sleep from his eyes warily.

"Thank you, my dear," says Fazal with a faint smile, while looking lovingly at his wife. The aroma of the steaming chai and the mouth-watering smell of a freshly made lunch please his senses. He eats without delay.

"My dear husband, you don't look good. I see you're even more depressed and withdrawn than yesterday. I have the feeling that Sialkot's situation isn't very good. You don't have to tell me everything. But I do want to know if your friend Jamal is all right."

"He and his family are okay, but Sialkot is a mess."

"I don't want to know. What will be, will be. You have to move on. You haven't opened the shop for days now. We're running out of money. You must start thinking about yourself and your family." After a few moments, she asks, "Do you know what day tomorrow is?"

"No, I don't."

"Tomorrow is *Juma*. You usually don't miss the Friday prayer. It has been weeks since you went to the mosque. Even Mr. Shafkat asked me about your absence. I suggest that you gather up your strength and show your face at the mosque. Are you aware that a number of *Muhajireen*—Muslim refugees from India, have come to Rurkee and have settled on the south side of the village?"

"I had the feeling. But I wasn't sure."

"Yes. About five families have made Rurkee their home, and some of the men go to the mosque, especially for Friday prayer. I beg you," pleads Rakhi, with a sober smile; "Go there tomorrow, meet the poor refugees and make some new acquaintances and customers."

Fazal nods slowly. "I know you're right. I need to move on and get on with my life. I miss my friends, Aneel Gill and Sher Singh, and I know that Karim misses Makhan dearly. Even though I'm terribly upset by the horrors of partition, I must stay strong, if not for myself, for our family, and especially for our children."

"Yes, if not for our sake then for the futures of our son and daughter. I'm glad you are listening to me."

The next day Fazal washes up, performs *woozoo*—ablution, and selects one of his best outfits. He wears his silk *kurta*, draped over a fine, cotton *dhoti* that touches his curl-toed silver sandals. He dons his favorite, rich indigo turban and, looking into a hand held mirror, adjusts it several times, seeking a comfortable fit. He sits down on a cot in the courtyard and waits for the *Muezzin's* call to prayer. His wife secretly admires him, as she has not seen him this well dressed since Vaisakhi.

"*Allah Ho Akbar, Allah Ho Akbar,*" repeats the message from the mosque.

"Time to go, Rakhi. I'll see you after the prayers."

The mosque sits at the edge of the village, next to a pond whose water level fluctuates with the sporadic rains. One of the few structures built from brick, the mosque is a short walking distance from Fazal's house. The simple building consists of a dozen steps leading to the open courtyard that fronts the covered veranda, which is supported by horseshoe arches going into the main prayer room. At the top of the steps, in a corner, a hand pump provides water for washing and ablution.

In the middle of the prayer room wall, and in exact alignment to Mecca rests the recessed *mihrab*, from which the Imam leads the prayer. Next to the *mihrab* stands an ornate *mimber*—a railed three-step high wooden podium, from which the Imam delivers the sermon. Four tall minarets unite the four corners of the mosque, rising gracefully, high above the village and in view from some distance—as far away as Shafkat's well.

Across from the mosque, on the other side of the pond, is an abandoned Sikh temple that was once equally beautiful. On clear sunny days the shimmering reflections of both the mosque and the temple intertwine, revealing an abstract spiritual oneness. Fazal walks up the steps and joins thirty or so other worshipers. He instantly takes in a half dozen unfamiliar faces.

"*Aslamo Elaikum* Fazal Sahib," greets Shafkat, smiling and extending a handshake. "We haven't seen you in Friday prayer for weeks now. You look good, very good. Come, sit by me." Fazal acknowledges Shafkat's warm welcome and sits next to him on a wide prayer mat. He half listens to the Imam's sermon. He occasionally scans the worshipers, glancing at the new faces. He wonders where they came from, and imagines them passing his Sikh friends who are on their way to the new India.

"See those refugees. They are the ones who fled India and have made Rurkee their home. They have suffered, and arrived here penniless. I'll introduce you to them after the prayer," whispers Shafkat, cupping his hand next to Fazal's ear, hoping that nobody will blame him for disrespecting the Imam's sermon. He feels the urge to talk, knowing that if not a sin, it is certainly improper to utter a single word during the service. The Imam delivers his message in

Punjabi, punctuated with occasional Koranic verses. He ends with a final thought before stepping down from the podium.

"Whether we like it or not, partition has become a reality," pronounces the Imam. "India has been divided. Punjab is split in two. I know people of all faiths have suffered immensely, especially the Sikhs and Hindus in Rurkee. However, despite the tragedy, maybe it's better and perhaps it's Allah's will that we have our own independent nation, where Muslims can practice their faith freely, just as Sikhs and Hindus can practice across the border. Today, here in the mosque among us, are Muslim brothers who, along with their families, have fled India and are now destitute. After prayer, talk to them, make them welcome and help them as much as you can. I know they have nothing, but in having you, they have everything. Praise be to Allah, and may Allah and his Prophet Mohammad—Peace Be upon Him—show us the right path and give us the courage to do good deeds. Let us get ready for the prayer."

The *Muezzin* calls for the prayer once again. People stand shoulder to shoulder in straight lines, regardless of their color or status, behind the Imam, and quietly declare their intent to pray, folding their hands below the chest. The Imam recites the prayer in Arabic; the worshipers follow the Imam's Arabic cues—to bend at the waist, kneel and prostrate themselves by touching the forehead to the ground; rise again and repeat until the ritual is complete. The entire prayer is in Arabic and hardly anyone understands the exact meaning. Regardless, the prayer provides hope, and is comforting, soothing and peaceful. After the prayer, the worshipers raise their hands and ask Allah's forgiveness and personal blessing.

The mosque is more than a place to pray. Here, Muslims interact socially, especially after the Friday prayer or other religious holidays. The attendees shake hands, hug each other and inquire about families and businesses. Community news and gossip mix freely with talk about religion and politics. Today the focus is on the newcomers. Most of the people have left, but a few remain huddled around Shafkat and Fazal, who are talking to the refugees. Following the lead of Shafkat and Fazal, the worshipers give whatever money they can afford to help the newcomers. Misty eyed, the recipients acknowledge the help with gratitude, except for one young man.

"Are there any Sikh or Hindu families left in Rurkee?" he interrupts.

"No. Everyone has left except for one Hindu family," answers someone in the crowd.

"Where does this Hindu family live?" asks the refugee.

"On the west side, in a small two-room house by the big banyan tree. It's not that far away from here. You haven't seen them because the family is lying low, almost in hiding. After the exodus of Sikhs and Hindus, they decided to wait, hoping the situation would become normal. They stay indoors to avoid being seen."

"They're very frightened," chimes in another, "and I would guess they'll decide to leave sooner or later. Why do you ask?"

"No special reason, just curious," says the young man.

Fazal and Shafkat, along with the others sit down with the Imam to talk about the well-being of the refugees and the future of Rurkee. They have barely begun the discussion when someone comes running into the mosque screaming. "Mr. Shafkat. Mr. Shafkat, please help. The refugee who asked about the Sikhs and Hindus is holding Sohan and his family hostage, threatening to kill them all."

Fazal and the Imam hurry down the stairs with the others, running as fast as they can in hopes of getting to the house by the banyan tree in time. In minutes, they arrive at the house and are shocked to see that Sohan's hands are tied behind his back, while he sits against the wall. The refugee, his jaw clenched in anger, holds a kitchen knife against Sohan's throat, shouting incessantly, "I'm going to cut your throat and sacrifice you like a lamb. You butchered my sister and her family. I won't rest until I cut you into pieces. You killed her, her husband and her innocent child. When I finish with you I'll get the rest of your family," he yells, pointing towards the room that he has bolted from the outside.

"No. No. Please listen. Don't do this. Allah wants his servants to help people, not hurt them," pleads the Imam.

"When did he kill your sister and her family?" yells Shafkat. "This man never left the village and you or your sister never resided in Rurkee. How could he have killed them?" yells Shafkat.

"That may be so, but I'm convinced that both Hindus and Sikhs are responsible. They butchered my sister and her family along with scores of others and dumped them all under the Canal Bridge near Chubara. I was supposed to be a part of that Muslim caravan that left for Pakistan. I could not keep up with them because my wife was sick and we had to take frequent rest stops. I was less than two hours behind, but when I approached the canal and saw the carnage I knew my sister and her family were among the dead. I was selfish and too much a coward to even stop and look, let alone give her the dignity of a burial. I was terrified and weak, thinking about my own family only; we hurried past those who'd been murdered; walked nights, and hid in fields during the day, until we arrived here. It took us a whole week to get to Rurkee," screamed the refugee.

"Sohan didn't harm your sister. Despicable men, who happen to be Sikhs and Hindus, carried out that horrific act," reasoned Fazal.

"But it is the *kafir* like him who murdered those Muslims, my sister among them. I know he was not responsible, but he is a Hindu nonetheless," argued the refugee, loosening his grip on the knife slightly.

"Each of us is responsible for our own actions," stresses the Imam. "Blame the ones who carried out those ghastly acts on the innocent, fleeing Muslims. The evil deeds they committed will remain on their conscience forever. This man, Sohan, has done nothing wrong. If you kill him, you'll take the life of a blameless man and inflict unbearable pain on his family, depriving them the love and protection of a father and husband. I know you seek retribution. As your Imam, I appeal to you to drop the knife. Allah Almighty loves those who offer forgiveness and refrain from revenge."

The young man struggles to take in the Imam's words and square them with the revenge he has been seeking. His enraged face turns pale, his hands tremble, as the truth washes over him. "I'm sorry," he wails, falling to his knees. "I don't know what came over me. When I heard, at the mosque, that one Hindu family lived in Rurkee, all I could think about was revenge. Please forgive me," he begs, dropping the knife. The Imam pulls him up and gives him an empathetic embrace. Fazal picks up the knife. Shafkat unbolts the door, freeing the frightened family. He turns to face Sohan and declares, with determination, "Sohan, for your family's well being and safety, pack up and get ready to leave. First thing tomorrow morning, I'll personally help you make the journey." Sohan nods. The next morning Shafkat and Fazal arrive at the house. No one is there. The family had fled in the middle of the night.

Fazal speaks with a heavy heart. "Mr. Shafkat, let's spread the word that Rurkee is free of infidels, Punjab is All-Muslim and Pakistan, as the name implies, is on its way to becoming the 'Land of the Pure.' We can do no more. We tried, but couldn't make a difference. I'm going to attend to my shop, take care of my family and make sure that Karim finishes his education. I'm going to find a good and loving husband for my daughter, Parveen."

"I agree, Fazal. We did our best and that is all we can do. Don't be too hard on yourself. Let's tend to our business, rebuild our beloved Rurkee and help bring back some of the peace and harmony we all once enjoyed.

—21—

Partition

Prime Minister Attlee proclaimed that Britain needed to part with its colonial crown jewel, India. Lord Mountbatten, Queen Victoria's grandson and the last Viceroy to India was dispatched to preside over its independence.

Political leaders, the urban elite and feudal landlords thought Britain would quit India when World War II ended. Gandhi and Nehru of the Congress Party fought to keep India united. Feeling betrayed by the Indian Congress Party, Mohammad Ali Jinnah, a political advocate for Muslims, led the Muslim League, adamantly demanding a separate homeland: Pakistan. Rumors of freedom and the division of India had circulated for over a year. The British dragged their feet in setting an exact date. Finally, they announced India would be handed to the Indians "sometime" before June, 1948. Independence Day materialized in August, 1947, ten months ahead of the previous declaration.

The government officials, politicians and some of the people in the big cities knew about the partition. However, millions of people, living in villages, had no idea they might be forced to leave their homes and join fellow believers across an unknown border, yet to be marked on the map. The official mapmaker, British Judge Cyril Radcliffe arrived on July 8, 1947 and stayed six weeks, carrying out the demarcation duties. He never left his office, and without a single field visit, using the 'Majority' and 'Minority' census, he created two countries, hastily marking borders on a map. Sadly, the map did not get to the press or the people until two days after the official Independence Day, August 14, 1947.

Most of the elite, regardless of their religious affiliation, managed to move and relocate across borders with relative ease, unharmed. The masses, without knowledge of the split, lacked the means and plunged into a whirlpool of violence. Horrific atrocities, including rape and murder ran rampant, uncontrolled. Biased and unauthenticated news blared over the radio on both sides of the border. The rumors that fueled brutality and hate spread across Punjab, becoming a prophetic reality.

The people of Rurkee were not aware of the impending Indian independence after World War II. When Fazal and Shafkat helped Aneel and Sher escape, they guessed and hoped they had left them well beyond the phantom line. Fazal was angry, bereft and numb from the religious riots, death and destruction he had seen. However, he would never know that for each Patel girl who was raped at knifepoint in Lahore, there were thousands more elsewhere who were raped and murdered. He would never know that more than seventy thousand Muslim, Hindu and Sikh women were abducted; most never seen again by their families. He would never know that for each refugee he encountered there were twelve million others; ten million in Punjab alone fled their homes to unknown destinations. The largest peacetime mass migration in history happened at his front door.

For each Dalair and Sarita cut down in their prime, nearly two million and an estimated one million in Punjab never made it to the 'Promised Land.' They were brutally murdered either in their homes or enroute, looking for their new homeland. Like the victims on the terror train, witnessed by Jamal, there were scores of others on buses and bullock carts, forcefully detained and subjected to terror, rape and mass murder. For each family who abandoned their village, there were hundreds of caravans consisting of men, women and children stretched for miles attempting to escape. Their tense bodies moved like robots at a snail's pace in opposite directions, occasionally looking at each other with hate; haggard and hungry, not knowing what would happen next. Muslims, Sikhs and Hindus suffered equally, not realizing that they were perpetrators as well as victims. Perhaps it was a blessing that Fazal remained unaware of the full extent of atrocities committed during partition; it would have been more than he could bear.

Amidst this tragedy, on August 14, 1947, the green and white crescent flag flies high in Karachi in front of cheerful noisy crowds marking the independent and sovereign nation of Pakistan. Mohammad Ali Jinnah, the first Governor General of Pakistan salutes the flag and waves to the gathered multitude.

The next day, August 15, 1947, in Delhi Fort, Jawaharlal Nehru, the first Prime Minister of India salutes the flag and jubilantly waves to the crowd, marking the freedom of India. During and for a long time after the ceremonies, riots continue. The carnage persists for over a year.

Fazal is sad and withdrawn. He has lost hope. With a heavy heart, he decides to pay attention to his business. He opens his shop. His priorities are his family, Karim's education and his daughter's well-being.

Part II

—22—

Surprise

Growing up without Makhan leaves a hole in Karim's heart. Despite the teasing and ridiculing, Karim refuses to remove the *kara*—steel bangle Makhan had given him at the well as a symbol of his friendship. He misses him terribly, especially when, at age sixteen, he receives his high school diploma in June of 1952. With limited job prospects, he reluctantly works with his father running the shop. For four years he bikes to Sialkot, getting supplies, visiting Uncle Jamal and looking zealously for employment opportunities in the big city. He hates running the shop and living in the village. Secretly, he has a plan for his future.

"Father, we're low on shop supplies," says Karim. "If it's okay, I'd like to bring them on the bike from Sialkot."

"Son, I suggest that you leave the bike at home and hire a tonga. It's getting pretty hot these days."

"I'd like to visit Uncle Jamal for a day or two," suggests Karim. "While I'm there I can use the bike to see some of my friends."

"That's a good idea. Jamal always asks about you. Leave first thing in the morning, and stay as long as you want."

The next morning Karim takes off on the bicycle, with plans to stay two or three nights. "Have a good time with your friends, Karim."

Fazal waves. Karim nods without looking back. He pedals strongly, negotiating and weaving his way through wheat and mustard fields on this fresh late spring morning. Although he enjoys the low, lush greenery and the cool musky air, his mind is on the job interview he has secretly scheduled. As soon as he arrives in Sialkot he is swept into a stream of pedestrians, cyclists, tongas and donkey carts. He threads his way through the swarming city bazaars and within an hour reaches the main Cantonment bazaar.

"Sir, could you point the way to the Sialkot Army Recruiting Office," Karim, smiling nervously, asks a shopkeeper.

"Son, go about half a mile straight, take a left by the tonga stand, go another mile and take another left. After the Army Signal Division there's a series of barracks on the right. You'll see an army hospital on the left. Across from it is a row of large bungalows. The Army Recruiting Center is at the end. You can't miss it. Today is recruitment day. A large number of young men like you'll be outside."

"Thanks. I'm much obliged."

Karim pedals to the bungalow where hundreds of young men are scattered in small groups, waiting on the lawn. He walks his bike inside the walled compound and leans it against the first tree he finds. He locks it, puts the key in his *kameez*—shirt pocket, and sits on the grass surveying the grounds.

The bungalow, located in the middle of a huge rectangular parcel is bordered by a tall brick wall. At each end of the long frontage wall, iron gates provide a one way entrance and exit, secured by military outposts, and manned by a twenty-four hour uniformed armed guard. A shrub-lined horseshoe driveway meets the bungalow entrance portico. Up six steps, a veranda stretches along the front of the building. Clay pots of jasmine, marigolds, and small roses stretch between the veranda posts.

Karim closes his eyes and imagines what the bungalow looked like when he was a boy, and the English lived on the property. Ornately carved double wooden doors open into a spacious foyer that leads to a series of rooms on each side: a living room on the right, a den and library located on the left. Family and game rooms follow. At the end of the hallway are four bedrooms, including a master suite with an attached *water closet*—bathroom. Ten-foot wide cloth ceiling fans connect to a rope and pulley system for hand operation in the larger rooms. In the searing, dusty days of summer, the fan pullers sit outside, working the fans back and forth, providing a minimally comfortable breeze for residents. Expensive English décor has created a sophisticated ambiance. A covered breezeway connects the kitchen to the back of the house. English meals are prepared and the butler serves the Sahib and his family English-style—on English-time.

High brick and stucco walls support the flat roof, under which large semi-arched glass windows and heavy tan draperies filter the light. The glass ribbed ventilators release stale hot air, a life saving feature on sweltering summer days. Stained wooden shutters fold to block out both rainy and hot weather. Bougainvilleas climb the walls, framing the windows, nearly touching the roof.

Close to the stables, against the back wall of the property, stand quarters for the resident domestic help. The cook, housekeeper, gardener, peon, fan operators and the horse handler, some with families, live in these cramped dwellings. They are at the 'beck and call' of the privileged *Angrez* family residing in the bungalow.

Giant deciduous trees offer shade in summer, and small ornamental shrubs scattered throughout the lush compound give the character of a well-manicured British garden. Plush green lawns and scores of flowerbeds lay with mathematical precision, connected by compacted gravel walkways. A mini-country estate has been created in Sialkot.

"*Aslamo Elaikum, Bhai,*" says a young man. "Hey brother, are you here to join the Army? Open your eyes. They're about to call our names," he explains, while shaking Karim's shoulder.

"*Wa Elaikum Asslam,* who are you?" inquires Karim, shaking off the catnap.

"I'm Omar. My village Perth is very close. It's just at the edge of the cantonment area. I walked here this morning to enlist."

"I'm Karim and I live in Rurkee."

"Nice to meet you, Karim." Omar plunks down next to him, extending a handshake. "That's pretty far. No wonder you're tired. What were you thinking about?"

"Oh, not much; I was imagining how this place looked when *Angrez* lived here."

"How can you picture that? Just like me, when they were here you were too young to know."

"When I was little, my father told me about these *kothees*—bungalows. He told me so many times and in such detail that it's etched in my mind. He often visited a friend who was a cook in one of these mansions. It's hard to believe the size of these bungalows, and it's amazing how *Angrez* lived here so regally. The place is larger than a village, or at least more than most land holdings of poor farmers in Punjab." Karim exaggerates.

"Does it look the same? The same as when *Angrez* were here, I mean."

"No. Not really. It's not what my father had pictured for me. It's run down, hasn't been kept up and looks dilapidated. I guess that our new nation is poor and doesn't have money for repairs."

"Karim, how many years did you go to school?"

"I graduated from high school four years ago."

"*Ma Sha Allah*, That is Allah's will."

"What about you?"

"I'm embarrassed. I had only four years of schooling. I dropped out to help my father run the farm."

At ten o'clock the place comes to life. An armed soldier opens the gate for the approaching jeep—open, and olive-drab in color. The driver slows down a little, while an officer in the passenger seat, holding the roll bar in one hand and a swagger stick in the other, acknowledges the guard's salute by nodding his head. The jeep suddenly halts under the portico. With an air of authoritative importance the officer gets out. He acknowledges more salutes, runs up the veranda steps and swiftly walks through the doors that are held open for him. Judging by everyone's behavior and the young recruits' stares, there is no doubt that he is the one in charge.

After partition, Pakistani military officers replaced the English residents in these mansions, which were converted to army offices. This bungalow has become a recruitment center. Scores of army and civilian personnel come to work at the center each day.

Soon, the door opens again and a military staff person steps out onto the veranda. The anxious young men stand up quietly and move forward to hear him. He glances at the youthful crowd, pauses a moment, looks down at a clipboard and calls ten names from the list.

"Gentlemen, come forward," orders the young man, pointing at two wooden benches placed on either side of the office entrance. "Have your interview letters ready and wait here until you are called in. When we are through with this batch we'll call the rest of you, in groups of ten. Be patient; it may take all day. I warn you, if you don't answer the call, your name will be struck from the list," he stresses, with a serious smile, tapping the clipboard with his index finger before disappearing behind the door. Like the rest of the crowd, Karim and Omar sit back and wait. In about two hours, the officer calls Karim's name. He springs up, takes the letter from his pocket and asks Omar to watch his bike. "It's locked but it's still a good idea if you keep an eye on it."

"Sure. I'll be happy to. Good luck."

"Thank you."

Karim follows his guide to a spacious office. The officer leans back in a comfortable swivel chair behind a green felt-draped wooden desk. He sips a cup of coffee—a status drink preferred over chai by aspiring military officers. A large yearly placemat calendar rests between two 'IN' and 'OUT' baskets. The black and red crystal inkpot set holding two nib pens lines up next to a blotting pad. The officer's hat and a Parker fountain pen have prominent positions on the other side. Uniformed assistants on stiff wooden chairs flank the desk. An old Casablanca-type ceiling fan creaks slowly, blade by blade stirring the stale air. From the back wall, a framed picture of Mohammad Ali Jinnah, the father of Pakistan, clad in *Shirwani*—a round collar jacket and a *karakul*—sheep skin hat, watches over the office patriotically.

"What's your name?" asks one of the assistants, looking up briefly, while scanning Karim's name in the file.

"My name is Karim, sir."

"What is your father's name?"

"Fazal Din, sir."

"You live in Rurkee."

"Yes sir."

"You look pretty thin. Are you physically fit enough to serve in the army?"

"Yes sir. I am. I play soccer and I'm the best *kabaddi* player in Rurkee."

"Karim, you graduated from high school four years ago. Why didn't you join the Army then?"

"Sir, I was helping my father run the family business, a small general store."

"Why are you leaving your family business?"

"There isn't enough business for both my father and me. Besides, I want to see other places and experience different things. I thought I could do that while serving my country."

The officer seems to pay little attention until now. He takes the last sip of coffee, places the empty cup in the saucer and leans forward. "Son, I see that you have a high school diploma. You know what that means?"

"No sir," says Karim.

"You are only one of three applicants who has a high school education. If you are selected, you may have a remarkable career with the army."

"Yes sir," says Karim, with a pleasant yet controlled smile.

"With your education and hard work you can earn respect, quick promotions and the good salary that comes with it." He takes his fountain pen, slides off the cap and puts his signature on the paper set before him by his assistant. He hands it to Karim with his left hand and offers his right for a firm handshake.

"Welcome to the army, son. Tomorrow, you go across the street to the army hospital for your medical. Get the package from the clerk next door."

"Thank you, sir. Thank you very much," says Karim cheerfully, while raising his right hand for the first time in an Army salute. He collects his package, walks out briskly and runs to Omar, almost shouting, "I'm in. I'm in."

"Congratulations. That's good news!"

Omar is surprised and touched when Karim tells him that he is going to wait for him to see if he too makes it through the interview successfully. Nervously, they wait. Omar's group is the last one to be called. Within ten minutes, Omar comes out running and waving the appointment letter like a victory flag. Karim smiles. They give each other a celebratory embrace. "See you tomorrow at ten," says Omar, with a full smile as he starts his short walk home.

Karim nods and climbs on his bike. Elated, he pedals his bike to Jamal's, whistling all the way.

"How are your friends Karim? Did you have good day?" asks Jamal with a welcome smile, when opening the front door.

"Yes. Uncle, this is one of the luckiest days of my life. I wasn't quite honest with you. I didn't go to see my friends. I went to the army recruiting center and signed up. Tomorrow, I go for a medical and within two weeks I'll be back in Sialkot Cantonment for training."

"Karim, I'm very happy for you, but does Fazal know about this?"

"No, my parents don't know. I am keeping it a secret. I'm afraid they might object."

"You're going to tell them, when you get home, aren't you?"

"Of course Uncle, I'll tell them. That's my plan."

"Well, tell your parents that I not only approve, but I'm confident that you'll have a great future in the army."

The next morning at ten, Karim meets Omar, who along with other candidates, waits outside the Army Medical Corps hospital. Just before noon, the army declares them healthy and fit to be soldiers. Karim heads back to Uncle Jamal's, loads up the waiting supplies and hurries home, rehearsing how best to break the news. He arrives slightly before dark, unloads the merchandise and joins his parents for supper.

"Son, what's new in Sialkot?"

"Father, I've joined the army."

"Army, why in the hell did you do that?" Fazal yells, stopping right in middle of dinner and pushing his food away. Never had his father been so angry or used such strong language.

"Fazal, calm down please. Let him explain," pleads Rakhi turning to Karim, "Son, why did you take such a step? Aren't you happy here?"

"It is not a matter of happiness, Mother. I've been working with father for four years. We all know that business hasn't been good for some time now. We barely make enough money to survive, especially since the refugees opened up two other shops. There isn't enough work for both of us."

"Not enough work for both of us! Who's going to help me? Who's going to run the shop when I'm old, or gone? I don't understand."

"Father, honestly, I want to get out of this village and pursue other options. I yearn to see different people and places. The army is the only ticket to my dreams. I can go places, do different work and experience places other than Rurkee. Besides, I hate running the shop. I want to do something different."

"Different. Did you hear that, Rakhi? He hates running the shop. He has decided not to follow in his father's footsteps."

"Fazal, listen to what you're saying. You didn't follow your father's profession. Being a dyer was back breaking, and a bad paying profession. You wanted to open your own shop and your father gladly agreed."

"I changed my profession but I didn't run away from my ancestral village. I stayed in Rurkee. Remember that."

"Father, I am not leaving for good. This is my birthplace; I will not forget my roots. Like a magnet, Rurkee will always pull me back. The Army will pay me thirty-five rupees a month. That's as much as we make from the shop."

"That's all! Only thirty-five a month? How do you plan to live on that?"

"Yes, thirty-five but there aren't any expenses. I can easily save most of it. I promise to send most of it home. Father, almost everything is free. They'll pay my room, board, food, uniforms and even laundry and barber services. Uncle Jamal thinks it's a good idea," says Karim. "Thirty-five is just a start. You'll be proud that I was one of only three—from hundreds of candidates, who have a high school diploma. The officer-in-charge was really impressed. He told me, personally, that with my education and discipline I could earn quick promotions and the salary to go with it. That's what I intend to do. Work hard, stick with the army and experience the whole country while serving my nation."

"Son, I had an inkling you'd been up to something," says Rakhi. "Fazal, our son wants to be a soldier. We should be happy and pray for his success. I can tell you one thing, Karim; you will be the most handsome and bravest soldier that the Pakistani Army could ever have." Her expression reveals mixed emotions. "I look forward to the day when you will come and visit us in your khaki uniform and a green beret." Karim kisses his mother's cheek before embracing his father fondly. Fazal prolongs his hug while turning his face away from his wife to hide his teary eyes, knowing that his son has chosen a dangerous profession. Both mother and son know that Fazal's cheeks are wet with tears. They know that he is the most caring, tenderhearted person they have ever known. "Son, if that's what you want to do. Then that's what you should do. May Allah be your protector."

Two weeks later Rakhi invites Shafkat and his family to an elaborate farewell feast. The following day, Karim packs a small steel trunk, loads it onto a tonga and arrives at the army training center in Sialkot.

—23—

Boys to Men

Karim stands in front of the iron-gated entrance to the Sialkot Military Training Center. Above the gate hangs a solid brass insignia of *Pak Fauj*, Pakistan Army, a crescent and a star flanked by two crossed swords embossed on a dark green plate. Two armed guards, straight and stiff, stand watch.

A *Naik*—Private First Class, steps out from the small reception cabin. Karim hands him the recruitment letter. He glances at the letter, looks at Karim and smiles, "Welcome to the Punjab regiment, *Jawan*—young man."

He waves him through the pedestrian's revolving gate and directs him to a complex, pointing. "See those Pakistan and Armed Forces' flags?"

"Yes sir."

"Pass those flags, turn right and go to the office that is on the far right and present your papers there."

"Thank you," Karim smiles and heads to the huge complex. He stops for a moment to admire the impressive flags. The white crescent and starred Pakistani flag on a green background sways atop a forty-foot pole, while the Pak Army and Company flags fly gracefully, slightly lower on either side. The poles thrust skyward from an earthen

oh good - the military religious... *is deeply*

mound filled with assorted petunias, pansies and marigolds. In the middle stands the army motto in big bold brass letters: "*Iman, Taqwa, and Jihad Fi Sabilillah*—faith and piety, to strive in the path of Allah." He walks into the reception office, greets the waiting clerk and hands him the appointment letter.

"What's your name?" asks the clerk without responding to his salutation.

"Karim, Sir."

"What is your father's name?"

"Fazal Din, Sir."

The clerk scans down the clipboard, checks off his name and hands him his nametag 'Karim Din' and a manila envelope.

"You're in barrack number four, space five. See the quartermaster for your gear and supplies. Training starts on Monday. The Captain will address all of you at ten in the morning on the soccer grounds. Don't be late. Settle in and familiarize yourself with the center and its facilities. Make sure you find the mess hall. That's where you get your meals."

"Can I ask you a question, sir"?

"Yes, of course," the clerk looks up.

"Is there somebody in our group by the name of Omar?"

"Yes. One young man, named Omar, checked in this morning."

"Is he from Perth?"

"No, he's not from Perth."

"Thank you," says Karim, striding out of the office, feeling disheartened that his new friend Omar from Perth is not there. He wonders why.

Karim picks up his gear: two khaki uniforms, two brass buckled belts, four pairs of socks, two felt beret caps, and steel-toed black boots, along with other army articles.

He arrives at the block-walled barrack number four, finds space five, and drops his belongings alongside folded sheets and a blanket on a steel framed cot. Next to the cot is a chair and small table; underneath rests a sizable gray steel trunk with his name, 'Karim Din,' stenciled in glossy white. Seeing his name so boldly lettered gives him a few seconds' pause. His ten by twelve-foot open space is one of ten, clearly marked with white paint on the gray cement floor along the wall. Another ten spaces lay exactly the same against the opposite wall.

A mirror hangs above the communal cold-water washbasin at each end of the sleeping quarters. He notices two dangling wires that disappear into the wall from the round, rusted electric alarm bell secured to one of the ceiling trusses that supports the corrugated tin roof. The clean, white-washed interior gives a sense of army protocol. He makes up the cot and meets his fellow barracks mates as each one saunters inside. Hungry, the recruits proceed to the mess hall.

Karim takes a moment to survey the center from the flag area and admires the spacious complex of barracks, classrooms and offices. Hedged walkways, shade trees and a patchwork of shrubs and flowerbeds connect the buildings. The soccer and hockey fields are located in two wide green quadrangles on each side of the flag area. Amazed at the scale of the center, he is excited, yet feels apprehensive about the path he has chosen for his future.

On Monday morning at nine-thirty, like a mini fire alarm, the electric bells go off in each of the ten barracks. At exactly ten a.m., the recruits, along with the training staff, line up on the soccer field and wait patiently for the center's commanding officer to arrive.

"Atten—shun!" bellows the Company *Havildar Major*, who heads the training staff.

Each trainee stands straight, shoulder-to-shoulder, with stiff arms stretched down along his sides, looking ahead. Captain Khan plants himself in front of the two-hundred young men standing alert in rows of twenty. Dressed in a crisp khaki uniform, he holds the leather swagger stick in his right hand. Silence prevails on the field. The Captain stares intently, scanning each row as if to gauge the potential of each trainee. He takes a deep breath and addresses the recruits:

"*Aslamo Elaikum.* First, I'd like to congratulate you on having been selected to join the Pakistan Army. Second, as Commanding Officer and on behalf of the entire staff, I welcome you to this reputable facility." The Captain takes a long pause and continues, "Pakistan is a very young nation, not even eight years old. The *Angrez* shortchanged us in the 1947 partition, both in civil and military resources. Within a year after the creation of our Muslim homeland, we were forced to fight a war in which we defended our borders bravely."

The Captain raises his voice a notch and declares—while tapping his swagger stick on his left palm for emphasis: "Your predecessors were ill equipped, and had no training, but fought bravely in the 1948 Kashmir war. Since then, we have been committed to building our armed forces, making it the number one priority. You're very lucky that today we have resources for training and are fully capable of providing you with the best available equipment. By the time you leave this center, you'll be physically and emotionally fit to defend your country against all enemies, both foreign and domestic. I'll leave the rest to the Sergeant Major. Work hard and feel proud to be part of our family, the *Pak Fauj*. Good luck to you all."

Soon after the Captain leaves, the *Havildar Major*, Sergeant Major orders, "At ease." The recruits relax, fold their hands behind their backs and listen to the Sergeant Major. "You heard the Captain. Although you are enlisted men, I guarantee you that hard work and discipline will earn you promotions and bring honor to you and your family. I myself enlisted some twenty-five years ago in the Indian Army that was run by the British. Look at me now—I'm Sergeant Major. One day you could be standing here in my place. You come here as young men, but by the time you leave I promise we will have turned you into soldiers; proud soldiers, becoming a part of the *Pak Fauj* family.

"Today is your first day here. Now my sergeant and corporals will split you into squads. They'll give you handouts and explain your training program over the next nine months. I know most of you can barely read, but instructions are in simple *Urdu* with many photographs and sketches. We'll have *Urdu* classes, as well. For now, do the best you can and link up with fellow recruits who can help you with the written material." The Sergeant Major steps aside quickly while his assistants take over. They split the recruits into squads, pass out the training booklets, and explain the overall purpose and objectives; then go over the details for the first four-week schedule. As soon as the corporals finish, the sergeant addresses the group:

"Today is your last day of leisure. Get to know the facilities, go over the first week's program, and if nothing else remember this: never be—and I repeat—never be a second late for the morning PT, physical training. It's almost noon; lunch is waiting. You are dismissed until the five-thirty morning whistle."

At nine p.m. the barracks go dark. Lost in thought, Karim is in bed staring at the rusty old alarm bell, dimly lit by a naked, low-powered bulb, screwed into the wall socket.

It was good growing up in a small village and working with my father in his shop. How I loved teasing Makhan and Dalair on our long walks to Chowinda School, thinks Karim. Then his mind slips into more somber thoughts. *Why were Dalair's and Sarita's innocent lives cut down in their prime? Where is Makhan? I wonder if his dream of becoming an important government officer came true. I hope he was not like so many other desperate and destitute refugees, who never had a chance. Maybe my father was right; I should have stayed and helped my family. But the fact of the matter is that Rurkee is too small and isolated. I had no future there. I have made the right decision. I am lucky for this opportunity that no one else ever had in my village. It is the right path and I must work hard and shape my own future.*

The alarm bells come alive at five a.m. The drillmaster blows his first whistle at five-fifteen and by five-thirty, all two hundred trainees line up before the second and the last whistle is blown. Once the physical drill is over, Karim runs back to his barrack; shaves, cleans up, puts on his uniform, looks into the mirror and proudly adjusts his cap before joining the recruits for breakfast in the mess hall. Exactly at eight a.m., he joins his platoon in a classroom where the instructor, a corporal, leans against a table.

The students sit on long wooden benches; the instructor has an old table, a chair and a plastered blackboard on the wall in this simple classroom. A few posters tacked to the wall border the blackboard. Classes go until mid-afternoon, with an hour lunch break. The trainees move to the soccer ground and split into small groups where they stay until five p.m. In a relaxed atmosphere on the grassy grounds, they study, learn teamwork strategies, do homework, ask questions and engage one another in group discussions. Participation in at least one track and field sport is mandatory for all recruits. Karim signs up for soccer.

Instructors spend the first four weeks teaching Pakistan history, its defense needs, Pakistan Armed Forces structure, and the critical nature of the Pak Army to which they all belong. They are not only trained to be physically fit, but are taught how to wear and care for their uniform, proper salute etiquette, keeping their space and barracks clean and preparation for inspection at a moment's notice. Karim, having a high school education enthusiastically offers to help others with reading, writing and homework. Within a month, he is an official assistant to his corporal.

Three months into the training, the most vital phase starts—firearms. In classes, they are shown different hand held weapons, and demonstrations on their use. Special emphasis is placed on the firearm and the personal rifle assigned to each soldier. Karim has never seen a gun, much less fired one. It is all new to him, as it is with several others. He cautiously, but diligently studies the 303 Enfield rifle, figuring out its operation and safety. Provided blank cartridges, the trainees spend days learning how to carry, march, maintain and safely keep the weapon. Finally, the time to fire one arrives.

On a warm June morning, ten green camouflaged transport trucks line up along the main road. The recruits climb onto the canvas-covered trucks, take seats on the wooden benches and head to the firing range. Before taking their positions for target practice, the squad leader gives the final directive.

"Plant yourself solidly, lift and hold the rifle firmly against your shoulder, close one eye and line up the other with the target and the cross hair, hold your breath, and squeeze the trigger." The squad leader demonstrates by firing a bullet that pierces the target center, embedding itself in the mound behind it. He orders the men to line up and wait for his orders.

When Karim's name is called, he moves forward and runs through the instructions in his head before pulling the trigger. He misses the target completely; the force propels him backward, causing him to lose his balance. The vigilant Corporal comes to his rescue, preventing him from falling flat on the ground.

"Karim, lean forward and keep the weapon firmly pushed against your chest. Do not, and I repeat, do not pull the trigger. You must learn to 'squeeze' the trigger," says the Corporal emphatically, while holding Karim by his shoulders. By now Karim is embarrassed and nervous.

"You've had enough instructions," suggests the Corporal. "Don't mark them off in your head, especially you, Karim. It has to come together in an instant. Eventually, you'll shoot instinctively. Don't worry. We'll make sure you develop that instinct. Marksmanship is nothing but practice, practice and more practice. We'll do this until you are the best, and make perfect shots."

Once a week target practice goes for half a day. After a field lunch, they sit in small groups under the watchful eyes of the leaders to inspect, clean and polish their rifles. They talk animatedly about improving their performance for the next time; some performed worse than Karim, and go over their mistakes, making verbal adjustments to their stance, their shoulders, and ways to "squeeze" the trigger.

Karim has no time to travel to Rurkee, so occasionally he visits his Uncle Jamal in Sialkot. Omar, he discovers, is in Sialkot Training Center No 2. They are able to see each other only when playing soccer during inter-center skirmishes. Their usual regimen goes six days a week, except Sundays when they have free time and permission to go off grounds. Having become close friends with Omar, Karim visits Perth and meets Omar's parents, who are genuinely taken with him. On one such visit, as the two friends are about to leave, Karim asks Omar's father, "Why did Omar drop out of school, Uncle?"

"Because, I didn't have the brain for it." Omar forestalls the answer, apparently uncomfortable with Karim's question.

"No, that's not the case," argues Omar's father. "Omar is really a very smart boy; smartest in the family. Karim, I'm a poor sharecropper and couldn't do all the farming by myself. Omar decided to quit school and help me on the farm so that we could feed our family."

"Father, please stop. You don't have to tell our family secrets."

"Son, Karim is your friend and I consider him part of our family. Please don't be upset. We are so lucky that he joined the *Pak Fauj* and that you became his friend. Omar has a respectable profession now, with a bright future. I want him to be happy and safe. I want him to come home, get married and start a family."

"Okay, Father, we gotta go," says Omar.

"You watch out for each other."

"We'll do that," says Karim.

"Father, see you in a couple of weeks and *Khuda Hafiz*," says Omar as he and Karim leave together and head to their separate training centers.

The alarm bells sound, PT drill is completed, classes held, equipment and tactics demonstrated, target practice and marksmanship routinely performed. Uniformed recruits are trained to walk proudly and confidently; singly, in twos, and as a unit in the military parade. In the ninth month, training is almost over. The last and most important parts remaining before the commencement exercise in November are boot camp exercises and final assignments. The final and ultimate tests for graduation—field exercises and a thirteen-mile cross-country run requirement are on every recruit's mind. In the middle of November, they are broken into small groups, ordered to run or sprint through mud and water, climb and swing on ropes like Tarzan, scale walls and hurdles in an allotted time. Fully uniformed, armed with a loaded rifle and carrying a sixty-pound backpack they run, crawl on their knees and elbows, belly slide through razor sharp barbed wire while live ammunition is fired all around them. A week later, they run the cross-country over the dry hilly terrain.

On November 30th they stand on the soccer ground where they began, waiting for the Colonel to arrive and deliver the commencement speech. Karim stands confident, combat ready and proud in his military formation. There are one hundred and eighty graduates. Twenty of the recruits have dropped out or failed the nine-month ordeal. The calm, cool and sunny day, under a deep blue sky, provides a scenic backdrop for the occasion. The graduating class is positioned in front, facing the podium on the three-stepped, high wooden stage. Hand-made woolen *kalins*—rugs cover the stage. In front, the officers sit on low cushioned chairs, while regular folding chairs line up behind, four rows deep for the center staff. A canvas awning hangs overhead. A ceremonial and celebratory atmosphere prevails over the field. The military band stops playing, signaling the arrival of the Colonel, with Captain Khan at his side.

"Atten—shun!" shouts the Sergeant Major.

The Colonel quickly steps to the mike. "*Aslamo Elaikum, Jawans of Pak Fauj.* I extend my sincere congratulations to you all on this important day. You've worked very hard for the last thirty-six weeks. You must be proud. Under the direction of Captain Khan and his staff, you have acquired knowledge, trained well, and are mentally and physically fit to be Pakistani soldiers. This institution has transformed you from juveniles to *Jawans*—soldiers of high moral value and excellent character. You've demonstrated strength, discipline and faith. Stand tall; keep the chin up, shoulders wide, chest puffed with pride, stride mindfully and aim high. This army needs you. Pakistan needs you. Welcome to the *Pak Fauj* family. God bless you and Pakistan *Zindabad*—long live Pakistan."

"*Jawans*, stand at ease," commands the sergeant. The soldiers embrace and congratulate each other. The corporals pass out the diplomas. Once dismissed, they rush to the mess hall for a special graduation feast. The officers and staff join them as the band plays patriotic army tunes. Karim visits Omar's family that afternoon, before going to Uncle Jamal's house.

"Karim, you boys must take care of each other," says Omar's father, issuing his favorite mantra as Karim leaves.

"Yes, of course. We will sir," replies Karim without revealing that they'll be at two different cantonments that are almost a hundred miles apart.

Later, Karim is welcomed warmly at his Uncle Jamal's home. "I'm very happy for you, Karim." says Jamal affectionately. "I'm sure your parents will be proud to see you in this uniform. Take this basket of sweets for my sister Rakhi, and don't be a stranger. This house is your house. Whenever you're in Sialkot, come see us."

"Thank you Uncle," says Karim with a firm soldiers' handshake, before climbing onto a tonga.

As Karim's tonga arrives on the outskirts of Rurkee, the children run alongside, admiring the young uniformed soldier, while shouting, "Sepoy, soldier Karim is here."

The word spreads. A couple of teenagers run atop flat adobe rooftops and alert Karim's parents of his homecoming. Fazal closes his shop, Rakhi scurries for her *dupatta*; Parveen, who has been married for six months and is visiting from Sialkot, follows her mother onto the street to welcome Karim. They wait in front of their house, where neighbors have already gathered into a small crowd.

When Karim arrives, he climbs from the tonga and gives a quick hug to his mother, father and sister before stepping back a couple of feet so they can get a good look at him. Karim is not scrawny anymore. His broad-shouldered, five-foot-nine inch frame is taut with muscles. He stands erect with his chest puffed out. Above his fuller and pencil-thin mustache, his piercing gaze exudes confidence. The brass belt buckle and the Punjab Regiment insignias on the shoulder epaulets add authority to the perfectly pressed, starched khaki uniform. His steel-toed army boots are polished to a mirrored sheen. The green beret, decorated with the Pakistan Army badge, adorns his crew cut head. A juvenile has turned into a *Jawan*.

"Son, you look so handsome in this uniform," says Rakhi, pursing her lips with motherly emotion, while extending her right hand for *piyar*. Karim hastily takes off his military beret to feel his mother's tender touch, which he has missed terribly for nearly a year. Taking her son's face into her hands, she plants kisses in quick succession on his forehead and cheeks.

"Parveen, you look so different," says Karim.

"Yes, I'm a married woman now *Bhai Jhan*—brother." She smiles blushingly.

"We didn't know when you were coming home Karim. I found a good match for your sister. She is happy and soon you are going to be an uncle," says Rakhi proudly, pointing to Parveen's belly.

"Married, and baby on the way," says Karim cheerfully. He picks up his little sister, twirls her around a few times and gives her his congratulations. "When do I get to meet your husband?"

"Soon, you'll meet him, soon."

"What's this white stripe, son," inquires Rakhi, changing the subject and pointing to his shoulder.

"Oh, I forgot to tell you. My high school education and hard work have already earned me my first promotion. They call me *Lance*

Naik—private first class Karim Din. Mother, you'll be happy to know that this stripe is worth fifteen rupees a month more."

"Do you really have to earn them or can I sew some on your sleeve? This way you can get more money."

They giggle and laugh. His father, beaming with pride, has been watching until now, and pulls Karim to his chest in a bear hug. He holds Karim's shoulders while smiling broadly and announces, "Look at him. He's my son. He's *Lance Naik* in the Pakistan Army." He shakes hands with other well-wishers who are utterly surprised at Karim's transformation and look at him as if he were a general.

Two weeks pass quickly, until the day a tonga arrives to take Karim back to Sialkot. A small crowd surrounds the tonga, while Karim bids farewell to his family and friends.

"Here, Mother, this is for you," says Karim, handing his mother a bundle of rupees.

"What is it son?" asks Rakhi.

"Hundred rupees—the money I've saved for you during my training period." He turns to his father and tells him about the financial arrangements. "On the tenth day of each month you can collect thirty-five rupees at the post office in Sialkot. *Abu*, this is the Army and it will not be a day late."

Karim's parents hug and kiss him, saying "*Khuda Hafiz*" repeatedly with teary smiles. A military travel voucher in hand, he gets on the tonga with his metal trunk that boasts "*Lance Naik* Karim Din" in glossy white letters.

"See you in a year and *Khuda Hafiz*," shouts Karim, looking away to hide his emotions, while half the village waves goodbye.

—24—

Mind over Muscle

On a cold December evening, a black steam engine, pulling an old passenger train, crawls out of Sialkot Railway Station, taking Karim to his assigned military base in Rawalpindi—two hundred miles to the northwest. It is the last train, leaving behind a deserted platform, where a single lamp flickers from a food stall, and a couple of bewildered dogs look around momentarily before bedding down behind a freight car. Karim is snuggled against a window, cramped between scores of passengers and their luggage, in a third class compartment—in spite of a red stenciled sign that reads 'Maximum Capacity—30 Passengers.' Karim continuously watches the pastoral countryside, dimly lit by the full moon. This is his first train ride, and the two hundred mile trip to the north is nothing but the adventure of a lifetime.

The slow moving train—on a single track, is frequently side-lined, yielding to oncoming express trains. By daylight, the train has covered less than half the scheduled distance and waits for a long time at the Kharian Railway Station, which teems with military personnel and equipment. The morning light and the loud screams of food hawkers awaken Karim. He murmurs to himself while rubbing sleep from his eyes, "It must be Kharian. Omar will be posted here on his first assignment."

Karim orders a small breakfast. No sooner does he hand the vender his money, than the train steams off, lumbering from the platform, whistling. The old train is not comfortable, but it is convenient. The long wooden compartments have paneled doors opening to both sides at each end. The heavy, sliding glass windows rise vertically above the framed benches. Passengers, dangling their legs and clutching their belongings, sit on the luggage racks that hang from the cabin wall, secured by steel chains suspended from the ceiling. The train chugs along as the cars sway from side to side. The steam engine hisses, and the rail line click-clacks—breaking the silence, while the doors and windows are partially open to the outside elements. The noise constantly changes with the train's speed through the open countryside, closed tunnels and the varying topography. It sounds faster than it is actually going.

There exists a stark contrast between upper and lower class cars. While upper class cars are nearly empty, the third class compartments are packed with people—like sardines in a can. Passengers cramped in the open area by the doors stand on the steps, hanging dangerously by the door handles.

A thin man in his mid-thirties enters the compartment, and stands astride the aisle, smiling. His high cheek bones accentuate his lips, reddened from chewing crushed beetle nuts, lime paste and tobacco, wrapped in a green leaf that produces the mild habit-forming high of a *Paan*. "Hello to everyone, *Aslamo Elaikum*." He hollers. "You're very lucky that I'm here today. I have with me a tonic that has been in our family for generations. It cures every disease and ailment. I assure you that this is the magic potion you've been waiting for all your life.

"My name is Shifa and I'd like a few minutes of your time so I can show you what I have in my bag, and what it can do for you or your loved ones—loved ones who might suffer from one of many ailments. This miracle medicine's formula was handed down to my great-great grandfather in the Himalayan forests by a hundred-year-old Yogi on his deathbed. It cures all kinds of aches and pains," he claims, scanning the passengers with a persuasive gaze, while holding up a white powdery sample in a small glass bottle.

"Take a spoonful and the stomach pain goes away. Rub it on an aching tooth and gum, the toothache is gone. If you have a fever, take it twice a day and the fever will leave the body for good, never to return. If you feel weak and tired, just take a spoonful for a week with milk and you'll feel energetic and years younger. If anyone here has a pain, any pain! It doesn't matter what kind of pain or ailment. Speak up."

Nobody speaks. Dead silence fills the car.

"Come on. There must be someone who has a problem," says the vendor.

"Hey, you've been complaining about your terrible toothache since we boarded the train in Kharian," shouts an older man, pointing to a younger middle-aged man sitting across the aisle. "Why don't you speak up and ask for the sample. No harm in trying the miracle medicine. It's free." The man slowly raises his hand, challenges the vendor's claims and asks for a sample. The red-gummed peddler happily obliges. As soon as the man rubs the powdered remedy on his gums, the toothache miraculously disappears. "I'm cured!" he says, and buys five rupee's worth.

"Who would like to buy this wonder potion before I get off the train at the next station?" Five people raise their hands, while feeling their pockets for the money. The vendor gleefully collects twenty-five rupees and waits for the next station. Karim, impressed by the vendor's sales, looks outside thoughtfully. Another vendor selling candy, small toys and trinkets for kids appears, pushing his merchandise. It is usual for vendors and beggars, both authorized and unauthorized, to come aboard and peddle goods, while constantly playing cat and mouse with the railway authorities.

"I have beautiful toys and sweet candy for your children. It's half the price you'll pay in the bazaar. Hurry, take out your money and buy before I go to the next car," says the trinket vendor. As he waits, eagerly scanning the crowd for customers, a teenage boy steps up and pitches his plea for money.

"*Aslamo Elaikum*, my dear Muslim brothers. I'm a *Muhajir*—refugee. Hindus killed my whole family while leaving me for dead during the partition. They chopped off my leg and one arm," says the young man, showing his leg and hand stumps. Please help me. Half a rupee, one rupee or whatever you can spare. I'll be happy even to have some change." The candy vendor pushes him aside, causing him to collapse onto a seated passenger, and proceeds to yell, "This is my car. I was here first. Disappear and never interrupt when I'm selling my wares. You *Muhajirs* have made our lives miserable." Karim observes the scene, still trying to understand how one medicine can work for almost every ailment, when he hears the beggar's scream. He bolts upright and grabs the candy vendor by the throat as if to kill him. The vendor gasps and pleads with Karim to release his grip. Karim relaxes his fingers slightly and orders him, "Don't you dare bother another crippled person ever again, especially a *Muhajir!*"

Passengers intervene, telling Karim to let go. He releases his grip on the vendor, whose frightened, wide-eyed face turns pale.

"I'm sorry. We haven't treated you with dignity," says Karim to the shocked beggar, who leans against the wall, resting his face atop a crude crutch, equally frightened.

"You should thank the *Muhajir*. We all should," says Karim. "We're indebted to people like this refugee, whose sacrifice and suffering made Pakistan a reality. *Muhajirs* paid dearly. Their sacrifices brought us a Muslim Pakistan."

Whispers turn into loud approval for Karim's act of kindness. His khaki army uniform undoubtedly helps him earn the crowd's respect. There is silence in the car, causing the noise of the train to seem louder. Karim cannot believe he acted so impulsively. He steps through and over people to get to his seat. He looks outside and thinks of his friend, Makhan Singh. He asks himself. *Did he and his family survive the ordeal? Did any of them lose a limb?* Karim adjusts himself one more time on the bench and looks outward, as the train halts at the arched, colonial one-room station. He squints to focus. His jaw drops as he sees the medicine man and the afflicted patient with a toothache sneak around the building through the breached fence, smiling and shaking hands, celebrating the perfect con.

The train chugs along the winter wheat, barley, maize and sugar cane crops—speckled with *sheesham* and acacia trees that stretch to the horizon. The countryside is dotted with small villages. Thick plumes of smoke, rising from the wood and cow dung-fired hearths into the gray December cold, indicate that women are preparing breakfast for their families. The schoolchildren, who run along the tracks jump, wave, make faces and grin with excitement at the passing train. The farmers, cattle and equipment work the fields. The passing scene reminds Karim of Rurkee; from the train it seems idyllic and serene. He knows though, that like in his village, the people who live here till, toil and work the land endlessly, just to make a paltry living.

The train crosses the Chenab and Jhelum, two of the five rivers in the Punjab—literally meaning *Five Waters,* and heads into the Pothwar plateau. Karim welcomes the rising terrain. The train snakes through rocky canyons, straddles the tabletop plateau and hugs the sparsely forested semi-arid scrub foothills, steadily climbing to 1700 feet above sea level at Rawalpindi.

This city, dating back to the fourteenth century, stands firmly at the crossroads of the Grand Trunk and Silk Roads, having been destroyed and reconstructed numerous times after subjugation by transient invaders—from Alexander the Great and the conquering Mughals, to the colonizing British. In the nineteenth century, the British turned the city into a large military base by building a major cantonment, whose mission was to defend and extend its power into the northwest frontier. From partition to this day, the general headquarters of the Pakistan Army are in Rawalpindi.

Karim disembarks the train, collects his luggage and hops onto the back of a military truck, joining a dozen others. The new soldiers are quickly whisked away to their assigned quarters. In less than a week, Karim is ordered to wait outside the lieutenant's office with nine other men. When called, he enters and stands at attention, after saluting the officer, while the *Subedar Major* sits in attendance.

"What is your name, *Jawan?*" asks the lieutenant while glancing over his file.

"Karim, Sir."

"No, you are not Karim. You are *Lance Naik* Karim Din."

"Yes sir."

"You earned not one but two stripes before finishing basic training. It's very unusual. You should be proud."

"Thank you, sir."

"Do you know what your superiors in Sialkot said about you?"

"No sir."

"You're one of the few enlisted soldiers who has graduated from high school. You have great comprehension, an inquisitive and analytical mind and possess a natural aptitude for problem solving. It's all here in black and white in your personal file. It doesn't mean you aren't a good soldier, but it seems to me that the Army can use your mind more than your muscle."

"Thank you, sir."

"Based upon your education, accelerated promotions and aptitude, I'm transferring you to the Army's Intelligence Division. I hope you're pleased with that."

"Yes sir. I am very satisfied, indeed."

"Congratulations and keep up the good work," says the lieutenant while extending his hand.

The timing is right for Karim to follow a new course. The army has transformed an idle young boy into a man. He is prepared for challenge and adventure. He is thrilled to be a part of Pakistan Military Intelligence and reports excitedly to the PMI School. He learns English, math, and geography, as well as land formations, mapping and compass reading before he is transferred into an advanced training class that takes place more than 100 miles into the Himalayas, a secret training school, nestled into the mountainside, 7,000 feet above sea level.

—25—

The Letter

"Postmaster Sahib, here comes our friend Fazal of Rurkee," says the clerk looking through a tiny window within the lone two room Sialkot Post Office. The flat roofed, brick building, located in the center of a spacious lot, is surrounded by a green lawn and shrubbery. The barely legible hours of operation are painted in black on a weathered wooden board, which hangs precariously above the window.

Post Office Hours
Summer 7:00 a.m. to 2:30 p.m.
Winter 8:00 a.m. to 3:30 p.m.

Most people can't read, and even if they could, would not pay much attention to the hours, as their visits are infrequent and full of anticipation. They come as they please, meet friends and acquaintances, assemble on the lawn enjoying the greenery and flowers, gossip and catch up with life happenings. Through a small window, the people of Sialkot and the surrounding villages buy stamps, post cards and government bonds. They collect their pensions. The shrewd ones, who have extra money, build up savings accounts, since the post office is a bank as well. Fazal is, as usual, early, and the first one to arrive.

He leaves his bike at the stand, rummages through a gunnysack that dangles from the handlebar and picks out a small package wrapped in a cloth napkin.

"*Aslamo Elaikum,* Uncle Fazal. We haven't seen you for two months. Everything is all right?" inquires the clerk while the postmaster joins him, greeting the visitor with a big smile.

"Everything's okay. I'm just getting old and don't feel like pedaling the old wheels more than I have to. Another shop has opened up in Rurkee; business has dropped and I don't need many supplies. It's fortunate that I don't need the money. Karim sends me more than I can make from the shop. The shop keeps me busy and out of trouble." He stops talking and hands a package to the postmaster with a gentle grin.

"Here, Postmaster Sahib, my wife had enough rice flower, flax seeds, walnuts and brown sugar syrup, to make *Ulsi Piniees*—flax seed balls for you and your wife. These are power balls. It'll make you and your wife young again." Fazal winks at the postmaster. "I hope you have my money. Not one but two month's worth. I should be getting seventy rupees."

"Of course we have the money, Fazal Sahib. It's eighty rupees, not seventy. Karim must have gotten a raise."

"If he keeps this up, I might just close the shop and retire."

"Here are eighty rupees. You also got a letter from your son. I'll tell the clerk to get it for you."

"A letter came? That's the first. I haven't heard from him since he left." Fazal collects the letter, tucks the crisp new rupees in the secret pocket Rakhi has sewn inside his shirt, secures the letter and hurries to Jamal. He cannot wait to share the letter with his friend.

"*Aslamo Elaikum,* my dear friend. Karim sent me a letter."

"What does it say?"

"I haven't read it yet. I hurried from the post office so I could share it with you. First, here are some *Ulsi Piniees.* Rakhi made them for you." They sit down on the rattan bench, a permanent fixture of Jamal's shop. Fazal takes the hookah from Jamal and takes a big drag, slowly letting out puffs of smoke into tiny circles. Jamal sends the shop

boy for chai. "Make sure it's hot and bring fresh spicy potato *samosas*."
Fazal opens the letter. "It's a long one, almost two pages."

"Well, go on. Read and tell me what our Karim is up to."

"It is dated September 25, 1958," says Fazal, holding the two pages before him.

My dear Abu—Father *and Amiji*—Mother . . . *and anyone who is listening.*

"That's me," exclaims Jamal.

Aslamo Elaikum. This is the earliest I could write. So much has happened since I left home. I arrived in Rawalpindi over nine months ago. Within a fortnight, I was offered and eagerly accepted a position in the Pakistan Military Intelligence (PMI). I really love it because I can use my mind to its full potential, which I never did in high school. The Pakistan Military has given me a second chance.

I was in PMI School for a full year. They taught us many subjects: English, Geography, Mathematics, Geometry, Trigonometry and Statistics, to name a few. I've learned to draw and read maps. With these maps and a compass I'm able to find my way anywhere. Since finishing the PMI School in Rawalpindi, we were sent to a location—the name of which I can't disclose, for advance field training. It's a secret military site. The only thing I can tell you is that a long winding road through the pine forest leads to an impressive facility tucked high in between two big pahars—mountains. I'm in the pahars you used to show me from Rurkee. They're snowcapped and have real berf on them year around. Every time I look at them, it reminds me of my Uncle Nazir, who never saw these majestic mountains, but convinced customers that the ice parrots of paradise indeed came from the Himalayas. This is all I can tell you. I'll be here at least a year. I'll write to you. I don't have a real address, but if you wish, you could write to me and send it in care of Military Headquarters in Rawalpindi.

I have sent money each month, and hope you've been collecting it from the Sialkot Post Office. My remittance has increased from 35 to 40 rupees since my promotion. I'm so excited about what I'm doing. There is much to see and do. I miss Rurkee but this is an adventure I've come to love. I don't exaggerate when I tell you that this is a different world. It reminds me of the stories you used to tell me when I was a little boy—about the hunting expeditions of kings and princes in the mountains and jungles of far-flung places. I miss you, yet I'm indebted to the Pak Army for introducing me into a new world; opening doors for different experiences. At times I feel that I'm one of the lucky young men from the dusty plains of Punjab who's been launched to the heights of the Himalayas, where I'll be trained for a profession that's both daring and dangerous. At times its nerve wracking, but I assure you that I'm enjoying the experience with a [sic] *sense of guarded exhilaration.*

Salaam, to my ever-smiling mother and sister Parveen and her growing family. Please pay my regards to Uncle Shafkat. When you see Uncle Jamal tell him that I'm very happy in the army. In couple of months I'll write again.

Until then,
Your loving son,
Karim

"Well, our Karim has come a long way Fazal. You should be proud."

"Daring and dangerous," repeats Fazal, looking at Jamal, while inserting the letter back into the envelope.

"Yes Fazal, there's nothing to worry about. All young men going into soldiering say the same thing. They can't help but feel thrilled to be around danger. Our Karim will be fine. You and Rakhi can be proud."

"Yes. Yes, Jamal I'm very proud. I know his mother is. She is the rock of our family. You better tell your son to fill my short and light order, as I can't wait to get home and share the news with Rakhi."

Jamal's son takes the list from Fazal, packages the listed supplies, stuffs two gunny sack bags and secures them on each of the bicycle handles. Fazal climbs on the bike, saying, *Khuda Hafiz* without looking back and pedals home energetically, impatient to read the letter to his wife. He is elated, and has not felt this good in a long time.

"I don't understand all those fancy courses our son is taking, but I'm happy he is gaining knowledge and getting smarter," exclaims Rakhi.

"Of all the classes he's taking, the two I understand are mathematics and English."

"What are mathematics and English?"

"My dear, it's the same arithmetic I've been doing to run the shop all these years, and English is *Angrezi*."

"Oh, *Angrezi* is the tongue of *Angrez*, isn't it?"

"Yes."

"Maybe someday I'll meet an *Angrez* and Karim can be the go between," chuckles Rakhi. "Fazal, we need to get him married off. He's getting old. A few families, some actually quite nice and rich, have offered their daughters for Karim. I know we're poor but he's a good catch. It's him, not us, they want. I don't know what to say. We need to ask him. I haven't seen him for a year now. Write him a letter and ask him what his wishes are, and next time he's home, he should be engaged."

"You're right. He should have been married by now. His sister has been married for over two years and she is much younger. I'll write to him and ask when he's coming home, and tell him that his mother has chosen the most beautiful, educated and rich Punjabi girl for his wife." Fazal teases Rakhi with a smile.

"Just ask him first. Would you?"

—26—

Disciple

Upon completing his advanced field training, Karim takes a month off before returning to the Military Intelligence Division in Rawalpindi. Once home, he must disappoint his anxious parents by telling them that he is not ready to settle down. "I love my job. I've learned so much from the experience. Now, I'll be working in Rawalpindi as a Defense Analyst. The Army has given me many promotions. I'm so grateful. Mother, do you know that I'm a *Subedar Major* now?

"But, my son you disappoint us. You're getting old. I wish you'd get married. I want to see my grandchildren before I die."

"Mother, I'm not that old. I'm only twenty-three, and besides, you're not dying any time soon. I know you're going to have a very long life. I'll not consider marriage until I finish my four-year assignment in Rawalpindi."

"Rakhi, I see his resolve," says Fazal. "He's an army officer now and speaks with authority. He's not going to change his mind. Give him some time. He'll come around." Fazal smiles and winks at his son. Realizing that Karim is standing firm, his parents put aside their questions about marriage for another time.

For the next four years, from 1958 onward, Karim pours his heart and soul into intelligence work. He constantly updates graphs, tables and charts for his superiors. He is good at what he does, but he gets bored and longs to return to the field. He yearns for action. In the summer of 1962, the Army sends him to Kargil, a military outpost near the Indo-Pakistan border in Kashmir. His assignment is to collect information regarding the strength and movement of Indian troops along the Line of Control—a "temporary" border negotiated by the United Nations and accepted by both India and Pakistan. Putting his training, tools and techniques to use—gathering and supplying data, undercover, for the defense of his country, inspires him. He disguises himself as a young spiritual seeker and asks one of the holy men to accept him as his disciple.

"Son, you're a handsome young man. Men of your age should pursue their worldly dreams," counsels the spiritual leader. "You should choose a career, or start a business; make money, get married and raise a family. Why do you want to join our *Silsila*—group of devotees?"

"Since I was a child," replies Karim, "I always dreamed of becoming a devotee of a great spiritual teacher. I've come a long way from the plains of Sialkot to the inspiring Himalayas, in hopes that *Baba Ji*—the old sage would take me into his fold." Karim lowers his eyes respectfully, toward the old man. He wears plain, civilian clothes as they sit facing each other in the open courtyard of a beautiful, century-old mausoleum, the burial place of Baba Ji's great grandfather.

A garlanded white marble headstone marks the grave where the name of the old sage, and the date of his death, along with Koranic verses, are etched and inked in black. The tomb is a square room bordered by a verandah on all four sides. A dark green, onion-shaped cupola sits on top of the square brick building. From the center of the dome, a long bamboo pole, from which a myriad of colorful flags flutter in the mountain breeze, thrusts into the deep blue sky. Inhabitants living and working in the valley below can see the mausoleum from miles away. Many believe this revered old saint converted thousands of idol-worshiping *kafirs*—infidels, to Islam, not by force but merely by his charm, sweet tongue and personal example of tolerance, fairness and compassion. People travel long distances to pay respect, make offerings and ask the saint's blessings in curing their pains and ailments.

"What is your name?" asks Baba Ji—the holy man.

"Karim, Your Holiness."

"Karim, look at me." Karim looks up at Baba Ji's face nervously.

"You'll be asked to shun worldly pleasures and live a simple life; grow a beard, let your hair grow long, and wear simple clothes and sandals. Oh, yes, you'll carry a *kasa*—a begging bowl, and swear a solemn oath to serve Baba Ji whole-heartedly and without greed. Soon, you'll look just like me." The holy man points to his own long hair, while stroking his white beard. "Are you willing to do that?"

"Yes, I'm willing to do whatever is asked of me. But can I ask for one small favor, Your Holiness?"

"Surely, what is it, my son?" Karim takes out Makhan's *kara,* which he has carried in his pocket. "Can I wear this on my wrist?"

"Of course, *Pirs* and *dervishes* love to wear the iron bangles and encourage their disciples to do the same." Baba Ji rises, telling Karim that he's very happy to have him join the *Silsila.* He congratulates him and pulls him to his chest in a bear hug. "Welcome, Karim. This is your home. You'll live here with us to serve Baba Ji."

"Thank you, Your Holiness. Thank you very much indeed."

Karim settles in with a half a dozen other young disciples, who greet visitors, accept offerings and arrange visits with Baba Ji. Like missionaries, they go to small villages and hamlets, sparsely dotted along the Indo-Pakistan border, spreading the Islamic faith and the good teachings of Baba Ji. They encourage villagers to visit the tomb, come for the annual *Urs*—the convention of devotees, and gladly accept food and money for the center. Karim, well disguised in his shabby, sacred cover, wanders throughout the mountain countryside, observing, collecting and dispatching information to the military headquarters in Rawalpindi. At first apprehensive, he surprises himself and acknowledges that he likes the adrenaline rush that danger brings.

People on both sides are Kashmiris and have friends and relatives going back and forth, without knowing where the border lies. They are aware that a line exists somewhere and, at times, Pakistani and Indian soldiers rattle each other by firing guns and artillery. Most go about daily living and fail to understand the conflict. They ignore the ruckus, always hoping that no one they know is killed or maimed by the shells that occasionally miss the mark.

Walking between adobe mud and stone dwellings that rise from terraced fields along the mountainside, Karim slips in and out of Indian territory through the porous border, which is difficult to protect due to the rugged mountain terrain. With a photographic memory, he observes and surveys Indian posts, the troops' strengths and their movements. His contacts provide him with important secret military information.

On one of his missions, he walks leisurely along a narrow path, unaware, that he is being followed, when he hears an abrupt order: "Stop right there Yogi. Hands above your head and turn around slowly." Karim obeys and turns around to face two Indian soldiers. With pistols cocked, they carefully approach, ordering him to stand still while they search his body for weapons.

"What's wrong? What did I do?"

"Who are you and where are you going?"

"I'm just a wandering dervish, who visits *pirs*—spiritual leaders throughout Kashmir. This time I'm on my way to Balakot to attend the *Urs* of *Pir* Kaku Shah. You know *Pir* Kaku Shah in Balakot. Don't you?"

"Shut up and don't say a word. We know who you are. You're a Pakistani spy," yells one of the soldiers, while pistol-whipping Karim about his rib cage.

The soldiers tie Karim's hands behind his back and take him to a nearby military post. Unable to extract information, or his identity, his captors rough him up, lock him in a room, and wait for their superior officer to arrive. The next morning an Indian Sikh Lieutenant drives up on a motorcycle, surprises the sleeping soldiers and scolds them for neglecting their duties. In an instant, the officer confiscates their guns, releases Karim and orders him to jump behind him. The motorcycle speeds off, its driver shouting over his shoulder to Karim,

"I'm taking you to headquarters." Shaken, the young soldiers watch the motorcycle disappear around the bend.

The driver delivers Karim safely into Pakistani territory. "You should be careful," he says. "Karim Sahib, next time you may not be so lucky." He peels off his fake beard, turban and uniform, revealing himself to be Anwar, Karim's Indian counterpart. He tosses the beard and uniform into the stream flowing through the canyon, thousands of feet below.

"Thank you, Anwar," says Karim gratefully. Without an answer, Anwar, turns around and vanishes; racing full throttle, in hopes that he won't be caught.

Karim works in the hamlets another two months, providing daily reports about the location and number of Indian patrols. Impressed, his superiors select him to head up an espionage cell in Muzzafarabad, the capitol of Azad Kashmir. Muzzafarabad is held by Pakistan, and presumably autonomous from the Pakistan government. At Karim's previous post, in Kargil, Baba Ji, occasionally curious about what happened to Karim, does not truly miss him, for it is common at the shrine to see devotees come and go.

The Headmaster at the Muzzafarabad High School gathers his staff to welcome Karim. "Let me introduce you to Mr. Karim, who is with the Pakistan Ministry of Education. He comes to us from Lahore. The Punjab Provincial government has been generous enough to send him here to help with student recruitment. Shamefully, at present our literacy rate is less than ten percent. Parents don't send their children to school, for a variety of reasons. They have not attended school themselves, and feel that education is irrelevant. More importantly, they need the children's help on their meager farms, raising crops and cattle. They are unaware that primary school is not only free but is mandatory. Mr. Karim is here for an outreach program. He has the expertise, supported by government funding, to spread the word about the importance of education in rural Kashmir. His mission is to convince parents that their children must go to school."

Clean shaven, and with his hair fashionably trimmed, Karim stands in front of the teaching staff clad in a white shirt, blue striped tie, black trousers and polished shoes with matching socks.

"Thank you, Headmaster Sahib, and thank you all. I'm happy to be here. Soon, three more educators will join me in the outreach program. With your help, I'm sure we can increase the student population. The Azad Kashmir government plans to open new facilities next spring. All of us must work very hard to fill our new schools with first graders."

Within a month, three more educators arrive, while Karim continues to prepare for his dual job of education and espionage.

Heading to a village nestled in a canyon high in the remote mountains, he negotiates his Triumph motorcycle over the steep dirt trail and arrives at a small alpine meadow that offers magnificent views of two peaks towering over 18,000 feet. He settles on a large boulder and eats his lunch, admiring the imposing pinnacles, when he hears a voice. He ignores it, believing his ears must be buzzing, but the barely audible voice becomes a series of raspy whispers, interspersed with painful moans.

"Anybody there? I'm hurt. Badly hurt. I heard a motorcycle. Motorcycle man can you hear me? Please come. I need help. *Maddad karo.* I need help. *Maddad karo.*" The utterances indicate a person whose *Urdu*—Pakistani language skill is limited. A series of whistles chirp in quick succession.

Karim stops chewing, holds his breath and cups his ear in the direction of the voice, and concentrates. He can hear, but cannot make out the words. More whistle sounds. Someone is in trouble and needs help. He runs in the direction of the whistle, up a hill, through the pine trees and jumps over the shrubs as fast as he can. The whistles become more frequent and desperately shriller. He climbs about 200 feet and follows a natural trail down to a rock outcrop, coming upon a shocking scene.

A young girl lies barely conscious next to a backpack, under the rock overhang. Her bruised hands, colorless face and swollen black and blue ankle are streaked with blood. A whistle strung around her neck is still in her mouth. Her glazed eyes flicker, and focus on Karim, who leans over her, wondering what to do? Karim realizes that she is English. Karim's understanding of English is good, yet he struggles with his wording.

"You alive *Mem Sahib*—English lady. *Inshah Allah*—God willing everything okay. No worry."

"Please, help me. *Maddad karo*—help me. I need a doctor."

"Wait. I take you hospital. I get motorcycle. I get water. I get medicine."

As Karim heads back to get his motorcycle, the girl faints; her head tilts to the side and the whistle hangs loosely in her mouth. Karim retrieves his motorcycle and races to the scene, grabs the first aid bag and crawls backward down to the site.

"Are you okay, Mem Sahib?" There is no answer. Panicked, he fears that she has died. He takes her pulse and listens to her heartbeat. "You're alive, Mem Sahib, you're alive. You are in shock."

His first aid and military emergency training goes on autopilot. He gently props her up, encourages her to drink water and gives her pain and fever tablets. He reinforces the ankle and leg bone with flat wooden splinters, and repositions her to a comfortable position, while constantly assuring her that everything will be all right.

"Mem Sahib, you be okay. *Inshah Allah*, God willing. I'm here. My name is Karim."

It takes over an hour for her dehydrated body to regain enough strength to open her eyes. She looks at Karim and whispers, "*Shukriya*—thanks. Please . . . can you take me to the hospital?"

"Yes, yes. Mem Sahib. I take you hospital."

Karim carefully carries her to the motorcycle. He straddles her on the back seat; tentatively holding her upright, he slings a shawl under her arms, adjusts his position in the front and ties it around his chest. He drives the girl downhill slowly, checking all the time to be sure she balances safely on the seat. He carefully maneuvers around the hairpin turns on the road, to the Civil Hospital in Muzaffarabad.

"Hurry hurry! Mem Sahib badly hurt. Please get doctor," Karim cries at the entrance to the hospital. Word spreads quickly. The doctor and other hospital staff who live on the campus, rush to help the girl off the bike.

"Miss Kaye, are you all right?" says Dr. Salim. "What happened to you? I thought you went for a walk. Kaye, I've told you so many times that these mountains are dangerous. You shouldn't be out there alone."

"I'm sorry. I should've listened," whispers the girl.

"I'm sorry too Miss Kaye. I didn't mean to yell, but it upsets me just thinking that you could've been killed," says Dr. Salim, turning to Karim. "Thank you very much, Karim Sahib, for bringing Kaye back safely. She is a valued member of our staff. You may go on home now and rest up after your heroic rescue, for which we are grateful. We'll take it from here." He orders his staff to attend to Kaye's medical needs.

"I'll come back and see how she doing, Doctor Sahib," says Karim.

"Of course, that'll be fine," says Dr. Salim, still shaken from the thought of what might have happened.

As Karim turns to leave, Kaye opens her eyes and squeezes his hand, sending a chill through his body. "*Shukriya*—thank you," she whispers, struggling to speak; "And one more thing."

"What's that?"

"I love the mountains. Next time, I'll follow doctor's orders and ask you to be my guide."

"I'd be happy to, Miss Kaye. I know these mountains like back of my hand."

—27—

The Penthouse

Kaye Peterson, bandaged and sedated, lies motionless on a cushioned *charpai*—cot, in a two room, mud-floored hospital guesthouse, recovering from the accident. During her occasional moments of consciousness, she reflects on her former life as a nurse in a Denver, Colorado hospital.

She lived a simple life, residing in a small studio apartment in Denver. She worked long hours and enjoyed hiking in the Rockies. Like young Americans at the time, she was independent, enjoyed 'rock n' roll' and was infatuated with the young president who challenged her generation to serve their country by serving the world. She believed deeply in the ongoing civil rights movement, and was troubled by the escalating U.S. involvement in the Vietnam War. She was restless, and thought constantly of doing something different; something out of the ordinary.

In 1961, Kaye decided to celebrate the Fourth of July with her parents, who lived on a small family farm east of Denver. On the morning after the fourth, enjoying a leisurely breakfast on the patio, they overlooked a stream that meandered through the lush green meadow. For years, the Petersons had tapped and diverted its waters to raise acres of alfalfa. Kaye sat quietly, took a few bites of scrambled egg, and pushed her plate away, gazing at the horizon that seemed to touch the vast prairie.

"Kaye, since you were a little girl, you've always enjoyed sitting on the patio admiring the green meadow and the alfalfa fields. Today, under the warm morning sun, our farm looks like an oasis. Doesn't it, honey?" said her mom, sensing something was on her daughter's mind.

"Mom, I'm answering President Kennedy's call. I've decided to join the Peace Corps."

"You're going to do what?" Her parents said in unison, caught by surprise, dropping their forks and looking at her in disbelief.

"Are you out of your mind? Leaving such a well paying job in America for a pittance, and putting yourself in danger in some awful faraway place," yelled her father. "What about Bob? Have you talked to him?" His face reddened with anger. "We were hoping that after he finishes his residency, you might get married and raise a family."

"Honey, Bob is a good catch. You won't have to worry about money if you marry a doctor," advised Kaye's mom, with a soft smile.

"What gave you the idea that I was going to marry Bob? He's a nice guy, Mom, and I like him; but we are different, way different. I like to travel; he likes to stay put. I want to see other cultures; he refuses to leave Denver. I love to trek and hike the mountains, yet he hasn't once made an effort. We've been drifting apart for some time now."

"Have you talked to him, Kaye? Maybe he'll go with you for a short tour after his residency next year," suggested her mom.

"I've talked to him. He gave me an ultimatum. It will be over if I ever leave Denver, and he won't come looking for me. Mom, we've broken up," said Kaye as calmly as if it were of little consequence.

"We're sorry, Kaye. You've obviously made your decision, and there's nothing we can do to change your mind. Whatever you decide to do, I pray to God that you're happy and safe," said her mom, looking across the field, away from Kaye.

Several months later Kaye received a letter confirming her acceptance into the Peace Corps, and a date to report for training in Washington, D.C. Her family and friends, unable to convince her not to leave the good life and bright future behind, gave in and sadly hugged her good bye at the Denver airport.

In the spring of 1962 Kaye, with mixed feelings—sad and excited, flew to the other side of the world: Pakistan. After an orientation in Rawalpindi, she was on a bus to Azad Kashmir. The colorful bus bumped and spurted for seventy miles, taking hours as it snaked through the steep canyons of Pakistan's northwest frontier, arriving in Muzaffarabad, the state capitol, where she started her job as a Peace Corps nurse volunteer.

"Mem Sahib. Mem Sahib. Here's chicken soup and crackers," says Rashid, the hospital cook, shaking the cot and bringing Kaye's thoughts back to the present.

"*Shukriya*, thank you, I was really asleep. Wasn't I?"

"Yes, Mem Sahib, you were. Do you need anything else, Mem Sahib?"

"No, I don't. *Shukriya* . . . would you please open the shutters before you go? I like to look outside."

"Sure thing Mem Sahib. I'll check back in half an hour to see if you need anything," says the servant, quietly leaving the room, and bowing his head.

Kaye finishes the soup, plumps her pillows, and gazes through the open window for a minute; then picks up a pen and paper to write a letter.

Muzaffarabad, Pakistan
July 4, 1962
Dear Mom and Dad,
I'm lying on a cushioned cot called charpai, recovering from a near fatal accident. Don't panic. By the time you get this letter, I'll have totally recovered. I broke my ankle while hiking in the wilderness and lay in the forest for hours, drifting in and out of consciousness. If it wasn't for Karim, I would have died. I'm still in pain, but I'm recovering fast. Mom, in your last letter you asked about my living arrangements and what I've been doing in Muzaffarabad.

I live in a simple mud and rock dwelling that I call my "Kashmir penthouse." This two room guesthouse has a single wood-shuttered window that offers an incredible view of the tumbling Jhelum River, against a backdrop of snow capped Himalayas. A lamp on a small table, a chair, wooden armoire, make-shift book shelf of planks on bricks and a few floor cushions scattered on the thick handmade cotton rug called Dari make up the décor. A couple of outhouses and a water hand pump are on the campus for communal use. I get my meals from the cook who serves the doctor and his family. I consider this a luxury that I didn't have at home and must admit that I enjoy it without guilt.

I work with Doctor Salim who, along with his wife, lives in an official residence located on the hospital grounds. I'm training young girls to be nursing assistants, and teaching midwives how to handle birthing complications. It's a small ten-room, twenty-bed hospital with an attached pharmacy/equipment storage room. The doctor and the staff are still excited about the X-Ray machine that arrived six months ago. Other than my house and the doctor's residence, there is a sizable kitchen and half a dozen servant quarters.

It's warm and feels heavenly, as I'm surrounded by pine scented air, rushing cold clear river water and the tranquility of the mountains. What a beautiful sight! Right now as I look through the window I see a couple of sheepherders watching their flock grazing on the river terrace. They've been sheared and look so skinny, but have color markings signifying that they're literally 'sacrificial lambs' and will be sold for Eid, one of the two Muslim religious holidays. In about six weeks, at the end of August, people who can afford it will celebrate Eid by sacrificing an animal, distributing meat to the poor and having a big feast with the family and friends.

I arrived here just in time for Eid last year. Doctor Salim bought the lamb, one of the servants koshered it and all teamed up to skin and cut the carcass. They hung it on a tree branch, cutting it into small pieces, while children wore festive clothes and played in the compound.

That evening I had one of the best meals of my life. We sat in a circle, while the servants brought containers of spicy mutton curry, skewered lamb kabobs, aromatic basmati biryani, and fresh baked naans, along with—believe it or not—chilled Coca Cola drinks. My mouth watered as herb and spice aromas filled the room. As tradition dictated, I was chosen to go first, which I did gladly. Soon every one dug in and ate to their heart's content. It was certainly different than the turkey and mashed potato meal I was used to in Denver.

You are probably wondering, 'Who is Karim?' He's a teacher in high school and is working to recruit kids for first grade attendance. Ninety percent of the boys grow up without going to school. Girls are not allowed in school, since educating girls is considered dishonoring the family. Since my miraculous rescue, Karim has been coming to see me, always bringing me some treat. I think he likes me, and to be honest I like him as well. I miss him when he's not around. I'm hoping Dr. Salim invites him this Eid. Oh, I hear Karim's motorcycle. I'd better go.

Say hello to Brother Jeff and his family. It's exactly a year ago today that I told you I was going to join the Peace Corps. You should know that in the beginning I was anxious, but I'm fine now. Maybe you and dad can take a break from the prairie and visit me in Azad Kashmir, if only to experience the Himalayas.

Love, hugs and kisses,

Kaye

The cook runs to greet Karim as he kills the engine and climbs off his motorcycle. "Rashid, is Mem Sahib awake?" asks Karim, heading toward Kaye's house.

"Yes, I think so Sahib," says Rashid, following Karim closely.

"*Aslamo Elaikum*, Mem Sahib. How you doing? You feel better? Pain gone or not?" stammers Karim, his English less than perfect.

"I'm okay. I'm feeling much better, *Shukriya*."

Karim puts a bag full of apples and apricots on the table, muttering to himself, while avoiding Kaye's gaze. "Fruit healthy for you. Eat and you get well. Gain strength."

"Karim, have you ever had coffee?" asks Kaye. "You should try it. Rashid bring us fresh coffee. Make sure to bring sugar and milk, as well. It's American chai. People drink coffee in the U.S. just as we drink chai here." Kaye explains it all, while smiling at Karim. Rashid brings the coffee and Karim loads his cup with sugar and milk and sips slowly, pretending to like it.

"Thanks again for saving me," says Kaye, pausing. "I appreciate your daily visits . . . you haven't missed a day." Her eyes meet Karim's.

"Actually I look forward to your company and feel anxious when you're late."

"Mem Sahib." Karim says softly, his heart pounding.

"Call me Kaye."

"Yes, Miss Kaye. It's my duty to see that you are getting proper treatment and becoming healthier every day."

Karim keeps his promise to visit Kaye every chance he gets. In early August, after nearly six weeks, Kaye is fully recovered and has returned to her training.

"Miss Kaye. I be gone two weeks. The moment I back I come see you. Bring fresh fruit from the hills," says Karim reverting to his pattern of broken English.

"Two weeks? That's a long time!" protests Kaye.

"I go number of villages and see many parents. I'll see you when I return."

Kaye reaches out and touches Karim's hand. "I'll be waiting. By the time you come back, I'll be well enough to hike the mountains. Remember, you told me that you know the mountains like the back of your hand." Kaye's touch sends a shudder through Karim's body; he hurries out, relieved nobody is around, climbs on the motorcycle and speeds away, his heart pounding.

After two weeks, Karim is not back. Kaye, fully recovered, waits anxiously, wondering and worrying over what has happened to Karim. *Where is he? Is he in trouble? The countryside where he bikes is remote and dangerous. There have been torrential rains and mudslides. Will I ever see him again?* she wonders. *Is he even alive?*

—28—

K2

Kaye runs out of her room when she hears a familiar motorcycle thunder around the corner. Karim leans the bike against the wall of the hospital and dashes towards her, holding a basket of fruit "Miss Kaye. Miss Kaye. I brought you fresh fruit. I picked it myself. Good for your health."

"Karim, where the hell have you been? You were gone over a month. You should've been back a week ago! I was worried sick. I kept thinking you had an accident, or got killed . . . or something," shouts Kaye, hands on her hips, her face flushed with anger.

"Miss Kaye, you mad. Not my fault. I couldn't come back. Suspension bridge broke. Couldn't get across river. I wait for repair. Sorry," says Karim with a charming smile, his improved facility with English lapsing into fragmented sentences, as his excitement at seeing Kaye thoroughly flusters him.

She disregards the explanation and tells him how extremely happy she is that he is back safe and sound. She takes the fruit basket, and stares at him intently. "You promised to be my trek guide. I'll be ready for the mountains a week from this Sunday . . ."

" . . . and I will be your guide," assures Karim.

The Sunday hike takes Karim and Kaye back to the outcrop from which he rescued her. It is a cool, sunny morning, under a bright cerulean blue sky. The sun warms the atmosphere. The scent of pine wafts in the breeze, stirring the musky forest floor, rustling the leaves. Birds flutter, occasionally diving for food, interrupting the stillness.

Karim has not been able to shake Kaye from his memory, since the moment she squeezed his hand two months ago. He knows that fraternizing with a woman is prohibited, yet he took a chance by visiting Kaye as she recovered; and he offered to guide her on a hike. They decided to meet at the very site that nearly proved fatal for Kaye.

They sit quietly. Although Karim frequents the hospital to be close to Kaye, he still feels nervous and uncomfortable, reluctant to express his feelings.

"When I first met you, I thought you were from England, not America," Karim mentions, clearing his throat and looking down at the rock.

"I've lived near Denver all my life," replies Kaye.

"How big is Denver?" Karim avoids her eyes and looks into the distance.

"I guess I didn't tell you much about it."

"What are you doing so far from home?" asks Karim.

Kaye has been waiting for the question, anticipating Karim's curiosity. "I grew up in a small town on a family farm near Denver, Colorado. I've always loved the outdoors, especially the mountains. Trekking is my passion. I've hiked everywhere in the Rockies, which are tall and beautiful, but nothing compared to these mountains. These are the highest in the world. They seem to reach the heavens. Hiking in the shadow of K2 has been my life's dream."

"The doctor told me you're working as a nurse in the civil hospital in Muzzafarabad. Couldn't you find work in the United States? Wasn't there enough land for you and your family to make a living?"

"My family gets by on 120 acres, but I wanted to be a nurse, so that I could help people."

"One hundred and twenty acres! That's ten times more land than the richest farmer in my village owns," says Karim, surprised. He turns around and, for the first time looks at Kaye's face with adoration.

"My family has lived on the farm since the early nineteen hundreds, and has never traveled out of Colorado. My generation is different. Unlike our parents, we want to see, do and experience the world. After graduation I worked four years in a hospital before joining the Peace Corps. I was so thrilled at the offer to work in Azad Kashmir that I didn't even question the conditions, or the compensation."

Karim notices how Kaye's shoulder length brown hair sways when she talks, and how her green eyes move animatedly when she's excited. Her slightly upturned nose suits her oval face, marked with a tiny dimple on her left cheek that becomes more prominent when she smiles. At twenty-five, she has a willowy five-foot-eight inch frame and a healthy complexion, the result of spending time outdoors on the farm. Her smooth skin is a tawny colored *Pathani*—Afghani look. Her love of the outdoors is reflected in her casual manner of dress—sporty, and unpretentious.

"So, here I am," says Kaye. "Thank you, Karim, for saving my life." She reaches for his hand and squeezes it lightly.

"What happened that day? How did you hurt yourself?" Karim asks, looking away nervously, as she continues to hold his hand.

"It's embarrassing, but I'll tell you anyway. The accident almost cost me my life. Foolishly, without telling anyone at the hospital, I hiked up here the day before the incident. It was so exhilarating to spend a day in the woods. Near the spot where you stopped for your lunch, I decided to go around the hill and look at the view. Right there, see that flat rocky area." Kaye points, extending her right hand. "Stupidly, I walked right up to it. The view was tremendous. I became engrossed. Oblivious, I slipped and fell ten feet to the ledge below, fracturing my ankle. Bruised and in pain, like a rock climber I crawled back up. It took me over an hour; it seemed like an eternity."

"Oh, my God," says Karim, tightening his grip on Kaye's hand. "It's over a thousand feet straight down. You could've been killed; nobody would have ever found you."

"The ledge and you saved me. I sipped water, propped up my ankle, and took aspirin. I always carry a first-aid kit with me, and I made good use of it. As the evening fell, I had no choice but to close my eyes and wait. The next day I couldn't move. Every time I heard a sound, I yelled and whistled for help. I was going in and out of consciousness and just about gave up. I thought that was it for me. I vaguely remember hearing a motorcycle. You know the rest." Kaye shrugs and smiles broadly. "Enough said about me. Tell me more about yourself."

Karim tells her everything except his real profession. "I'm a teacher. I've been here nearly four months on assignment from the Punjab Education Department in Lahore."

"The way you handled my accident, I would have guessed you were a medic."

"I know these mountains, Kaye. I'd like to show you a beautiful spot not too far from here."

Karim jumps off the outcrop, extending his hand. Kaye slips her hand into his and slides down the rock. They walk side by side around the hill, up a gentle slope, through the tall pine and cedar trees. After less than half a mile Kaye sees the dramatic alpine meadow.

"What do you think?"

"It's gorgeous," says Kaye repeatedly, as she walks briskly down slope. "What a beautiful sight! What a stunning view! Come on Karim, come on." Karim sprints to join her. In front of them, a hundred feet below, lies the oval shaped alpine meadow, ringed with pine and cedar trees. A small, clear lapis blue lake rests serenely in the middle of the meadow, reflecting the white clouds. Green grass borders the lake and wild flowers march colorfully up the slope, almost hugging the tree trunks.

"Wow, don't tell me that's K2 in front of us."

"Yes, it's K2, the second highest peak. If we go further down the meadow, we can see a few more peaks, including *Nanga Parbat*."

"I can't wait." Kaye grabs Karim's hand and turns toward the lake, dragging him along. They come to a sudden stop and Kaye surveys the mountains. Astounded and humbled by the snow-capped peaks that are over 20,000 feet high, her eyes widen; her jaw drops. "Wow!

Gorgeous!" She exclaims. "What a sight! They're awesome, Karim. Those peaks look like tent poles holding up the roof of the world."

"I thought they were just big *Pahars*."

"*Pahars?*"

"In *Urdu* and *Punjabi*, we call them *Pahars*."

"What is that white ribbon below? That must be the river Jhelum," says Kaye, looking at Karim.

"Yes, it is one of the four rivers that join the Indus. It must be three thousand feet straight down. Don't look down, or slip now," says Karim, teasing.

"One of these days you're going to tell me your real profession and explain what you are doing here, racing around on your motorcycle? Maybe you're a spy or something," says Kaye, teasing in return.

"I told you," says Karim, taken aback at her comment concerning spying. "I work for the Pakistan Ministry of Education. My mission is to spread the word that education is the key that can free people from ignorance and poverty." He emphasizes his philosophy on education, but wonders if Kaye really knows the truth.

"I was just joking." She grabs his hand and they head through the flowered meadow around the lake and arrive at the edge of the forest out of breath. The breezeless summer weather makes the early afternoon pleasantly warm. The stillness is so intense they can feel their breath and heartbeats. Karim imagines that he and Kaye are like Adam and Eve in a wild garden spot. She touches his hand softly, his palm damp with nervousness. His body trembling, he looks at his feet. She lifts his chin and looks directly into his brown eyes. Her strong gaze touches his heart, and pierces his soul, sending a shock of electricity surging along his spine, like a bolt of lightning. It melts him. Holding both his hands, she pulls him gently toward her. He does not resist. She closes her eyes, offering her lips for a kiss. Her full lips meet his. They press against one another, while kissing tentatively.

"Kaye, no," says Karim, pushing her away gently. "We shouldn't do this. It's not right. Besides, it's not safe."

"Karim, don't you like me? Don't answer that. I know you like me. Moreover, what's this not being safe? No one is around. What's the danger?"

"I like you Kaye, but what if people find out. They'll banish you. They'll kill me. They could kill both of us," whispers Karim. Overwhelmed by his passion, he hopes Kaye will not take no for an answer. Kaye moves toward him, covers his face with a series of moist kisses, while holding him tightly. Karim's fear and his reason evaporate. The natural urge of young lovers to be one erupts like a volcano.

They undress frantically, peeling off their own and each other's clothes, while kissing and hugging breathlessly. Their hands caress each other until their bodies ache with desire. Karim lowers Kaye gently onto a bed of strewn clothes. He moves on top of her, kissing her gently; wrapping his arms under her shoulders. Magnetically, their bodies entwine, fusing together. Karim's passion matches Kaye's as she clutches his back, pressing her nails against his skin.

Sighs of ecstasy break the stillness, until, at fever pitch, they can no longer contain their longing for one another. Their union is blissful—as though they have tumbled down from the top of the Himalayas to rest in this heavenly spot. In each other's arms, they doze off, only to be awakened by the strong afternoon sun. Rising quickly, they pull their clothes on and sit against a towering cedar tree, whose graceful branches spread over their idyllic state of delirium. They lean into each other, hold hands and look across the open valley; their eyes fixed on the high peaks in the distance. The stillness returns.

"Kaye, do you know what *Nanga Parbat* means?"

"No, what does it mean?"

"The naked mountain."

"So I can call you *Nanga* Karim?" says Kaye slyly.

Karim laughs with slight embarrassment and swiftly pulls Kaye close to him and seals her mouth with a long kiss that prohibits her from further teasing.

Karim and Kaye meet when they can—secretly and discreetly, frequenting their favorite mountain lake where they made love the first time. On one of these occasions they are relaxed, sitting by the lake in the meadow, looking toward K2, shrouded in clouds. Karim is lost in thought.

"What are you thinking, Karim?"

"Just as K2 is covered with clouds, perhaps our future is like that also—cloudy and uncertain."

"Why? I love you. You love me. Don't you?" asks Kaye, perplexed.

"I don't know what love is, but I know I want to spend rest of my life with you," says Karim.

"That's love, Karim."

"I wish you could be my wife."

"I'll take that as a proposal, and I accept," says Kaye. "I want to marry you. I want to be your wife."

"But our culture, language and the religion are poles apart. We're so different."

"I agree that our culture, language and religion are different, but not us. You have to agree that we are the same, just two people in love. That's all that matters."

"We believe that a match is made in heaven," says Karim.

"Look around you, Karim. This is heaven; our match *is* made in heaven," she says, once again teasing.

"I have to persuade my family. It won't be easy. But I do love you and would like you to be my wife. I'll talk to my Uncle Nazir, who I am sure, can convince my parents. Let's keep this a secret. Here, parents arrange marriages," Karim explains. "Premarital visits between the sexes, let alone premarital sex, are strictly forbidden; young people pay with their lives if they are caught ignoring societal norms."

Kaye listens patiently about what she already knows. "We'll keep it a secret," she says. "You guide me and I will follow, until the match made in heaven has earthly blessings."

"Talking about secrets, I want to share another secret with you."

"What's that?"

"I'll tell you only if you promise not to tell anybody until the day you die. My job and life depend on it."

"I promise. I swear that I won't tell a soul," says Kaye, smiling and quickly sealing her lips with her fingers.

"I work for the Pakistan Military Intelligence. Education outreach is a cover for espionage. I hope I don't lose my job by falling in love with an American."

Kaye takes Karim's hand and puts it on her chest and looks into his eyes, then teases him with a gleeful smile. "I kind of knew you were keeping something from me. But really, I had no idea that you were a spy," says Kaye. "I won't tell a soul that Karim is a spy and is madly in love with an American."

"What about your family?" asks Karim. "Don't you have to have your parent's permission to marry?"

"No, I don't, but I definitely would like their approval. They'll be surprised—even shocked at first, but I'm certain that they'll be okay with it. They want me to be happy. If I'm happy, they'll be happy, too."

"I'm going to Lahore in a month or two," says Karim. "I'll talk to my uncle who is very understanding. I'll take him into my confidence and have him arrange for you to meet my parents. We'll do the marriage Pakistani style."

"Did I tell you that my time with the Peace Corps will be over at the end of the year, and I'll be reporting to my head office in Lahore? By the way, I have come to know a couple of families in Lahore. Aunt Nighat is like a second mother to me. Maybe she and Uncle Nazir can work together on my behalf."

"That's wonderful," says Karim. "I'll be transferring back to Lahore right about the same time. I expect to have a desk job and decent housing."

"How perfect. We'll get married then," says Kaye excitedly.

"I better get to work and convince my family that I want to marry the American nurse I met in the Civil Hospital in Muzzafarabad. I'll mention that she has an aunt in Lahore," says Karim, while planting a soft kiss on Kaye's cheek. "I have even more exciting news to share with you," he whispers, while kissing her ear lobe, his warm breath sending a shiver through her body.

"What's that?"

"Eid is less than two weeks away and I'll be at Dr. Salim's for the big feast. He promised me that if I'm lucky, I'll get to meet the beautiful American nurse I rescued. Kaye, I think he knows. Maybe he can put in a good word for you."

"Put in a good word for me? You are the one who needs the help." Kaye turns away, prancing towards the lake, shouting giddily. "No one invited me. I'm not going to be there. Have a good time with the doctor . . . and don't eat too many *kabobs*."

—29—

Boundless Love

It has been less than six months since Karim met Kaye. He sits anxiously next to his Uncle Nazir, on a *charpai* in his modest home in Lahore, pleading with him to convince his parents to bless the marriage proposal.

"Uncle Nazir, Kaye loves our people and culture. She speaks *Urdu*, and in Pakistani clothes, she looks like a *Pathani*—Afghani girl, with fair skin, brown hair and green eyes. She grew up in a small town, much like Rurkee, in the United States. She's straightforward and smart. Did I tell you? She graduated from college in nursing and left her comfortable home to bring health care to the poor people of Kashmir. Uncle, if she is happy there, I'm sure she'll make an easy transition to Lahore.

"Uncle, are you listening? You haven't said a word. She's a wonderful, caring person and most importantly—we love each other very much. You've got to help me. You're my only hope."

"Is she willing to convert?"

"Willing to convert?"

"Is she willing to become a Muslim?" asks Nazir, turning to Karim, while spewing out a big puff of smoke. He has been nursing a hookah all this time.

"Yes, I'm sure she will. Uncle; yes, she'll be willing."

"Okay then, we'd better get busy. We've a lot of convincing to do." Karim and his uncle travel to Rurkee.

"You want to do what? No wonder you've been making excuses for avoiding marriage," fumes Karim's father. You found someone in Kashmir? Having a Kashmiri or *Pathani* daughter-in-law is hard to imagine. But no, you have to go for a Mem Sahib."

"Brother, just listen to Karim for a minute; let him explain," says Nazir.

"Listen to what? Our culture is different. Our language isn't the same. What about her faith? People will say our son is marrying a nonbeliever," shouts Fazal.

"Brother, in talking with Karim, I feel this girl will adapt to our ways. She's willing to become a Muslim. She has already lived many months in Kashmir, where conditions are much more difficult than here. She has spent a lot of time with Muslim families. She is a nurse and teaches women and midwives how to take care of babies and children."

"She's willing to convert? That's a good thing Fazal," says Rakhi, with a hopeful smile.

"How did you meet her, Karim?" Rakhi asks, and listens intently while Karim explains how he rescued the girl from a rocky ledge in the mountains.

"So you saved her life," says Rakhi. "She's a lucky girl."

"Mother, I'm fortunate, too, that I found her. If she becomes my wife, I'll feel like the luckiest man in the world."

"Karim, we're not in *Walait*—England. We can't adapt to English ways just like that." Rakhi snaps her fingers. "We'd like to meet her parents. Meet the girl and spend some time with her to see if she is good for you, and judge for ourselves if she's a good fit for our family."

"Sister Rakhi, I've already arranged that," says Nazir. "You come to Lahore at the end of March. We'll visit her aunt in Lahore."

"She has an aunt in Lahore?"

"This is her adoptive Pakistani aunt. She's like a second mother to her."

"Okay, we'll come to meet her in Lahore. We'll do this the proper way. Right, my dear Fazal?" says Rakhi, facing her husband. "There's no harm in checking her out. Our son has grown up as a responsible military officer. We'll give him our honest opinion. We don't know how he'll react, but the rest will be up to him."

"Thank you, *Amiji*. Thank you. I know you'll like her," says Karim, leaning over to kiss his mother's forehead with a sigh of relief.

By March, warmth embraces Lahore. Fazal dons his best *kurta*, *sarong* and a plumed turban. He holds a box of sweets. Rakhi wears her silky blue *shalwar-kameez* with a matching star speckled *dupatta*. Nazir, equally dressed up, waves down a rickshaw. "We're going to meet our future *Mem Sahib-in-law*. We'll go in style. We'll take a rickshaw today, not a tonga. Take us to Model Town," he tells the rickshaw driver, handing him a piece of paper. "Here's the address."

The three sit on a single bench seat just behind the driver, sheltered only by the heavy flapping plastic. Squished together, they bump up and down and swing sideways, as the driver negotiates his way over potholed back roads and through bazaars crowded with a stream of pedestrians, tongas, buses and donkey carts. The driver constantly changes gears, honks the horn and revs up the engine at every stop, circumventing cut-offs. Thick black smoke from the two-stroke Italian Vespa engine spews forth into the opaque air already saturated from smoke and dust.

"Here we are. 42-A Poplar Ave, Block B, Model Town," declares the driver, stopping in front of a small white bungalow.

"Thank you, Driver Sahib. It was quite a ride." Nazir smiles, handing him the fare.

"We should've hired a tonga," grunts Fazal nervously, already feeling uneasy about the visit to an upscale neighborhood.

"*Aslamo Elaikum*," chants the woman who greets the threesome at the door. "You must be Karim's parents and his Uncle Nazir. Welcome. Come on in. We've been expecting you," says Nighat, a short, plump woman with round cheeks and cropped gray hair, visible without a *dupatta*. She points to the velvet sofa situated in front of the *kalin*—hand-woven rug that is the centerpiece of the living room decor. A matching love seat and a single arm chair, with a footrest, sit on the opposite side. "Please be seated and do feel at home. I'm honored to have you in my home." The guests sit stiffly on the sofa, hands folded in their laps, pretending to be comfortable.

"Here is a box of sweets," says Nazir, breaking an awkward silence. "Where's our daughter Kaye? I hope we didn't make this trip for nothing."

"Oh, she's here. She and my daughter are in the kitchen making chai. They'll be in momentarily." No sooner does Nighat finish the sentence, than her daughter and Kaye enter the room with trays of chai, sweets and fruit.

"*Aslamo Elaikum,*" the girls say in unison and sit on the love seat. Wearing their *dupattas*, they appear quite modest. Both wear a fashionably patterned *shalwar-kameez*. It is obvious that Kaye is not accustomed to wearing the *dupatta*, as a pin secures the scarf to her hair. Kaye pours out tea, puts the cups on a small tray and offers them to the guests. Her friend follows with the tray of sweets.

"Chai *laein*—please take tea."

"*Shukriya, baytee*—thank you, daughter," says Rakhi giving her a *piyar*—a pat on the head.

"*Koi bat naheei*—no problem," says Kaye perfectly.

"She speaks *Urdu*," remarks Rakhi. "I only know Punjabi, and I'm from here. I guess I'll have to learn *Urdu* now," she says, clearly showing her acceptance of her son's choice. "What about her family, Nighat? Is it all right if she marries Karim? Will they accept us?"

"Oh yes, we've talked by phone several times. It's all right with them. They want their daughter's happiness. They might even come to Lahore for the wedding. If her parents aren't here, Kaye is like my own daughter. I would give her away in style, with a wedding that people will remember forever."

"I understand you are a nurse," says Fazal, addressing Kaye. "Are you going to work after the marriage?"

"I would like to help the sick."

"But, you are not going to work with men, are you?" asks Fazal. "It is not appropriate for a woman to work outside the home; and working with men would certainly be dishonorable."

"No, I'd continue to work with women and children. That's my specialty and that is what I did in Muzzafarabad. Everyone seemed to accept me, and I really enjoy working with kids."

Nazir springs up from the sofa. Knowing that the girl had rehearsed her lines well, he sneaks a congratulatory wink at Karim and tells Fazal, "Brother, enough interrogation. Karim is very lucky, and we are fortunate that Kaye is joining our family. Get up and give *piyar* to your future daughter-in-law. Rakhi, here's the ring. Put it on Kaye's finger and start learning *Urdu.*" They all laugh, relieved that the matter of Karim's marriage has been settled successfully.

Rakhi motions for Kaye to sit by her. She sits between Fazal and Rakhi. Rakhi slips the ring on and tearfully pulls her close for a warm hug. She gives Kaye her *piyar* and kisses her cheeks. Fazal picks up a piece of sweet and puts it in her mouth. "Welcome to our family and welcome to Pakistan," he says, choked with emotion. "You're a brave girl, making your home and future so far away from your family and friends. And, remember one more thing, *baytee.*"

"What's that?" asks Kaye, wondering what Fazal means.

Fazal leans closer and whispers in her ear, "You must convert and take a Muslim name before the wedding." Kaye nods her head in affirmation and says, "Of course." Nighat pulls out a small box and opens it up, presenting a ring for Karim. "This is for Karim. I hope it fits. If not, we'll get it sized."

The families congratulate each other, then hug and embrace Kaye, who in turn says, *shukriya.* Karim's family leaves. Filled with joy, Kaye runs to Nighat, wrapping her arms around her in a bear hug and squeals, "*Shukriya* Aunty, *shukriya.* You did it; we did it. I'll prove to Karim's parents that our marriage is the best for all of us."

Kaye and Karim are engaged—the first milestone toward the wedding is checked off. The fall days are comfortably warm, while cool nights and shorter days turn boulevard trees golden, making the arrival of Kaye's parents even more auspicious. Kaye has eagerly anticipated their visit, and looks forward to their meeting Karim.

"Welcome, Mom and Dad," calls Kaye, running to greet her parents as they move through the customs line at the Lahore airport. "I'm so glad you're here. I bet you'll be amazed at this exotic place."

"Welcome, welcome to Pakistan Mr. and Mrs. Peterson," says Nighat, as her daughter hands Mrs. Peterson a bouquet of flowers. Luggage collected, they quickly get into a Morris Minor yellow cab that merges into the traffic. The Petersons, who have never traveled outside Colorado, are weary from their long airplane trip to Pakistan. Through the back seat window, they gaze at the land of Rudyard Kipling, as the driver moves through scrub and dry countryside to the Pearl Continental Hotel, located in a relatively quiet and lush neighborhood of Lahore. The Petersons had insisted on staying in a comfortable air-conditioned place for their visit.

Nighat arranges the *Mehndi* for Kaye—a fun filled October evening that takes place the day before the wedding. It will remain etched in Kaye's memory forever. She has chosen a Muslim name, Kishwar. Nighat's daughter delicately decorates her hands and feet with vibrant, red henna, curlicue designs. Kishwar, the center of attention, gazes at the dozens of brilliantly costumed young girls, as they play a *dholki*, sing folk wedding songs and dance around her. Their joy and laughter make Kaye feel like one of them.

At the wedding, the following day, Karim, clad in *shalwar*—baggy pants, *shirwani*—closed-collar tunic and a fancy turban, sits next to Kaye, who is dressed in the traditional beaded and gold-embroidered, red satin bridal dress, and wears a sheer *dupatta*. Facing them, the invited guests assemble on plush cushioned chairs in the great room of the Intercontinental. The Petersons are seated in the front row with Karim's parents, his Uncle Nazir, and his sister Parveen, her husband and their five and three year old children.

"This is quite different from the weddings we have in our country. I've never seen anything like it," whispers Mrs. Peterson in Rakhi's ear. Someone translates quickly for Rakhi and with a smile, she turns and says, "Mrs. Peterson, I have never seen anything like this either."

The *Maulvi*—Muslim cleric recites a few Koranic verses, after which he guides the bride and groom in the exchange of vows. He asks three times, "Do you, Karim, accept Kishwar, as your wife?"

"Yes, I do."

"Do you, Kishwar, accept Karim as your husband?"

"Yes, I do."

They sign the wedding papers, duly witnessed by two people. The *Maulvi* asks the guests to raise their hands in prayer, bless the union and pray for their happiness and bright future. "Congratulations to you both and to your families. May Allah give you peace, happiness and many, many beautiful children." MALE

Karim and Kishwar are married. A band plays; the attending waiters bring out and serve trays of aromatic and colorful spicy food. Guests shower money gifts on the newlyweds and bring them gifts, as the waiters serve chai and sweets.

The wedding festivities end the next day when Uncle Nazir throws a traditional *walima*—reception party. A huge tent stands in his neighborhood community garden. Block printed panels—*kanats* enclose the sides, and *kalins* of vibrant colors and designs fully cover the ground. Nazir and Karim's parents welcome the guests, who are ushered to the decorated tables and chairs for a feast. The cooks, who have been preparing vats of food on site since dawn, are almost finished.

As the Petersons arrive, Nazir comes forward to shake hands with Mr. Peterson and proudly says five words that he has rehearsed so well in English. He puts one hand on his heart and points to the tent with the other, "Mr. Peterson, welcome to my Hotel Intercontinental."

The gregarious Uncle Nazir sees to it that the festivities last well into the night. In his heart, he recalls the days of Vaisakhi when Karim helped him sell the famous birds of paradise.

After the celebrations have concluded, the Petersons return to Colorado. Their neighbors welcome them home with a potluck dinner. Everyone wants to know all about Pakistan. They are curious about Kaye, Karim, and the wedding. The Petersons proudly show pictures of their unforgettable adventure. Mr. Peterson grabs a beer and sums it up for his inquisitive friends:

"It was an adventure straight out of National Geographic. Pakistan is different. The country teems with life. The culture, the customs and the costumes are rich, yet so different from what we know in America."

He pauses, taking a swig of beer, and glances at his wife. "Our Kaye is an audacious young woman. We hope that all her wishes come true and pray that she'll be safe in such a foreign land. Her wedding was similar to a Hollywood musical. My wife attended the *Mehndi* ceremony, which she says was just like a fairy tale." Mrs. Peterson nods in agreement and rolls her eyes. "The wedding ceremony itself was performed as if it were a scene in a movie, and the gala reception—held in an open tent, was right out of Arabian Nights."

—30—

Duty Calls

Extremely happy, Karim and Kaye move into a small bungalow in Lahore. He works in Intelligence Logistics, while she offers nursing services at the Mayo Hospital. Karim has an official military assistant, and Kaye loves having ten-year-old Sonia, a girl servant, living with them. Life borders on luxury.

The three-bedroom, two-bath house is on a quiet tree-lined street in Lahore cantonment. A six-foot security wall, providing privacy to the family, surrounds the flat-roofed, white stucco house. A reinforced metal gate, decorated with wrought iron, is the only access into the residential area, which includes a carport. Flowerbeds border a covered porch along the spacious, grassy courtyard, where a sole deciduous mango tree stands.

On weekends, the couple enjoys lazing in the sun—sipping chai and reading the newspaper. On weekdays, a military jeep chauffeurs Karim to work, while the staff van takes Kaye to the Mayo Hospital where she attends to the health issues or needs of many women and children. The newlyweds are contented with their first home and life together. Both are satisfied with work and sense that they are contributing to the country and its people. Their daily conversation centers around the base and hospital. Several friends frequent the house, enjoying dinners prepared by Kaye, who experiments with curried dishes, snacks and desserts. Most are surprised by the Mem Sahib's cooking abilities, which satisfy their curiosity, and delight their appetites.

In May, 1965, a secret closed-door meeting between a dozen top brass and civilian officials opens in the General Head Quarters (GHQ) in Rawalpindi. A three star general begins the session. *Two words?*

"We're here this morning to discuss two very important subjects: First, the aftermath of the Rann of Kutch battle over the disputed border area west of the Indian State of Gujrat, during the war with India. Second, an assessment of our military performance. We want to evaluate the successes and failures—the strengths and the weaknesses of our forces during the March-April engagement with the Indians. Remember, this is a matter of utmost importance. Our national security is at stake. We must be honest, as the future actions of our government depend upon a diligent and professional appraisal of our military capability. This is critical for solving the long, outstanding issues of Jammu and Kashmir."

The most senior official speaks for the entire group, while others listen attentively, perusing and flipping through their files. "Sir, we had a great success in Rann of Kutch. Our military and border police, although outnumbered by the enemy, were quick and precise; they took brave and decisive action, reclaiming significant disputed territory. Our men are well equipped and highly motivated."

"Can we repeat our performance in Kashmir?" asks the General. *of course, God is on their side..*

"Sir, I'm sure we can. *Inshah Allah*—God willing, our swift and well-planned action can achieve similar or better results," replies the spokesman.

"The Pakistan Government is concerned that India may absorb the disputed territory of Kashmir into her Union. Our government doesn't intend to start a full-scale war with India. The sole purpose of any operation, if ordered, will be to take control of occupied Kashmir as much as possible; thus forcing India to the negotiating table; and to solve the Kashmir issue for good. Come up with a workable plan, scrutinize it thoroughly, hammer out the details and be prepared to present it to the Chief of Staff. We'll meet right here in a week," commands the General.

A week later, in the same room, equipped with intelligence reports, maps, charts and graphs, a dozen or more senior military planners present the action plan—code-named 'Operation Gibraltar', to the Chief of Staff and the heads of the Armed Forces.

"Do we have enough motivated volunteers who are willing to cross the border for our good cause?"

"Yes sir, we do indeed. More than enough, ready and willing," responds the spokesman.

"What about locals? Would they join in the struggle?"

"The people of Kashmir are primed for uprising, as they've been discontented and displeased with the Indian rule for years. Their right to self-rule has been denied for too long. The local insurgency is well organized, and eager to join."

"If we're forced to launch 'Operation Gibraltar,' would the Indians keep the battle in Kashmir alone, or would they attack us somewhere else? Would they open other fronts; say further south in Punjab?"

"Sir, it is unlikely that the Indians would expand the war beyond Kashmir. We believe they would employ all their resources in the Kashmir sector, keeping the conflict in the disputed territory. It wouldn't be in their interest to violate the United Nation's mandate and risk the world community's displeasure by attacking across the international border. But if they do, we can certainly defend ourselves."

"Very well then, be prepared to act at a moment's notice. Wait for further instructions," orders the General as he walks briskly out the door.

A few days later, in Lahore, Kaye says good-bye to her husband. "How long will you be gone Karim?" she asks with an apprehensive smile.

"Six weeks, maybe eight at the most."

"I know that you can't tell me," whispers Kaye while holding him close in a prolonged embrace, "but I wish I knew where you were going. Take care of yourself and be careful, Karim. I'll be thinking about you every day."

Karim is dispatched to Muzzafarabad, in Azad Kashmir, joining teams of others who frantically gather new intelligence, validate the old and do field reconnaissance. Their assignment is to assess the chances of a successful incursion by the Freedom Fighters into occupied Kashmir. He spends seven weeks at Muzaffarabad before returning to his Lahore duty station.

During his stay at home, Karim's demeanor, quieter than usual, troubles Kaye. She senses something ominous, but asks no questions, knowing that he will not discuss his mission. She is relieved for the moment; glad that he is home with her. After his brief stay of two days, he must leave, telling Kaye that his parents may be coming to live with her while he is gone. "Please look after them while they're here," says Karim. "I don't know when I'll be back, but I want you to keep a low profile until my return. Stay strong. I promise I'll be back for this." Karim smiles, and rubs Kaye's bulging belly. *she's pregnant I gather...*

"You better." Kaye feels a knot in her stomach. She is sure that her husband is heading into harm's way. Lately, rumors and rumblings of war between Pakistan and India over Kashmir have been rampant.

"I love you, Karim," says Kaye, taking his hands in hers.

"I love you, too." Karim squeezes Kaye's hands one final time and turns to Sonia. "Take good care of my Mem Sahib while I'm gone," he says, lifting the girl's chin lovingly before hopping into the waiting military jeep.

Karim is part of a small unit deployed along the Punjab border, less than fifteen miles from Lahore. Rurkee is fifty miles to the north. He and his team wander through the porous border, blending in with locals; they gather information and report back to headquarters. The situation along the border seems relatively calm.

A couple of weeks later, on a hot and muggy August evening in Lahore, Sonia opens the front gate and yells with excitement, "Mem Sahib. Karim Sahib's parents are here." Kaye runs out and welcomes Fazal and Rakhi. Sonia and Kaye quickly relieve them of their belongings, as they are soaking wet from the hot and humid weather.

"*Aslamo Elaikum, baytee Kishwar,*" says Rakhi. She always calls Kaye by her Pakistani name.

"*Wa Elaikum Asslam.* Come in, please." *repeatedly translated*

They sit down on the *kalin*—hand woven woolen rug, directly under the continuously whirring ceiling fan. Sonia hands them the floor cushions, while Kaye serves them their favorite sweet pomegranate drink—chilled and refreshing *Rooaye Afza*. "*Amiji* and *Abu*, you brought a heavy load with you this time!"

"*Kishwar, baytee*, a few days ago, Pakistani soldiers came and warned us that India might attack Pakistan. Since we live too close to the border, they ordered us to vacate Rurkee as a precaution. Hundreds of villages, including Chowinda were ordered to do the same. They told us to take our valuables with us and lock up the houses. It won't be long before we can return to our homes.

"The military spokesman assured us: 'The Kashmir war won't last long. India won't cross the Punjab border and if it does, we will fight back hard. We don't want you be in the line of fire. Your houses and property are safe with us, We'll let you know when you can return.' So, here we are," says Rakhi, beckoning Kaye to sit with her. "I hope and pray for Karim's safety."

The situation is too much to handle. The only way Kaye can deal with it is to keep busy and occupy her mind with work, despite being seven months pregnant. With Rakhi appealing repeatedly for her to rest, Kaye immerses herself in the hospital work, caring for sick children and impoverished mothers. She feels fulfilled, knowing that she is making a difference; yet, she feels anxious and even depressed at times. There is too much suffering and too few resources to properly treat the sick and the destitute. They are neglected by society, afflicted with ignorance and poverty. Prematurely aged bodies and hopeless faces overwhelm her.

On August 15, 1965, Kaye comes home from work and picks up the Pakistan Times that awaits her in the living room. She barely finishes the headlines before collapsing on the sofa with a loud gasp.

India attacks Azad Kashmir; Indian forces cross the cease-fire line
*Pakistani Army helps Kashmiri Mujahidin
repel enemy's unprovoked aggression*

"Oh no," moans Kaye. "That's just what Pakistan and India need. Another war." She has been hoping the inevitable would somehow be avoided. Sonia runs from the kitchen with a glass of water in hand, while Rakhi follows. "Mem Sahib, are you all right?"

"India and Pakistan have started the war."

"Everything will be just fine Mem Sahib, I'll pray, *Inshah Allah*. Karim Sahib will be safe."

yep, that should do the trick...

Kaye pulls Sonia into her arms as if she were her own daughter. "Yes, of course, everything is going to be all right," she says. "We'll pray for Karim and all the other soldiers. We'll pray and pray hard that war will end soon."

No problem since God likes them best

Rakhi draws both Sonia and Kishwar into a three-way hug while giving them *piyar—love pats*, and says "We'll be fine. Karim will be home soon. Allah is our protector."

repeatedly translated — of course He is...

Should be italicized Kaye reads the Pakistan Times daily, both at work and at home. Her ears are tuned constantly to the BBC radio. In one of the broadcasts, she hears a BBC reporter detailing the Indian-Pakistani conflict:

Today is September 1, 1965 and this is a BBC Special World Report: The Indian Ministry of Defense has confirmed that its armed forces have crossed the cease-fire line, launching an attack on Pakistani held Kashmir. An Indian spokesman further claims, "The Indian attack is in retaliation for the massive infiltration by Pakistan's armed forces and Pakistan-trained insurgents across the Indian border. The provocation threatens the stability of Kashmir and poses a grave danger to Indian national security. After a prolonged battle, our forces have captured three mountain passes, including Haji Pir Pass, which is eight kilometers inside Pakistan. Although we are facing heavy resistance, we'll not stop marching forward unless Pakistan withdraws every soldier and insurgent from our soil."

Pakistan vehemently denies backing the insurgents. However, The BBC report continues, *a Pakistani spokesman claims that the August 15th, Indian attack was unprovoked aggression and therefore Pakistan had no choice but to launch a counter offensive. The Pakistan forces have moved into Indian Territory and are in control of the Tithwal, Punch and Uri areas of Indian held Kashmir.*

Kaye wonders if Karim is in Kashmir. Wherever he is, she prays for his safety. On September 6, 1965, Kaye again hears a report on the radio:

This is a BBC special Indo-Pakistan War Report: On September 1st, Pakistan launched 'Operation Grand Slam' in the Kashmir Theater. It is an all out attack on Indian held Kashmir. The operation's objective is to recapture the lost territory and take full control of the only road to Jammu, thus cutting off communications and supplies to the Indian troops in Kashmir. The Pakistan Army reaffirms that it has no territorial ambitions except for that of pressing India to withdraw to the UN established ceasefire line; and to earnestly consider a negotiated settlement for Kashmir. India, on the other hand, denies any Pakistani gains and this morning launched a full-fledged land and air attack across the international border into Punjab, possibly to relieve pressure on its troops in Kashmir. The Indian spokesman says its forces are backed by artillery and their tanks are pushing onward to Sialkot and Punjab's capital Lahore.

Kaye turns off the radio, and renews her prayers for Karim's safety.

By September 9th, the war is in full swing. India's First Armored Division, known as the 'Pride of the Indian Army' launches a two-pronged offensive toward Sialkot, only to retreat and retrench when it meets heavy Pakistani tank fire. Fifty miles south of Sialkot, Pakistan's own pride—the First Armored Division, pushes an offensive towards Khem Karan with the intent of capturing the holy city of Sikhs—Amritsar.

"Karim," announces his superior. "We've captured two Indian Army Officers who are wounded; they are being treated in our field hospital. I understand they might give us valuable information. I want you and your team to work on them to extract whatever intelligence you can. I want it fast," he orders. "I want it now! I expect a full and comprehensive report by 2000 hours. I would have attended to this matter personally, but I've been summoned by the commanding officer to handle another important matter."

"Yes sir, consider it done."

Amidst all the urgency and confusion of war, Karim leaves the field office with a leather brief case containing classified files. The waiting jeep whisks him to the MASH (Military Army Service Hospital) unit, less than a mile away toward the rear of the battlefield.

Machine gun fire and exploding mortar shells detonate in the distance, while fighter jets scramble, shriek and zoom overhead in both directions. Diesel fumes mixed with soot and dust hang ominously in the air. Karim feels—in his bones, the consequence of war. Death and destruction are rampant on both sides.

Karim and his two assistants walk into the makeshift field hospital, shored up by timber, tin and tent canvas. Red Crescent banners hang on four sides and atop the tent roof. Karim walks through the front entrance, flashes his security badge, and the military police quickly escort him into a small cordoned off space in the back. Here lie two Indian officers on camp cots, exhausted; their wounds dressed, their bodies medicated. A small tray of food, barely touched, lies on a small folding table between the cots. The officers, though well trained for such unfortunate circumstances, respond to Karim's hello with apprehension. As prisoners, they are unsure of their treatment.

"Are you from Punjab?" inquires Karim politely.

"Yes, we are Punjabis," says one of them, clearing his throat.

"Good, then we can speak Punjabi."

Karim spends about three hours with these prisoners. He is pleased with the interrogation. As he walks back to the entrance, exhausted, weaving through scores of cots occupied by wounded and maimed Pakistani soldiers, he pauses a moment to look around. The soldiers lie suffering from a variety of severe wounds—fractures, tightly bandaged in blood soaked-muslin dressings; limbs damaged beyond repair, necessitating amputation. A few patients appear to be clinging to life, with little hope of survival. The medical staff runs from section to section, continuously working, ignoring the nauseating smell of blood and antiseptic liquids.

Karim is about to dash out of the facility when his eyes rest on one particular cot. He stops in front of the cot. "Omar, is that you, Omar?" Omar's blood-caked, mummy-like body shocks him. His friend is barely breathing.

"Sir, they brought him last night. He hasn't spoken a word. He is gravely wounded. We are afraid he isn't going to make it," says the attending nurse sadly. Karim kneels down, holds Omar's hand and whispers, "squeeze my hand if you recognize me." Omar struggles to respond. Karim, like a sensitive instrument, registers the warm touch of Omar, whom he has not seen since they joined the army.

"Omar, can you talk? I know it's hard. Please try to say something. Even a few words would mean a lot to me. What can I do, Omar?"

"Ka—rim."

"Yes, Omar." Karim puts his ear close to Omar's mouth.

"Don't leave me here. Send my body home. I want my parents to know that I died for Pakistan." Omar takes his last breath. Karim pushes back his tears and regains the composure and resolve of a soldier. He orders the staff to make sure Omar's body is sent home to Perth. He then dashes out of the hospital, knowing he has a report to prepare.

On the other side of the border, between Chowinda and Amritsar, in a camouflaged tent, a captain and two lieutenants of India's First Armored Division lean over a map waiting for their commanding officer. Major Makhan Singh enters the tent. "What is the situation, gentleman?" asks Major Makhan Singh, acknowledging the salute.

"Sir, our advance has been stalled. We have retreated a bit. Not only are we facing anti-tank obstacles like trenches, underground tunnels, barbed wire, along with very effective anti-tank gunfire, but also many mines lie in the area. The Pakistanis are a lot better prepared than our intelligence led us to believe. We must re-evaluate, and plan to surprise them with a swift and fierce attack to disrupt the enemy's command, control and supply lines."

"How are we holding up at the front?"

"Sir, we are in a pitched battle with the enemy. For now, we are holding our ground. We have taken significant casualties and I'm sure Pakistan has as well. We must request additional air and artillery support while we regroup, clear land mines and rethink our attack plan."

"Okay, let's send word to our high command; give them our recommendations and request quick air and artillery cover." Major Makhan Singh looks towards the battlefield. The storm of dust, diesel fumes, and gun and mortar shell explosions is clearly visible. He can hear the rattling of armored vehicles and equipment, as well as the sonic booms of fighter jets overhead. His heart sinks. Chowinda is less than four miles away.

The war rages on for five weeks, causing thousands of casualties on both sides. Chowinda sector witnesses the fieriest tank battle since World War II. Pakistan defends Chowinda successfully, while suffering a loss of more than one hundred Patton tanks to the Indian Fourth Mountain Division, which halts and pushes back Pakistan's offensive, aimed to capture Amritsar.

The United Nation's mandated ceasefire ends the war on September 22, 1965. Both Pakistan and India claim exaggerated gains, while minimizing their losses. A day after the ceasefire, Major Makhan Singh accompanies his superiors in a helicopter, for reconnaissance of the ceasefire line. Chowinda is a ghost town. His old Alma Mater, Chowinda High School lies in ruins, testifying to the successful Indian Artillery firepower. He cannot stand it and looks the other way, only to see Rurkee just ahead of him. Makhan's thoughts turn to his childhood. He thinks of his friend Karim, Uncle Fazal and Shafkat, but especially of Karim. *Did he finish high school? Did he take over his father's shop? Did he leave Rurkee for a better future? Where is Karim today? Did he and his family have enough notice and time to leave and move to safety?* He imagines their lives since he left Rurkee.

"Makhan Singh, you haven't said a word since we've been airborne," shouts the commanding officer over the helicopter's noise. "Are you all right? What are you thinking?" he asks. "Are you disappointed that we failed to capture Chowinda? I'm disappointed too, but we've won the war. We fought bravely and kept a good portion of enemy forces engaged, resulting in a decisive and historic win further south, protecting our Golden Temple in Amritsar."

"Sorry sir, I was lost in my thoughts. I was thinking about the villagers below us. Did the villagers have a chance to leave? After all it is one Punjab and they are all Punjabis."

"Major, we are soldiers. We don't ask those kinds of questions. We leave that up to the politicians and our leaders."

"Of course, sir, we shouldn't ask those kinds of questions."

It is a late November evening when the military jeep drops Karim at his home in Lahore. Sonia runs out, opens the gate and Karim hurries in. He cannot wait to see his family. Fazal and Rakhi welcome him with hugs and kisses. Kaye, glowing with motherhood and smiling through happy tears for her husband's safe return, comes from the bedroom holding a month old baby. "We haven't named him, yet. I was waiting for you to come home." *[handwritten: oh thank Allah, it was a BOY!]*

"Amman, I want to name him Amman," says Karim, reaching for his child.

"Amman. Does it have special significance or meaning?" asks Kaye, while handing him the eight-pound bundle and hugging them both.

"Yes, it means peace."

"Then, Amman it is." *[handwritten: yes, even I now know what a kalin is.]*

A week later Rakhi and Fazal sit on the *kalin*—rug, their backs leaning against the living room sofa; they have found it more comfortable to sit on the floor. They are all packed, and ready to return home to Rurkee.

As they wait, the warm sun shines through the window, and the fragrant aromas of breakfast and chai waft toward them, making their mouths water. Sonia brings a tray loaded with plates of spicy omelet, a stack of buttered toast, jars of jam and jelly and fine silverware. Kaye follows her with a tray containing a ceramic teapot, covered with a tea-cozy; along with matching cups, saucers and milk and sugar containers.

"*Amiji*, here is your *Angrezi*—English breakfast, and English Chai."

"Thank you, *baytee*."

Rakhi nudges Fazal. He had dozed off in the sun's warmth. "Here is your *Angrezi* chai my dear. You have to mix it yourself," chuckles Rakhi.

Fazal looks at Kaye lovingly. "I have to tell you something. I can't believe that my dream has come true."

"What dream?"

"I haven't told anyone, not even my wife about the dream I had years ago. Karim was only ten and was in fifth grade then. One cold morning in Rurkee, just after Karim and his friend Makhan left for school, I was sitting in my shop waiting for Rakhi to bring me my breakfast. I fell asleep. I dreamed I was fancily clad and sitting in my son's living room in a beautiful bungalow, while Karim's driver was waiting in the driveway to take him to work. Karim's cook brought me a hot cup of chai. Once awakened by my wife, I realized it was just a dream.

"Look at me now. It's better than what I dreamed. I'm sitting in this beautiful bungalow. How lucky I am that my Mem Sahib daughter-in-law brings me hot English breakfast. How fortunate and honored I feel. May Allah give you a long life and bless you with many children."

"I feel lucky and honored as well," says Kaye. "Karim talks about his childhood memories. He speaks frequently about his friend Makhan Singh; so much so that I feel I have known him all my life. Finish your breakfast and have a safe trip home. You have a long way to go."

—31—

East and West

After two months the war ends, and the United Nation's mandated ceasefire is in place. Both India and Pakistan claim victory, while accusing each other of starting the conflict. The state run radios and newspapers minimize their losses, while glorifying their victories and territorial gains. These two impoverished nations can ill afford the incalculable cost of war. Approximately three thousand Indian and four thousand Pakistani soldiers have lost their lives, while the number of displaced and dead civilians will never be known. Fazal and Rakhi, like thousands of others, return to devastated villages, their homes reduced to rubble and pock marked with gunfire and artillery shells. The fields that farmers planted a few weeks before the war lay ruined; unattended and trampled by the army and armaments. The country landscape, scarred with military trenches and pitted with mortar shells has changed beyond recognition. Fazal rebuilds his house and the shop, but the emotional damage caused by the death and destruction of war will take a long time to heal. Karim's intelligence gathering slows down. He is assigned to the 1965 post-war defense analysis work. Unlike Omar and thousands of others who never made it back alive, he feels lucky to be unscathed and home with his family.

Kaye has continued to work at the Mayo Hospital, where there has been a surge of poor patients after the war. On a typically busy day, Kaye, struggling to keep pace with the influx of deprived patients, has asked to speak with the hospital administrator. Shortly after her request, she is summoned to the administrator's office.

"Come in Miss Kaye," beckons her superior, pointing to a chair in front of his desk. "Please have a seat." As a nurse, Kaye's exuberant dedication to helping sick children and poor mothers, along with her warm smile and diligent work ethic, commands special attention. The administrator rings the bell, instantly alerting a servant, who waits for the order respectfully, his head down and hands folded.

"Bring us two Coca Colas; and make sure they're chilled." The servant bows and promises to return.

"What's on your mind, Miss Kaye?" inquires the doctor.

"Dr. Javid. This hospital is swarming with sick mothers and children. Resources are stretched to the limit. We know that pathogens in the unclean water are the major cause of most of the diseases. The World Health Organization (WHO) estimates that over a million people die each year, worldwide, due to unsafe water supplies. Thousands die right here in Lahore. These diseases can be prevented—or at least minimized, if basic principles of sanitation and hygiene are followed. I propose that we make it mandatory, at least in my ward, for any patient who wants free medical care to attend a basic health class. I'll demonstrate how easy it is to avoid the diseases and ailments afflicting them and their children."

The servant returns with two Coca-Cola bottles. Dr. Javid takes one and hands the other to Kaye. "Don't you think we should include men as well?" smiles Dr. Javid, knowing that no man will accept such training.

"That would be great," says Kaye. "The more people we educate the better. However, women are the basic caregivers and they and their children are at high risk. We should start with them. Simple education, coupled with better hygiene and nutrition, should be a great preventive boost."

"I concur. Let me know what you need. I'll do the best I can to make it happen."

"Thank you, Dr. Javid." Kaye beams as she walks out of the office.

On a mission, Kaye assembles course materials and teaches scores of mothers twice a day. Her opening remarks are enthusiastic; yet convey the serious importance of clean water. "Your babies and young children are most vulnerable to ailments caused by poor hygiene. These childhood diseases are preventable. I want to teach you the basics of hygiene, nutrition and safe drinking water. The principles are very simple. When you pay attention to what I say, and follow the ideas you learn dutifully, your children will grow up healthy and nearly disease free. If they are healthy you'll be happy, and you will have more time to attend to other family matters." The statement invariably draws muffled laughs and shy giggles.

"Stomach pains, weight loss, bloating, vomiting, diarrhea and fever are symptoms of cholera, dysentery, typhoid, hepatitis and other awful diseases that are caused by unsafe water. Don't take a chance. I urge you to boil water for your babies and young children until they are, at least, four years old. Keep the babies clean and dry to avoid skin disease and lice. Feed them balanced and nutritious food. Protein is very important. If you can't afford meat, which I'm sure most of you can't, lentils are an excellent substitute." She conveys basic health knowledge at a level they can understand, while drilling them on ideas they can use at home. Their poverty is foremost in her mind, while she works diligently on methods they can follow with resources they can afford.

"Kaye, you look exhausted," Karim, remarks frequently when she comes home from work.

"Yes, I know that. Yet, I am happy being exhausted. Karim, some of the mothers are paying attention and are learning simple ways to take care of their family's health. I think we're making a difference."

"You are an angel, Kaye," Karim reminds her repeatedly.

President Ayub's ten-year military dictatorship ends on March 25, 1969 when he hands the country over to General Yahya Khan, who continues the standard military regime by imposing martial law.

On November 28, 1969, Yahya Khan addresses the nation, promising general elections and a transfer of power to the winning party.

Meanwhile, Karim's family has expanded, with the birth of their second child. Amman, now four years old, clings to his mother, while looking with a mix of admiration and jealousy at his baby sister, *Jasmin,* being nursed by her mother. With the birth of Jasmin, Kaye has stopped working, to be with her children. The hospital administrator, however, convinces her to return to part time work twice a week, supervising the basic health education program she pioneered three years ago.

Elections are held on December 7, 1970. East Pakistan's Awami League Party headed by Sheikh Mujib Ur Rehman wins the simple majority and demands formation of the government. Zulfiqar Ali Bhutto, the leader of the Pakistan's People's Party, wins the majority in West Pakistan and refuses to concede to Mujib. President Yahya Khan, facing civil and labor unrest in West Pakistan, fears the secession of East Pakistan. He calls in the military, made up largely of Pathans—tribal soldiers and Punjabis, to control the explosive situation.

By the middle of March, 1971, the temperate weather in Lahore is beautiful; warm enough to wear lightweight *shalwar-kameez,* and enjoy the outdoors. Families walk in the city parks, push children on swings and stop for ice treats. At sunset, children and adults practice flying kites on the flat rooftops.

While his neighbors live their days in peace, Karim cannot sleep. He tosses, turns, and lies awake, thinking about the civil unrest that threatens to erupt. He worries about Kaye, six-year old son Amman and two-year-old daughter Jasmin. He gets up in the middle of the night and sits down with a hot cup of milk. His mind races and his heart pounds with uncertainty: *How am I going to tell Kaye that I'm leaving for Dhaka in a week? How am I going to break the news to my children that I'm going away and may not see them for a while? What if Amman asks where I'm going and why? What am I supposed to tell him?* He is not afraid, but his head spins as he thinks about leaving behind his beautiful family and aging parents. *If something happens to me, what will Kaye do? She'll be alone in this foreign land. How she will survive? If I don't return, I couldn't blame her for going back to Colorado. But then our children will be in a foreign land and my parents will never see their grandchildren. I've got to make it back*, he tells himself.

Karim steps back into the bedroom where Kaye and the baby are sound asleep. He kisses them both and, for a few moments, caresses the baby's tiny arm that is wrapped around her mother. He gently closes the door behind him, walks across the hallway into his son's bedroom and plants a lingering kiss on Amman's forehead. Amman just rolls over on his side, unaware of his father's affection. Karim lies down on the living room sofa and falls asleep, only to be awakened the next morning by his wife.

"Karim, what are you doing here in the living room? Are you all right?"

"Next week I'm leaving for East Pakistan. An enormous and vital military operation is under way. East Pakistan is on the brink of civil war."

"I wondered when you were going to break the news. You know, I read papers and listen to the radio."

"I'm worried sick about you and the children."

"Don't worry; I'll take good care of them. You do your job and return home to us safely." Kaye throws her arms around Karim, securing him in a tight embrace and kissing him fervently.

"I don't say it very often, but remember that I've always loved you. I'll love you until the day I die. If I don't come back, you have Amman and . . ."

Kaye puts her hand on his lips and whispers, while the tears roll down her cheeks. "Don't say that. Your children and I will be waiting for you.

Dressed in civilian clothes, Karim sits among a planeload of his colleagues on one of the dozens of secret Pakistan International Airlines flights. His first flight on an airplane excites him. His eyes are glued to the window during the thousand-mile journey over Indian airspace to Dhaka, the capitol of East Pakistan. He thinks about his family and for a moment wonders about Makhan Singh and his family, who are out there somewhere. Two and a half-hours later, the undercover soldiers in civilian clothes are shuttled away from the airport to a base outside the city. Shiploads of the Pakistan Army's soldiers with their arms, armaments and tanks had already sailed from Karachi to Chittagong.

History will show that March, 1971, was a month of madness that touched off communal riots and lit a powder keg of hatred. Bottled up anger exploded. Any possibility of turning back ended as the ensuing tragic events resulted in horrific human suffering that changed the geopolitical landscape forever. Now, believed to be true, Bengalis initiated bloodletting that cascaded into an orgy of rape, murder and arson. They killed, raped, burned and looted, victimizing over 100,000 innocent West Pakistani civilians and non-Bengali Bihari Muslims. The Pakistan government had the excuse it was looking for.

President Yahya Khan appointed Lieutenant General Tikka Khan as governor and chief martial law administrator of East Pakistan. Tikka Khan, ruthlessly determined, vengefully ordered his army to smother the civil disobedience. The army squelched every uprising and brutally eliminated most of the anti-state rebels and their leaders, in an attempt to restore peace in the province. Karim was among hundreds of military and civil intelligence personnel charged with thoroughly combing Dhaka to report the whereabouts and the activities of the anti-state elements; those the government would call 'secessionists, miscreants, rebels, extremists, mischief makers, criminals, saboteurs and infiltrators.'

Karim had befriended one of his Bengali colleagues, who was on a deputation in Lahore from the East Bengal Rifles. The friend had provided him the names of half a dozen people in Dhaka, assuring him of their patriotism and loyalty to the unity of Pakistan.

"Any one of them will be happy to work with you and more than willing to provide the information you might need," Karim's Bengali friend insists. Karim decides to use one of those contacts and dials the number. It is March 18, 1971.

"Hello," says an unfamiliar voice.

"Is this Mr. Rehman? This is Karim. I am a friend of . . ."

"I know who you are."

"Can we meet somewhere?"

"I can't talk on the phone. I have to be careful. I'll pick you up tomorrow just after sundown at the front entrance to the botanical gardens. I will be waiting in a motor rickshaw. Don't wear a uniform. You don't want to stand out. Besides, it's Dhaka. It's hot and sticky here. You Punjabis wear *dhotis*. A sarong, sandals and muslin shirt shouldn't be a problem for you. I look forward to meeting you."

"I'll see you tomorrow," says Karim, and hangs up the phone, which has already gone dead. The next day, just before sunset, Karim dresses in the suggested clothing. Holding a folded black umbrella, he stands by the gate, looking for Mr. Rehman. He scans the street, which is strewn with a dozen or so parked rickshaws. None of them is motorized; all are human powered. The scrawny drivers rest while waiting for fares. As darkness settles in, Karim starts to worry. He's about to leave when a motorized rickshaw pulls up right beside him.

"Mr. Karim," says a familiar voice.

"Yes. You must be Mr. Rehman."

"Yes, I am. Please get in quickly," says Rehman. "I'm sorry for being late. It is much safer in the dark." He orders the driver to go. Karim joins him in the back seat.

"Where are we going?" asks Karim

"We are going to see an ex-army officer. He has contacts. We'll get important and sensitive information about insurgents. People paid a heavy price for creating Muslim Pakistan in 1947. East and west are like two arms of a body that we can't allow to be severed."

"How far are we going?"

"It's not very far. He lives only a couple of miles outside Dhaka."

The rickshaw speeds through Dhaka and enters a narrow, pot-holed soggy dirt road. "We are almost there. Our contact lives in that house," says Rehman, pointing to a dimly lit house across the rice fields. The driver gears the two-stroke engine down and bumps ahead on a sinuous trail along the rice paddies, coming to an abrupt stop in front of an old thatched dwelling built on stilts. Two young Bengalis jump out with loaded guns pointed directly at Karim. One of the gunmen orders, "Get out. Put your hands above your head and step out slowly." Karim complies. The other guard searches Karim and removes the pistol Karim had wrapped under his sarong.

"Welcome to Bangladesh, Mr. Karim." Rehman laughs derisively and orders the driver to take him back to Dhaka.

"Bangladesh?" questions Karim.

"Shut up," orders one of the gunmen. "You heard me. Yes, you're in Bangladesh and not in East Pakistan. Remember that."

Karim, his hands tied behind his back, is ordered to walk up a flight of wooden stairs, while the gunmen follow close behind. At the top of the steps, a long veranda provides entrance to six small rooms. His captors kick and push him into one that is windowless. "Have a good rest, Mr. Karim. We'll see you in the morning," says one of the guards before closing and locking the door from the outside.

In Lahore, Kaye wakes up screaming, trying to shake off a terrible dream. She has not slept well and has had nightmares since Karim left for East Pakistan. The dreams come frequently, each more intense and frightening. Tonight she dreamed that an armed mob was chasing her and her children. She yelled out for Karim but he was nowhere to be seen. She ran as fast as she could, away from the mob, until she could not breathe.

She finds herself sitting at the edge of her bed, frightened; gasping for air. She darts to the children's bedroom and is relieved to know that they are safe, sleeping soundly. She kisses them both and whispers, "I wish your father were home."

Karim sits in the dark room on a bamboo mat and leans against the wall. He hears yelling and screaming all night. He prepares himself for the worst. At dawn, the door opens and a middle aged Mukti Bahini, a Liberation Army leader enters the room. The interrogator sucks in a final draw before throwing his cigarette butt on the floor; he stamps it out quickly with his heavy army boot. He takes two more cigarettes out of the package, puts one in his mouth while offering the other to Karim, "Cigarette?"

"No, thanks, I don't smoke."

The interrogator packs one away while lighting the other. "You came here on an intelligence mission. I suggest that you use your intelligence and give us all the information you have," says the leader slyly.

"I don't know anything. I just got here last week."

"I know that. I want you to write down anything and everything you know about Pakistan's army positions and plans in Kashmir. You were in Kashmir, weren't you? You have only one day. It's up to you. Your cooperation will earn you our good hospitality. If you don't cooperate, or try to fool us you won't live to see your family." The interrogator stamps out the cigarette, while handing Karim a clipboard and a pen. "If you need more paper just knock at the door. You have 24 hours. I'll see you tomorrow morning. Looks like you can use some food. Someone will bring in the breakfast."

At the Mayo Hospital in Lahore, Dr. Javid sends for Kaye. "You wanted to see me?" she says as she enters Dr. Javid's office.

"Yes, Yes. Come on in and please do sit down. Two cups of chai and biscuits," orders Dr. Javid, before a servant closes the door. When the tray arrives, Dr. Javid removes the tea cozy, pours the well-steeped dark tea into two fine bone china cups, pours the hot milk and looks at Kaye. He offers biscuits, along with the tea, and looks at Kaye with concern.

"Kaye, I've been watching you," says Dr. Javid. "You look tired. More than tired, you look weak, almost spent. I'm asking you to take some time off. You've a lot on your mind. It has to be very difficult for you, with Karim gone and two children at home. I urge you to take a leave of absence from work. It would do you good."

"No," resists Kaye. "I don't want to take any time off. Actually, I've been thinking about asking for more work. To keep my sanity, I've got to keep myself busy. While I work, I don't think about anything, not even Karim. It's therapeutic."

"I thought I'd try. I can tell you one thing; you are not putting in more hours." Dr. Javid pauses and smiles. "The real reason I asked you in was to invite you to dinner this Saturday. I don't want 'no' for an answer. Mrs. Javid has already made the arrangements. She's looking

forward to seeing Amman and Jasmin. Bring Sonia, as well. I'll send
the driver at 6:30 in the evening."

"Thank you. That will be wonderful. We'll be ready and
waiting."

Dr. and Mrs. Javid are middle-aged upper class professionals
who live in Gulberg, an upper echelon Lahore neighborhood. Their
two grown sons live in England, pursuing educations in engineering
and medicine. Mrs. Javid, perhaps missing her own children, waits
anxiously all day and runs to the door when the chauffeur pulls into
the driveway. She and her husband treat Kaye and Karim as if they were
their own children. The two families are very close, often visiting each
other. Mrs. Javid enjoys having Amman and Jasmin over, loving their
precocious, yet well mannered personalities. Dr. Javid frequently tells
his wife—although he barely mentions it to Kaye—"This American
Peace Corps woman, with her passion for making things better, and
her perseverance, has single-handedly done more for poor patients
than most of the doctors on my staff have done in years. She has made
a profound difference by teaching poor young mothers the dos and
don'ts of basic hygiene, sanitation and nutrition, thereby preventing
many childhood diseases."

"Welcome, Kaye," says Mrs. Javid, holding Amman's slender
shoulders excitedly, and placing kisses alternately on both of his
cheeks. Kaye carries Jasmin, while one of the servants holds open the
door. Dr. Javid welcomes Kaye and teases the children, who quickly
withdraw and reach for their mother and Mrs. Javid. After being
treated to spicy snacks, the gathering moves to the dining room where
a lavish feast awaits—arrayed on a large dining table, under a garishly
expensive chandelier.

"You must be worried about your husband," says Dr. Javid. "I
would be, too, if loved ones of mine were in harm's way. However, I'm
very pleased and happy that our proud soldiers are putting down the
rebellion in East Pakistan. Mujib is a traitor. He and his rebels should
be taught a lesson," he declares while sipping his chai.

"Traitor?" repeats Kaye, looking at the doctor in disbelief. Mrs.
Javid has wisely taken the children and Sonia outside, inviting them
to play a game of croquet.

"Yes, Mujib is a traitor. So far as I'm concerned all those Bengalis who don't submit should be swatted like mosquitoes. That's what they are, just mosquitoes. Mujib and his Mukti Bahini liberation army are nothing but low class troublemakers who never really accepted Islam. The fact is they never became true Muslims. They look like and act like Hindus. That's the reason they want to break away from Pakistan and join Hindu India."

"Dr. Javid. Those are very strong words," asserts Kaye; "and, I might add, they are surely not based on facts. Your statements sound not only biased but also seem to stem from a preconceived notion of self-superiority, and a wrongly held belief that East Pakistanis and Bengalis are inferior to West Pakistanis. I never thought in my wildest dreams that you would hold such hateful feelings about your own fellow Pakistanis. Indians maybe, but not Pakistanis." She looks squarely and passionately at Dr. Javid. Surprised by Kaye's forcefulness, Dr. Javid leans back, his white knuckles gripping the chair arms, and listens intensely. "I have to tell you that your fellow Pakistanis in the East, although in the majority, have been treated like second class citizens. Not only have they been under-represented in the government, but they have suffered economic inequality since the creation of Pakistan in 1947. Moreover, what's this about Mujib? He and his party have won the simple majority in open and honest elections, yet Bhutto and his Party refuse him the right to form the government. In November 1970, when East Pakistan was hit by a catastrophic cyclone, that killed more than 200,000 people, it took your president over a week to declare the disaster region 'a major calamity area.' It's clear that from the top down, you in the West consider your fellow Bengali Muslims not as your brothers but—as you have called them yourself, mosquitoes."

Mrs. Javid enters the dining room with tired but happy children. "Miss Kaye, the good doctor is at it again," she says, smoothing over the exchange between her husband and Kaye. "He's giving you a bad time. I know he has strong feelings about East Pakistan. I don't know anything about politics, and I have not been to Bengal; it is over a thousand miles away. All I can do is pray for peace. I want the war to end so that Karim may come home, and people can go back to their normal lives." Mrs. Javid has apparently had to intervene in her husband's political discussions many times. "Miss Kaye, maybe we should not talk politics, but stick to our real passion; healing the sick."

"We should," agrees Kaye, relieved to have the evening end on a pleasant note.

"Miss Kaye, here we are," says the driver, startling Kaye as he opens the car door in front of her house. Kaye has been lost in her thoughts, wondering and worrying about Karim. *Where is he? What's he doing? Will he come home at all?*

Kaye has good reason to worry, for Karim is in Bangladesh; imprisoned; subjected to daily interrogations and brutal beatings. Each day of his captivity, an interrogator with an armed assistant enters the room in which Karim is being kept. A cigarette habitually dangles from the man's mouth, twitching as his lips move. "Mr. Karim, what do you have for us?"

"I'm sorry. I don't know anything," Karim replies. "I was in Kashmir in 1965. That is over six years ago. Besides, why would you be interested in Kashmir?"

"It's none of your damn business." The interrogator becomes furious. "I ask the questions here, not you. You just answer," he yells, while slapping and punching Karim. Karim covers his face and head with his arms while taking the beating. The interrogator stops for a moment and turns to his assistant. "He's a high value detainee. I know that he knows more than he's telling us, not about Bengal but about Kashmir. I'm under great pressure to extract important and usable information for our Indian friends and allies. Don't kill him; just soften him a little. When I come back, he better be talking; telling us what the Pakistan army is up to in Kashmir. Is that understood?"

The interrogator storms out the door and two men enter the room, each carrying a rope. They tie Karim's hands, loop the two ropes over the pulleys secured in the ceiling and hoist him well above the floor. Karim squirms and screams under the painful weight of his own body. They kick, beat and hit him relentlessly until he passes out. They lower him and throw a bucketful of water on his face, only to bring him back and repeat the same process, until he is unable to regain consciousness. Locking the door behind them, the captors leave him sprawled on the floor, bruised and bloodied.

The interrogator and his armed assistant return the following day. The interrogator pulls up the only chair that is in the room and sits squarely, resting his arms on the slatted wooden back. He and his armed assistant look at Karim, curled up in a fetal position, half-dead.

"Do you know what your people did yesterday while we were showing you our hospitality?" Karim can barely open his eyes. The chain-smoking interrogator grits his teeth and turns vengeful eyes on his prisoner. "Let me tell you about the brutality that your army inflicted on our innocent people," he shouts. Karim, in pain, opens his eyes halfway. He looks at his questioner submissively, in an attempt to comply with the demands.

"Perhaps, you have lost track of time. Yesterday was March 25th, 1971. At midnight, your army, our own Pakistani army with its American built tanks, followed by hundreds of Punjabi and Baluchi soldiers, rolled into Dhaka University. Without warning the tanks and troops fired, indiscriminately killing scores of students and forcing the rest out from their dormitories. The cruel butchers didn't stop there. They ordered the unarmed and innocent students to come forward in groups of ten with their hands on their heads. As students came out, they were ordered to line up and, at the wink of an officer, shot dead, making room for the next group. Group after group chopped down like carrots. One hundred nine students shot dead along with their professors. All mowed down by their own military, just because they were Bengalis."

"I'm . . . . I'm . . . . ashamed, really sorry," pleads Karim.

"You're sorry! It was a well-planned, premeditated murder of students and intellectuals by their own army."

Karim struggles to keep his eyes open, while sprawled motionless on the floor. Through clenched teeth, the interrogator continues, "Your army has gone mad. They are on a rampage of killing, a full-fledged massacre and genocide. Your army has taken our leader Mujib, and millions are fleeing to India." The interrogator's voice hardens. "I want you to recover, so that you can think clearly and tell us about your army's cowardly intentions in Kashmir. We will see that you get medical treatment. We'll nurse you back to sanity for one reason only—so that you can tell us the truth without our resorting to torture."

Karim nods his head. The interrogator gets up and paces around the room. He finishes his cigarette, extinguishes the butt by rubbing it into Karim's chest and walks out, threatening, "You better have something good for me when I return." Karim lets out a scream and struggles to say 'yes' as the door is locked shut.

The East Bengal Regiment, the East Pakistan Rifles and the civil police, pledge support for Mujib and his Awami League Party. They proclaim Bangladesh an independent country from a small village on the Indian border. Pakistan insists that its military is in control. India and the international community accuse Pakistan of using the army to commit mass murder and genocide. Two million refugees cross the border into India and by June, the number swells to six million.

On November 23, 1971, while the world and the United Nations debate the civil war in East Pakistan, Indian troops cross the international border at several points. On December third, the Pakistan Air Force attacks Indian airfields. India responds and war expands on the Western front in Rajasthan, Punjab and Kashmir. The UN General Assembly passes a resolution to stop the war. The Indian Army closes in on Dhaka. On December sixteenth, the Pakistan Army surrenders, handing over 90,000 prisoners of war to the allied forces of India and Bangladesh, jointly known as *Mitro Bahini*, one of the largest surrenders since World War II.

About 4,000 Indian troops were killed and 10,000 were wounded, while the number of Pakistani soldiers wounded and killed remains unknown. The large number of dead and wounded civilians, the real victims of war, were hardly remembered and ended up as a footnote in history books.

The 1971 protest that started as a small civil disobedience had grown into a full-scale civil war and metastasized into a bloody international military conflict. One to three million people lost their lives, hundreds of thousands of women were raped and nearly twenty million people became refugees. Neither a colonial foreign power nor non-Muslims inflicted the atrocities. Their own race and fellow believers conspired and wreaked the savagery. No brutality, killing or ethnic cleansing ever makes sense but such acts carried out by one's own are impossible to fathom. The second partition was complete. East Pakistan became Bangladesh, gaining independence from the tyranny of fellow citizens, at least for the time being. *op-ed*

Karim is totally unaware of the course of history while he has been held prisoner during the civil war. He has been talking to his interrogators, who are pleased with his cooperation. He has not supplied any useable information. Torturous beatings along with food and sleep deprivation have numbed his body and mind. He tells them everything—everything they want to hear. He either makes it up or truly tries to help his captors. He doesn't know the difference. The only thing that keeps him from going mad is the love of his wife and children. His mental mantra is *I must survive and sustain myself for them.*

Physically and mentally broken, he is one of the 90,000 prisoners taken by the Indian Army and transferred to a POW camp somewhere in West Bengal, inside the Indian border.

—32—

The Camp

Sonia runs to the gate and holds it open for Dr. Javid, who steps out of the car and heads toward the front. It is January 2, 1972.

"Sonia, it's really cold today," says the doctor, while rubbing his hands. "Where's Mem Sahib? I need to see her immediately," he tells eighteen-year-old Sonia, patting his hand atop her long, thick hair, extending *piyar*. How she has matured since the tender age of ten, when she came to live with Kaye.

"She's in the kitchen feeding Amman and Jasmin breakfast," replies Sonia, while running ahead of the doctor to open the front door.

"Kaye, sorry to bother you this early, but I'm here with very good news."

Still holding a dishtowel, Kaye rushes from the kitchen into the living room and faces Dr. Javid. "I can use some good news; we all can," sighs Kaye, looking gaunt. Worrying about her husband has taken a toll on her.

"Karim is alive. He's all right. He's in camp number 15."

Sonia, so well trained and perceptive, takes the children into the back bedroom and shuts the door behind her. Kaye puts her arms around Dr. Javid, resting her head on his shoulder, and cries hysterically. The tears come in a flood, dampening the doctor's shirt. "Are you sure?" she stammers.

"Yes, I'm sure. This morning, I spoke to one of the army majors I know. He's absolutely certain that Karim is on the list of POW's that are being held in camp number 15 in West Bengal."

"You've been like a father to me," says Kaye. "Thank you so much for looking out for us, especially while Karim's been away."

Dr. Javid is unable to contain his emotion. He wipes his tear-filled eyes and urges, "Let's go. Sonia, bring the children out of the bedroom. Hurry, hurry, Mrs. Javid is waiting. We're going to celebrate. Sonia, lock up the house. You're spending the night with us."

Camp number 15 is one of the POW facilities holding thousands of Pakistani prisoners. It encompasses a large area, fenced in by barbed wire, and punctuated by watchtowers that are equipped with searchlights manned by armed soldiers. Guns cocked, they look out constantly, eyes sweeping the area, ready to shoot any prisoner who dares to escape. Under the watchful eyes of armed guards, the entrances and exits are checkpoints, where every person logs in and is scrutinized carefully. The compound is a small city, dotted with makeshift barracks and tents providing cramped detainee housing.

Clearly marked dining facilities, scaled down athletic fields and living quarters stand close together for use by the military and civilian staff that manage the camp. A small army field hospital provides care for the sick and wounded. An Indian flag flies atop a sizable office, where two armed Indian soldiers stand guard. A sign reads:

Colonel Makhan Singh, Commanding Officer POW Camp No. 15

"Today we'll inspect the medical facility. I understand some prisoners are still recovering from war injuries," announces Colonel Makhan Singh, bolting from his office and walking toward the hospital, while his staff follows him dutifully, holding files and clipboards. "How are our guests, Doctor?" inquires Makhan Singh as soon as he enters the facility.

"They are doing well, sir, but we certainly could use more medicine and manpower, especially in the treatment of trauma and distress. Most of them have healed physically from their wounds and diseases, but some are suffering terribly from the guilt of being taken prisoner and from worrying about their uncertain future."

"Doctor, we aren't here to treat mental diseases. Our mission is to provide basic health care, until we know what to do with the prisoners. I'll see what I can do to provide you more resources."

"Thank you, Colonel Makhan Singh." As the Colonel is about to leave, he stops in front of a cot on which a POW lies half-unconscious.

"What's on your wrist soldier?" asks the Colonel, pointing with his swagger stick. The medicated prisoner is too weak to answer. The doctor hastily stoops down and nervously shakes the patient, "Can you hear me soldier? Colonel *Sahib* wants to know what's on your wrist."

"It's nothing. It's just a simple *kara*. I've had it for a long time. It's nothing. It's just a ring of steel. Don't take it away. Please let me keep it," pleads the soldier in a halting, raspy voice as he struggles to keep his eyes open.

"Nobody is taking it away, Karim. Colonel *Sahib* just wants to know where you got the *Kara*?" repeats the doctor.

"His name is Karim! Are you sure that his name is Karim? Double-check your records."

"Yes sir. I'm sure his name is Karim Din, POW number 52," confirms the doctor, looking at the chart. The colonel takes the doctor aside and whispers into his ear. "He's most likely one of our high value prisoners. I want you to treat him well. Clean him up. Attend to his medical and nutritional needs. Make certain that he has fresh clothes before you send him to my office tomorrow evening."

"Yes sir, tomorrow evening he'll be at your office."

Despite flickering doubts, Makhan is almost certain that prisoner number 52 is his childhood friend, Karim. He spends a restless night thinking about possible scenarios.

Karim is a common name for Muslims. Sometimes Muslims of the Sufi faith wear kara. But, he's too young to be a Sufi, and besides, he's in the Pakistani army. The army won't let him wear such a thing. Maybe the prisoner is cunning and shrewd and the bangle is merely to gain sympathy. But what if he's my childhood friend and the kara he's wearing is the one I gave him when I left Rurkee?

Evening finds Makhan still speculating on the possibility that the wounded soldier is his childhood friend. There is a knock on his door.

"Sir, the prisoner Karim is here," announces a guard.

Karim enters the room, somewhat rested. He exhibits the common reticence of prisoners to speak, unsure of what to expect. Makhan Singh stands anxiously, leaning against his desk, trying to conceal his nervousness.

"Karim, are you from Rurkee?" begins Makhan. "Is your father's name Fazal Din? Does he own a shop in Rurkee?"

Karim stands quietly, tongue-tied. Recovering from the traumatic interrogation near Dhaka, he has been shut off from the outside world for over nine months. Having been through so much, he trusts no one. His body is weak, his spirit is broken, and his mind is muddled. His memory fails him. *Maybe I am being tricked*, he reflects, to himself.

"Karim, do you remember me?" urges Makhan. "I'm your childhood friend from Rurkee. You must have been through hell if you don't recognize your old friend. Don't be afraid. Test me. Ask me questions. You'll see that the *kara* you are wearing is the one I gave you twenty-five years ago."

Karim, nearly delusional, concentrates hard and manages to blurt out two simple questions. "How many sisters do you have? What're their names?"

"Karim, I had only one sister, who never made it to India; and a cousin named Berket. Remember . . . Sarita was married to Dalair, and both she and her husband were brutally murdered. Remember the evening at the *Khoo*. I gave you this *kara* as my token of friendship before they dragged me away to India. Try to remember that day."

Karim collapses into a chair, dazed, with tears rolling down his cheeks. Makhan pulls him up and enfolds him in a long hug, until his ribs hurt. The Colonel cannot contain himself and he too breaks down. Makhan's eyes gleam with joyful tears, while Karim laughs aloud, as if he has gone mad.

"My dear friend, I can't believe it! What a destiny! Karim, I'm going to send you back for tonight; prison camp protocol. Besides, I don't want others to get suspicious. Tomorrow you'll have decent quarters and care. I'll make damn sure that you're not only comfortable here but that you're fully healed before you go home. I've so much to tell you and I'm sure you have much to say, too. We'll visit."

After a week of arduous effort by the doctors, and the personal attention of Makhan Singh, Karim regains partial strength. Makhan often invites Karim to his residence for dinner, pretending to question him, when actually they talk about old times.

"Colonel Makhan Singh, I've told you everything," says Karim. "Now it's time that you bring me up to speed. I want to know about you, your family and, of course, your parents. The last time I saw you, you were on our favorite donkey cart and Tez was pulling you away from Rurkee, nearly a quarter century ago. Don't leave anything out, I want to know everything."

"After Uncle Fazal and Shafkat left us in Chubara," says Makhan, "we traveled another day and crossed the canal bridge into Rahim Pura, a small village that was well inside the Indian border. We moved into one of the homes owned by a Muslim family that had fled to Pakistan. My parents never recovered from the shock of leaving Rurkee and losing everything. My father made a meager living, as a sharecropper with quiet dignity, while my mother never forgot Sarita. My mother felt Sarita's absence even more when my cousin Berkat was married, and left home to go live with her husband and in-laws near Amritsar. Her memories of that brutal murder consumed her like termites chewing wood."

"Obviously, you graduated from high school with honors or something."

"Yes, I was first in my class and had high enough marks to get a college scholarship. After I finished college in Delhi, I joined the army as a commissioned officer. I was in the military academy in Dhera Dun when Mother passed away. I knew she had lost her zest for life when Sarita left us—a long time ago. Still I was shocked and devastated."

"Oh my God, I'm sorry," says Karim, toying with the *kara*.

"After earning the commission," Makhan continues, "I was posted in different cantonments and bases. Father stayed with me wherever I went, until he died—ten years ago. He talked about Rurkee as if he had never left. Soon after, I married my beautiful wife. Our eight-year old son's name is Karim Singh. I hope you don't mind."

"No, not at all Makhan, I'm honored. Where do they live?"

"In Amritsar. I've built a nice house there. Did I tell you I was in Chowinda sector in the 1965 war?" Makhan asks. "I was a Major then. I saw our school reduced to rubble. I could not believe that I would be responsible for destroying the very school that gave me my start."

"But it wasn't your fault."

"It hurts nonetheless."

"I was there in Chowinda as well, Makhan. Only I was on the other side, fighting to defeat India. I never thought we'd be enemies. One of my best friends, Omar, was killed there and I had to send his body home. It was very painful."

"Well, that's enough. By a twist of fate, we're both here now," says Makhan, smiling with affection for his friend. "Let's have dinner."

The Colonel's orderly serves the dinner, while Makhan and Karim share many memories of the past. At one point, Makhan turns to the orderly and says with pride, "This is *Subedar Major* Karim, my childhood friend. We grew up in Rurkee together. Did you know that Rurkee is in Punjab, across the border in Pakistan?"

"No sir, I didn't." replies the orderly, quietly withdrawing while the two friends pursue their reunion.

When the time comes for Karim to return home, Makhan Singh waves a warm good bye and shouts, "One of these days I'm coming to see you; I want to meet your Mem Sahib and your son and daughter."

Some days later, Karim smiles as he boards the Pakistan Army transport. "Makhan Singh is dreaming," he remarks to himself. "Two countries at constant war with each other? Punjab divided into two; a Muslim Punjab and a Sikh Punjab? It's impossible. I'll never see my friend again."

In early 1972, India released all but 200 of the 90,000 Pakistani prisoners. India wanted to try the 200 for war crimes, based on the brutality and genocide in East Pakistan. Yielding to international pressure, and in an effort to create a long lasting peace in the region, India abandoned the idea and freed the remaining prisoners, as well.

—33—

Coming Home

Karim, along with thousands of Pakistani soldiers, comes home defeated and depressed. Pakistan is split in half. East Pakistan has become Bangladesh. Bengalis welcome Mujib as father of their new nation. President Yahya Khan is under house arrest, while Zulfiqar Ali Bhutto assumes power as Prime Minister of the remaining half of Pakistan. West Pakistani's false sense of superiority, reinforced by state media and manipulated by political leaders, is in full force. Rather than admitting defeat and defaults, the politicians blame treachery by rebellious Bengalis, calculated Indian aggression and a lack of help from Pakistan's staunch ally, the United States of America.

Karim is not the same person who left home more than a year ago. He is weak, has little appetite and frequent nightmares. His confusion and anger reveal that he suffers from Post Traumatic Distress Syndrome (PTDS). Slowly he improves, but at times his mind and memory play tricks on him.

"Kaye, I've been home almost a month. I've been asking you about my parents. Are they still in Rurkee?"

"Yes dear, they're in Rurkee." Kaye lies. "I forgot to tell you that your sister Parveen in Sialkot sent a message that they'll be coming here in a few weeks to visit us," she adds from the kitchen. Kaye

feels apprehensive, and suffers quietly. She and Dr. Javid are aware
of Karim's condition, and have decided that he will require a lengthy
recovery time. She prays, gives him space, and listens to him talk
about East Pakistan and his dear friend, Colonel Makhan Singh.
He is most happy when he plays with his children and shares stories
about his old friend. Kaye and Dr. Javid encourage him to spend as
much time as he can with the children. They do everything possible
to help him become Karim, once again. After a few months, he feels
better, almost normal.

After a pleasant dinner at Dr. Javid's, Karim's renewed sense of
happiness pervades the room. "I've decided to go to Sialkot and Rurkee
to see my sister and my parents," he announces. "I haven't seen them
for two years. Kaye, you come along and see a real Punjabi village. I
can't wait any longer. I have to see them now and let them know that
I'm still alive; that I've survived the war." Kaye looks at Dr. Javid, who
nods his head. Mrs. Javid calls for her servant, who takes the children
outside, setting them up with a game of croquet.

"Karim, I have to tell you something," says Kaye. "I'm afraid it's
bad news. I want you to be strong." Kaye inches closer to her husband
until she can lean against him. She holds his hands. With pursed
lips and teary eyes she speaks softly in a raspy, scarcely audible voice.
"Karim, Abu—father is dead."

"He's dead! No, it can't be. Why didn't you tell me?" demands
Karim. "Why did you keep me in the dark? You should've told me the
day I came home. I should've known that you were holding something
back from me." He bows his head in silence, while struggling to absorb
the news. "How did he die?" he asks. "Did he die a natural death, or
was he a casualty of war, too? I know hundreds of civilians died in
Sialkot during the conflict."

Karim looks at his wife, and then to Dr. and Mrs. Javid. They
are all in tears; their concern for Karim somehow lessens his pain;
releasing tears of his own that stream down his face. "Please, will
someone tell me how he died?" he pleads. "I want the truth. I'm a
soldier. I can handle it."

Dr. Javid begins. "In early November, 1971, the army ordered
most of the villages along the Indian-Pakistan border to evacuate.

They told the villagers that it was unlikely that India would attack, but in case they did, it would be safer for the villagers to move some distance westward."

"Let me guess. Abu didn't leave. He never wanted to leave his ancestral village."

"It is true, Karim; and Fazal was not the only one. Most of them stayed. They didn't feel threatened, since the protests and the war were a thousand miles away in East Pakistan. Then on December third, the Indian infantry crossed the border with armored vehicles and tanks, and headed west towards Rurkee at a calamitous speed. There was panic, confusion, and chaos. Your dad was among throngs of people fleeing westward."

"What happened then? Did he make it to Sialkot?"

"Yes; he loaded his bike with the family valuables, took your mom in tow and dragged his famous transport to your sister's house in Sialkot."

Kaye picks up the story and continues. "Your sister Parveen and her husband welcomed your parents warmly. Their ten-year-old grandson and six-year-old granddaughter were excited to have grandparents for company. As you know, your father could never sit still. He had to be doing something. Besides, he didn't want to burden your sister. He ignored his daughter's requests to relax. He worked with her husband daily, selling vegetables in the bazaar. He shadowed him all day. They went to the main market and bought seasonal provisions: potatoes, cauliflower, carrots, mustard greens, onions, turnips, green onions and stocks of cilantro. He arranged the vegetables on the cart, showcasing their colors and quality. He pushed the cart, hawking and vending the merchandise." Kaye smiles affectionately at Karim, while she calls up colorful images of his father. "He constantly listened to the tiny transistor radio he kept on the cart. Talk of the war was everywhere. He listened to Pakistan radio and eagerly shared the news of Pakistani soldiers bravely fighting the Indian aggression both in Kashmir and in East Pakistan. Karim, he would tell every customer proudly that his son was fighting in Dhaka to squelch the civil war that India had instigated."

"Abu was optimistic. He had faith in the United Nations," interjects Karim. "He was a big fan of the UN. He always talked about how the United Nations could solve or settle world problems and national conflicts. It was just like the 1965 war, he'd say. It would soon be over. The United Nations would get involved, a ceasefire would be declared, India and Pakistan would sit down at the negotiating table and this time would resolve the Kashmir and Bengal issues peacefully without bloodshed." Karim's voice trails off, just as Dr. Javid picks up Fazal's story—seamlessly, as if Kaye and the doctor had rehearsed the sequence.

"One morning your dad took your nephew to the bazaar for a breakfast treat. Everyone in the bazaar knew your father. Abu pedaled his bike, while his grandson sat behind him on the back seat, wrapping his arms around his grandpa's waist. The shopkeeper who served him breakfast that fatal day remembered him telling his grandson that he should know that his Uncle Karim was fighting the enemy so they could be safe. After they finished their breakfast, your father ordered a dozen thin deep-fried *puris* and two pounds of *halva* for the family. He told the waiter that he worried about his son every day and prayed that he'd come home soon.

"Fazal secured the take out breakfast in the back seat, helped his grandson get on the front bike bar and merrily pedaled home. Suddenly, there was a thunderous noise. People in the bazaar looked up to see two Indian fighter jets disappear into the blue sky leaving only the sonic boom behind. Within seconds, the two jets reappeared and came toward the bystanders, fast and low. A series of explosions shook the ground. Fazal lay wounded next to his grandson, jagged pieces of shrapnel in his right leg and stomach. Semiconscious and lying in a pool of blood, he opened his eyes, only to see his grandson sprawled, motionless next to the mangled bicycle; his grandson's blood mixed with his. It was like a battlefield. Scores were dead or wounded. Houses were ablaze—spewing out foul smoke. Bright lights flashed, and the wail of ambulance sirens filled the air. In terrible pain, Fazal mustered the strength to lift himself up, but his blood-drained body collapsed to the ground.

"A day later Fazal awoke in the hospital. Your sister held his hand and tried to get him to talk. He didn't speak. Doctors had removed the shrapnel and dressed his wounds. They allowed Parveen to take his morphine-infused body home. He lay on a cot for two days, while the family stood watch over him. Your sister asked him if he could speak. He opened his eyes briefly and asked about his grandson. Suppressing her grief, and with reluctance, Parveen told him that the child was dead.

"Fazal told your sister that he wanted to go home—home to Rurkee. 'Parveen send-me-home.' He breathed his last breath. Late that night, under the cover of darkness—while the war still raged—his brave friends and neighbors took his body to Rurkee. They buried him next to his father. Fazal was home, home with the ancestors that he never wanted to leave."

Karim rises shakily and screams, "My father and nephew were innocent victims. They're just collateral damage. That's what we call it in the army."

"What do you mean by collateral damage, Karim?" asks Mrs. Javid.

"When innocent civilians die in the war, they don't count," shouts Karim, at the top of his lungs. "They're written off as collateral; less important than the combatants—said to be unfortunate casualties of fighting a war—just or unjust."

Karim walks outside and paces in the courtyard. Finally calming down, he hugs and kisses his children as if he were a child himself. Kaye, Dr. Javid and Mrs. Javid follow his lead, offering what comfort they can.

Life is not the same. Kaye has curtailed her hospital commitments, making more time for her children's education and Karim's welfare. Karim tries to expunge the war memories, and overcome the loss of his father. He has seen and suffered so much pain that life's essence has been sucked out of him. For weeks to come he is like the walking dead. He gradually recovers, and starts his life anew, taking a teaching position in the Pakistan Military Intelligence School.

It's spring of 1974. Nine-year-old Amman runs to the gate to answer the doorbell. What he sees scares him. He runs back screaming. "Daddy, daddy, there is a *jinn* standing outside our front gate."

"Calm down, Amman. I've told you so many times that there are no *jinns*. The evil spirit is only in your imagination."

"No, Dad it's not my imagination. I swear that there's a *jinn* at the gate for sure. He's tall, has a beard, big moustache and, a huge turban. I've never seen anything like it. He's scary." Karim goes to the gate and is stunned to see Makhan standing on the other side. Karim exclaims loudly and opens the gate.

"I told you that one of these days I'd come to see you. Here I am. I'm sorry I startled your son. I bet he's never seen a Sikh before," laughs Makhan while enclosing Karim in a bear hug.

"Come in," insists Karim. "Come in, please. Everybody come here; meet my friend, Colonel Makhan Singh." Kaye welcomes him with a smile; Rakhi gives him *piyar* and kisses him on the forehead, while Amman and Jasmin keep their distance, watching the newcomer warily.

"Makhan, look at you. How you have changed," says Rakhi. "You look just like your father. You've grown into a strong handsome man. What happened to your dimples? They must be under that thick beautiful beard." She gestures toward Makhan's cheeks. "Karim told me all about you. He said he stopped to see you in India when he was on his way to Lahore from Dhaka. You are a colonel or something." Karim's mother is unaware of her son's capture, and detention in POW camp number 15.

"Yes, Aunty, we did meet in India. We had a very good visit. Didn't we Karim?" says Makhan with a smile, sensing Rakhi's innocence.

During Makhan's brief stay, Amman and Jasmin slowly warm up to their father's friend, setting aside their mistrust, while maintaining a healthy curiosity.

"Dad, if Uncle Makhan is not a *jinn* then he must be spy," says Amman.

"Why do you say that?" asks Makhan, tickling the boy.

"You have long hair, a long beard and a big moustache; that makes you a spy."

"How do you know that the spies don't cut their whiskers?"

"That's what they say in school, Uncle. Real spies disguise themselves by growing long hair and beards. Only thing you've added is a big turban," chuckles Amman.

"What brings you to Lahore?" asks Karim. "How did you find me?"

"Karim, I've connections. I'm here to visit Sikh holy shrines, to celebrate Vaisakhi in April and most importantly to see my old friend and his family. Just for old time's sake you are going to Vaisakhi with me."

"I'm very grateful that you have come," says Karim. "I have thought of you so often."

Karim takes Makhan to Rurkee, where they visit Makhan's old house, the *khoo*—well and all the other familiar childhood places. They end the visit by praying at Fazal's and Shafkat's graves, and those of others who died in the war. They observe a moment of silence on the ground where Sarita and Dalair were cremated.

"Whatever happened to *Badmash*, rascal Rifaqat?"

"My father told me that just after one week of your leaving, Rifaqat was nowhere to be seen. He and his family fled Rurkee."

"Why, did he do something wrong?"

"We'll never know my friend." Karim had decided not to burden Makhan with the rumor that Rifaqat may have been involved in Sarita's and Dalair's murders.

After going to the Sikh holy places in Lahore, Makhan takes Karim and his children to Hassan Abdal to celebrate Vaisakhi, providing them a day of shared enjoyment and laughter. Afterward, Makhan stays one more day with Karim, before returning to India. The morning of his departure, following breakfast, Makhan wrestles with an emotional good-bye to Karim and his family. Kaye takes a long look at Makhan, recognizing a part of Karim in his bearing. Amman and Jasmin cling to his side as if they have known him all of their lives.

"Okay, that's enough," says Makhan, his voice catching on the words. "I'd better be going before this Colonel makes a fool of himself."

"Wait a minute Makhan." Rakhi beckons. "I have something for you. You'd better take it before you go."

"What is it, Aunty?" says Makhan, pushing back his tears.

Rakhi disappears into her bedroom and returns with two urns. "Take Sarita and Dalair with you," she murmurs, wiping away tears with her *dupatta*. "They've been with me for too long. It's time that they too go home."

Makhan grasps the two urns, kisses Rakhi, and raises the urns to his forehead. "*Sat Sari Kal, Rab Rakha*, God be with you. They're going home with me. Sarita will finally be with her mother."

Misty eyed, Makhan walks to the waiting taxi that will take him across the Pakistani border at Wagha, less than 15 miles away; into a community and a country that once was one, and so akin—yet now so estranged.

A Brief History of the Indian Subcontinent*

(3000 BCE to 1947 AD)

The South Asian Indo-Pakistan subcontinent takes its name from the Indus River. The area covers more than one and a half million square miles containing vast desolate deserts, unlimited river ribboned fertile plains and the towering Himalayan Mountain range whose peaks rise more than 29,000 feet above the Arabian Sea. Invaders and traders have traveled this land for several millennia. Some stayed developing great cultures and civilizations; some returned to their origins after plundering and pillaging, taking home with them enormous wealth and irresistible bounties. Others settled by assimilating local people into their culture, traditions and religion and over time to some extent they themselves were assimilated in the process.

Even the earliest residents, who settled along the Indus River banks and created one of the oldest and greatest civilizations the world has ever seen, were immigrants. Archaeologists believe that their ancestors were a Proto-Australoid and Mediterranean mix. The dark skinned inhabitants of this region lived along the Indus in well-planned cities. Harappa, Mohenja-Daro and other sites reveal that a sophisticated civilization prospered before 3000 BCE (Before Common Era).

These people had a written language, worshiped different deities that were possibly precursors to Hindu gods, developed a thriving irrigated agriculture economy, constructed granaries, built citadels for protection from water and warriors and conducted trade and commerce with the Sumerians. Around 1700 BCE, earthquakes and disastrous Indus floods ended the civilization entombing it under silt.

The next wave of Indo-Aryans arrived in India about 1500 to 1000 BCE. Descendents of the semi-nomadic barbaric tribes dispersed from the Black and Caspian Seas regions around 2000 BCE. The mass scale dispersion, theoretically, was due to natural calamities or foreign invasions, possibly by Mongol attacks from Central Asia. Primitive herding tribes stayed in Persia (Iran) for 500 years before pushing further east into India through the Khyber Pass over the Hindu Kush Mountains of Afghanistan. Along with their cattle and herding ways, they brought the Indo-Iranian language and over the next 1000 years conquered most of north India, establishing the *Mauryan* dynasty in 326 BCE. They either killed their predecessors, the more civilized *Dasas,* dark skinned people, or forced them deep into southern India. Learning farming and irrigated agriculture from their dark skinned forerunners, they increased food supply. The population exploded and the countryside became dotted with small farming villages and towns. Although the affluent Indo-Aryans worshiped gods and deities very similar to the *Harappans,* they either added or modified a very strict caste system into their socio-religious practices. Brahmin, the high priest at the top, they adhered to the following four distinct classes in descending status, each having specific tasks and places in the society.

Brahmins	Priests and academics
Kashatriyas	Rulers and military
Vaishyas	Farmers, landlords and merchants
Sudras	Peasants, servants and workers
Untouchables	Non-Hindus, lowest of all

Two major events in the subcontinent changed India's future, forever. First, the Indo-Aryans established numerous small kingdoms along the Ganges River and second, bore two religious philosophies, Buddhism and Jainism that were fundamentally different from classic Hinduism.

Siddharta Gautama, later known as Buddha was born around 595 BCE. He preached Buddhist principles and philosophy based on self-salvation rather than the inherent piety of a high priest, the Brahmin. A few years later prince *Mahavira* founded the order of monks who rejected the Brahmin's rituals and authority (ca 540-468 BCE). These two religious philosophies, especially Buddhism, took hold and flourished throughout India and Southeast Asia. It had profound socioeconomic, cultural and political impact on these same areas because the powerful kings and rulers converted and patronized the Buddhist religion.

Chandragupta defeated the warring tribes along the Ganges, consolidated his power and unified the small kingdoms into a powerful *Mauryan* Empire circa 324-302 BCE. In the spring of 326 BCE, Alexander the Great having conquered and pacified Persia, marched into India. Welcomed by the Raja of *Taxila Ambhi*, he defeated King *Porus* at the river *Jhelum*. His army refused to go further, so he returned to his homeland leaving the Mauryan kingdom unscathed. The Mauryan Empire grew stronger and more powerful by expanding westward. *Chandragupta* left his crown, converted to Jainism and fasted until his death.

His grandson, *Ashoka* (269-232 BCE) became a Buddhist. Ashoka declared Buddhism a state religion, built stupas and sent missionaries to Ceylon, Burma and Southeast Asia. *Guptas* lack of central authority around 320 AD, the Empire split into numerous independent monarchies. India continued trading with China and Rome, creating wealth along with intellectual artistic and cultural interaction. The next few centuries saw the reunification of North India with relative calm and further international trade created a classical Hindu state.

Muslims arrived in India about 711 A.D. The mission was not to conquer or expand Islamic faith, rather it was a retaliatory attack on the small Sindhi kingdom of *Brahmanabad,* modern day

Karachi, along the Indian Ocean whose army had looted and raped women of an Arab merchant ship. The Umayyad Governor of Iraq dispatched Mohammad Bin Qasim who quickly defeated the Raja of Brahmanabad. People were killed or converted to Islam. The Arab army left and Muslims became a minority. Islam lay dormant until the 10th century when invasions were launched from Afghanistan.

The Mongol invasion and China's expansion to the west drove nomadic Turkish tribes east to Afghanistan where the converted warrior *Allptigin* established an Islamic kingdom of Ghazni in Afghanistan. Starting with his grandson Mahmood, *Ghazanavids* were the first Turko-Afghan Muslims who launched a series of attacks into India (971-1030). The rule of the *Khiljis*, the *Tughluks,* and the *Lodis* followed culminating in the seizure of power by *Babur* in 1526, setting the stage for the most powerful Muslim dynasty, "The *Mughals"* in India. The Mughal emperors Akbar, Humayoun, Jahangir, Aurangzeb, and Shah Jahan ruled for more than three centuries (1526-1858), creating beautiful Muslim art and architecture along with leaving an indelible Islamic imprint on the subcontinent.

Like Buddhism and Jainism earlier, during the fourteenth and fifteenth centuries, many spiritual and religious philosophies developed that did not follow classic Hindu or Islamic orthodoxy, rather preached devotional and divine love for the creator. *Bhakti,* devotional Hinduism, *Satya Pir,* Truth Saint and perhaps the *Sufis,* Muslim saints are such examples. However, none had a more profound religio-political impact than Sikhism in the Hindu Muslim India.

Nanak in Punjab founded Sikhism. He was born a Hindu and was deeply influenced by the democratic principles of Islam. He rejected the caste system and preached loving devotion to "one God, the Creator" whose name was *Sat,* Truth, becoming the first *Guru,* divine teacher of the Sikh faith. The new liberal and peaceful Sikh religion flourished in Punjab drawing its converts mostly from the poor Hindu and Muslim peasants. Later, the Sikhs and their Gurus became the martial force that defended against the *Mughal* persecution.

The foreign invasions from the northwest and the rise of local Hindu rulers further weakened the *Mughal* Empire already fragmented by wars of accessions. On the heels of the East India Company, the British colonized India squelching the last Muslim uprising in 1857, adding Hindu Muslim India as another jewel in their colonial crown.

In 1858, the British Parliament enacted the Government of India Act, officially bringing India under direct control. The British Viceroys, the official representatives of the crown kept India pacified by increasing the number of English soldiers, recruiting the local martial races such as Punjabis, Pathans and Ghurkas, pulling them away from their homeland, a so-called divide and rule policy, and employed the Indian-English educated civil servants to run the huge government bureaucracy. Offers of generous land grants and concessions to landlords and princely state rulers cemented loyalty and alliances. Although Queen Victoria declared herself the Empress of India in 1877, the rebellion of 1857 had created a deep chasm of mistrust between white rulers and India's non-white native subjects. India always had foreign invaders that either left with the loot or settled to rule. Regardless of regional and religious differences, the natives were unhappy being ruled by white Sahibs living thousands of miles away in a country whose culture they never saw nor could understand. Indian nationalism and struggle for independence was always on the minds of Indians regardless of their creed, caste or color. It bubbled under the political subconscious; it lay dormant at times, but never died.

On December 28, 1885 in Calcutta, Womesh C. Bonnerjee presided over the first annual meeting of the Indian National Congress. The "Congress" would prove to be the first significant national movement for Indian independence. There were only two Muslim delegates in the first meeting. By the third annual meeting in Madras eighty-three out of six hundred members were Muslims. Muslim leaders joined Congress and politically fought for decades alongside Hindus demanding the British to end imperial rule.

Muslims, fearful of not getting fair representation, broke away from Congress. On December 30, 1906, delegates from all the provinces of India and Burma met in Dhaka and founded the All-India Muslim League.

WWI broke out in 1914, lasting until 1918. A large number of Indian soldiers lost their lives fighting side by side with their British counterparts, outside their country in faraway places on different continents. The Indian Congress and the returning soldiers were disappointed and disillusioned as the British tightened its grip on Indian rule. Politicians were jailed, demonstrators ruthlessly dispersed and governments' heavy-handed tactics in quelling any dissent were widespread.

On April 13, 1919 General Dyer, without warning, ordered the military to open fire on innocent men, women and children, mostly Punjabi Sikhs, who had gathered for a peaceful rally in *Jallian Wala Bagh* in Amritsar, massacring four hundred and wounding more than twelve hundred. Upon learning about the incident, the Governor of Punjab, Sir Michael O' Dwyer voiced full approval of the horrific action. People had had enough. The Congress abandoned its policy of cooperation and joined the masses to follow Gandhi's call for peaceful and nonviolent non-cooperation against the English Raj.

WWII (1939-1945) had a significant impact on the political future of India. The British expected Indians to help them fight against Nazi Germany. Indian leadership demanded freedom or at least a promise of freedom if their people were to shed blood for the crown. They were not ready to entertain the idea of Indian independence at a time when the survival of their own country was at stake. Over two and half million Indian soldiers served in different theaters on different continents, twenty-four thousand killed while sixty-four thousand were wounded. The end of the war reenergized the freedom movement.

Disillusioned and disappointed with Congress, the League was convinced that Muslims could not get fair representation in a united free India and would always remain a minority. The idea proposed by the great poet-philosopher Dr. Muhammad Iqbal in 1930 for a separate Indian Muslim state revived in Lahore at the 1940 League's annual convention. Mohammad Ali Jinnah who later became *Quaid-e-Azam,* the great leader, and founder of Pakistan, declared that India would be partitioned and Muslims would have their own free country. Some students under the leadership of Choudhry Rahmet

Ali in Cambridge, England had already coined the name of the future Muslim nation, *Pakistan*, the land of the pure. In August 1947, the British left, dividing the subcontinent into two countries: A Hindu India and a Muslim Pakistan.

Information derived from Stanley Wolpert's book, A New History of India, Sixth Edition, published by Oxford Press, Inc. 2000.

Glossary of Urdu and Punjabi Words

Allah Ho Akbar	God is great
Amiji	mother
Aloo	potato
Angrez	English
Angrezi	English language
Abu	father
Apu	father
Aslamo Elaikum	Muslim greeting 'peace be with you'
Babaji	sage
Baytee	daughter
Behn	sister
Berf	ice or snow
Bhabi	sister-in-law
Bhangra	Punjabi folk dance
Chai	cardamom, cinnamon sweet milky tea
Chapatti	tortilla like bread
Chapatti Plate	round hand woven straw plate
Chimta	metal tongs used as a musical instrument
Charpai	cot woven with jute twine

Churri	dagger or knife
Dal	lentil curry
Dehra	farm center
Dhol	large drum
Dholki	small drum
Dhoti	sarong
Dupatta	head scarf
Eid	Muslim religious holiday
Fakir	beggar
Fajar	Morning prayer
Gee Aiyan Noon	my heart welcomes you
Ghana	tasseled bracelet
Giani	Sikh priest
Goonda	hooligan
Gota	plaited silver ribbon
Grunth	Sikh holy book
Gurdawara	Sikh temple
Guru Grunth Sahib	Sikh holy book, last living guru
Goras	white people
Heer Ranja	Punjabi love story
Haji	one who has performed pilgrimage to Mecca
Halva	sweetened cream of wheat with nuts
Haridwar	sacred place on Ganges River
Hawaldar Major	sergeant major
Hookah	water pipe
Inshah Allah	God willing
Jalebis	sweetened fried pretzel
Juma	Friday
Jawan	soldier
Kabaddi	a tackle game
Kachera	sacred undergarment

Kafir	infidel or nonbeliever
Kalima	Islamic allegiance to God
Kameez	loose tunic
Kanga	wooden comb
Kara	steel bangle
Kasa	begging bowl
Kabobs	skewered grilled beef
Kes	body hair
Khaddar	coarse homespun cotton cloth
Khara	wedding bathing ritual
Koi batt Nahin	no problem
Khoo	water well
Khuda Hafiz	God be with you
Kirpan	dagger
Kothees	bungalows
Koran	Muslim holy book
Kurta	collarless tunic
Lassi	drink made from whey
Lathi	wooden fighting stick
Luddi	women's welcome dance for newlyweds
Maddad Karo	please help
Mem Sahib	Hindi/Urdu name for English or western girl
Ma shah Allah	Allah's will
Mehndi	henna
Mela	fair
Methai	sweets
Mihrab	prayer niche for imam, facing Mecca
Mimber	podium from where imam delivers sermon
Muezzin	Muslim person who calls faithful for prayer
Muhajir	refugee
Naan	leavened oven baked flat bread

Naik	private
Namaste	Hindu greeting
Namaz	Muslim prayer
Nanga	naked
Numberdar	government representative
Paan	narcotic: areca nuts and quicklime in a betel leaf
Pahars	mountains
Paeti	large metal trunk
Pakoras	deep friend fritters
Parbat	mountain
Pathani	fair skinned Afghani girl
Paratha	round layered pan-fried flat bread
Pinnu	doughnut shaped cloth head cushion
Pir Malang	Muslim holy man
Piyar	hand affectionately touching top of head
Puri	deep fried paper-thin tortilla bread
Raita	shredded cucumber in yogurt
Saag	spicy spinach paste
Sara	silver and gold tinseled face covering
Sardar ji	term of respect for Sikh male
Samosa	fried pastry filled with spicy vegetables
Sara banai	wedding ritual, placing of sara on groom's face
Sat Sari Kal	Sikh greeting
Shaitan	Satan
Shahnai	reed wind instrument
Shalwar	baggy trousers
Shamshan ghat	cremation ground
Shirvani	round collared coat
Shiva	Hindu god

Silsila	group
Sheesham	deciduous cottonwood-like tree
Shukriya	thanks
Tandoor	clay oven
Taviz	amulet
Tez	fast
Tibba	plateau, knoll
Tonga	horse drawn two-wheeled carriage
Tonga wala	carriage driver
Toofan	storm
Topi	cap
Ulsi Pinees	flax seed balls mixed with syrup and nuts
Urs	holy gathering
Vaisakhi	Sikh religious holiday
Veera	brother, term of endearment
Wa Elaikum Asslam	Muslim response, "and peace be with you"
Woozoo	Ablutions, washing ritual

Edwards Brothers, Inc.
Thorofare, NJ USA
February 27, 2012